BRANDI WEBB

The Unsound Mind

First published by Z.H. Publishing 2023

Cover Design: @custombyerikaplum

First edition

ISBN: 979-8-98-762030-4

This book was professionally typeset on Reedsy.
Find out more at reedsy.com

For my parents, who never once made me feel like going to therapy was something to be ashamed of.

Contents

Acknowledgement

Mom, Dad, Clayton, Oliver, Jovie, Milo, Ferris, Dana, Courtney, Wendy...Dr. Pepper Zero. I am forever grateful for the support. So many people helped make this book a reality and I appreciate each and every one of you.

Also, a huge thanks to the therapist that first recommended I try writing as a way of expressing feelings. *The Unsound Mind* took several forms over the years, but I don't think it would have happened at all had I not been given therapy homework.

To everyone who asked how my writing was going and received way too long of an answer, I appreciate you not running away and remaining strong for the duration of my rambling answer.

I truly hope those who read this book, whether dealing with a mental illness or not, will be able to understand the importance of finding happiness and hope whenever possible. Mental illness is hard, it's hard for those with it, and hard for their loved ones who watch them struggle. But, even though there are many times when all you can do is feel the pain and pray for it to pass-life it still worth living and celebrating. Mental illness may be a part of you, it's a part of me and many of the people I love, but it is never something to be ashamed of. Go to therapy and don't be afraid to talk about it. Take your medication and don't let anyone make you feel weak for doing so. Pray for help and pray for peace and surround yourself with people who will love and support you...find your Anders, your Bird, or your Walter.

Finally, a huge thank you to every one that reads my book. I am more grateful for you than you could possibly know.

Chapter One

New York 1933

Her name was Lina. She was small for her age. She was only four, but somehow she looked younger. Her red hair hung in two matching braids down her back, and her white nightgown had a large juice stain on the front – she had been wearing it all day long. Lina stood just outside the bathroom door as she watched her mother wash her hands over and over and over again. Had Lina known how to tell time, she would have been able to tell you that her mother had been washing her hands for 53 minutes. But Lina couldn't tell time in the traditional sense. She did, however, know that the pang in her stomach meant that it had been a long time since lunch.

Luckily, it wasn't long until Lina's father came home from work.

"Hello, my lovelies," he called out.

Neither Lina nor her mother responded.

"Hello?" her father called out again.

Lina heard footsteps coming toward her. Her father saw what was happening. He picked Lina up and kissed her on the head.

"Why don't you go play with your toys, little Lina," he said as he set her back down.

Lina didn't move. She was confused. She watched as her father walked and rested his hands on her mother's shoulders.

"Marie," he said gently, "I think they are clean."

She watched as her mother shook her head, tears in her eyes.

"They are *clean*," he said again.

He kissed the top of her head, just like he had kissed Lina's. He moved to turn off the water. Her mother instinctively pushed him away.

"Not yet," she said through tears.

Lina began to cry. She didn't understand what was happening, but everything felt sad. Lina's father saw her crying. His eyes were red.

"Lina, it's okay. Go play with your toys."

Still, she didn't move. She watched her father and mother. She looked at their red eyes. She had never seen both her parents with such sad eyes. It worried her. Her father started singing a gentle, quiet song to her mother until her mother turned off the water.

When her mother finally stepped away from the sink, her hands were red and bleeding. Her father led her mother to their room and laid her down on their bed. After that, he came and held Lina. They sat together in the hallway, and her father held her for a long time. He told her that everything was all right. He told her that mommy and daddy loved her. He told her stories, stories about princesses and fairies. He told her stories until Lina smiled. When her father saw Lina's smile, he smiled. He fed her toast and jam for dinner. He put her to bed. She fell asleep. A little while later he came back to the room. He picked Lina up.

"Mommy wants you to sleep with us tonight," he whispered to her.

Laying between her father and mother, with her mother's arm around her, Lina forgot about the sadness, she forgot about her mother's red hands, and she fell asleep with a smile on her face.

The next day, Lina's father stayed home from work. They went out for ice cream. A few different women came to their house, and her father asked them questions. Sometimes he called Lina into the room and had her talk to the women, too. The women were nice and smiled at Lina.

After they left, he said to Lina, "I think we are getting a nanny, little Lina. Someone to play with you and mommy while I am gone."

Lina smiled.

"Would you like a nanny?" her father asked.

Lina nodded. A nanny sounded fun.

Her father stayed home the next day as well. He took Lina and her mother on a walk. Lina noticed that her mother's hands were still all red. Later that day, one of the women Lina had talked to the day before came over.

"This is your nanny, Lina," her father said.

The nanny smiled at her. She was tall and had lots of curly hair.

"Hi, Lina. I'm Ruth."

"Hi," Lina said, and then she skipped away to her room. On her way to her room she passed by her parents' room. She saw her mother sitting on her bed.

"Mommy, a nanny came!" Lina said to her.

Her mother's eyes were all red again, but she smiled, so Lina wasn't worried.

Sometimes Lina noticed that her mother seemed very sad. She was anxious too, but Lina didn't know that word yet. To Lina, Mother had up days, when her eyes were light and full of smiles, and down days, when the light was gone. But, whether the day was up or down for Lina's mother, Ruth now came over every time Lina's father went to work. Ruth played with Lina and her mother, just like Father said she would. Some days Lina didn't see her mother much at all. On those days, Ruth was extra nice. She let Lina put bows in her hair, and she made her as many turkey sandwiches as she wanted.

Every so often, Lina would see her mother doing something strange. She would see Mother walk through the house and touch all the windows with one hand and then with the other. Her mother would do this several times in a row, ten to be exact, but Lina didn't know that because she wasn't very good at counting. Other times, she would hear her mother yelling at herself. She would hear her frustration and tears through the bedroom door.

When things like this happened, Ruth would try to keep Lina extra busy. She would take her outside to play, and she would shield Lina from things she could not comprehend. Lina did not know her mother was crazy. She wouldn't find that out until years later. She didn't think that there was anything strange about her life. Lina was happy. She loved her mother and father. In her young eyes, they were perfect.

Lina slept with her mother and father every night. She liked that. Her father would tell her stories while her mother would cuddle her close and tell her she loved her. Sometimes her mother would cry and Lina would kiss her on the nose. That made her mother smile every time.

Bedtime was Lina's favorite.

* * *

For nearly a year, nothing changed in Lina's world. Life was good. Life had a routine. Lina loved her routine. It kept everything the way she liked it. But tonight, for the first time in almost a year, Lina's parents were breaking the routine by going out. Lina would not be sleeping with her mother and father. This made her sad. Tonight her parents were going to a party, and Ruth was going to stay with Lina while they were gone. When Lina saw her mother all dressed in her party clothes, she thought she looked like one of the princesses from Father's stories. She was particularly mesmerized by her mother's white gloves. She thought they were the prettiest things in the world. She rubbed her cheek against the silky fabric of the gloves. She didn't know they were hiding the wounds on her mother's hands and wrists. Lina's father twirled her mother around the living room. Lina laughed. They looked like people from a movie. Her father picked her up, and together the three of them danced all through the house.

When they stopped dancing, Lina clapped her hands joyfully, and her parents gave her kisses. Her father tickled her and she snorted. It made her mother smile. They told her they loved her. They told her they would see her in the morning.

They walked out the door.

In the middle of the night, Lina was suddenly pulled from a deep sleep. She'd been dreaming about being a princess with white silk gloves. Her Uncle Clark, her mother's brother, was standing at her bedside. He told her that Mother and Father were gone. She didn't understand. There had been an accident, he said, and they were gone. Lina was confused and scared. She called out for her mother and father. Her uncle told her they weren't coming. They were gone. She saw Ruth standing by the door. Lina ran to her and held her tight. She cried into her nanny's nightgown. She asked Ruth when her parents were coming home. Ruth kissed her head and hugged Lina very close to her. Lina let out hard sobs that shook her tiny body. She sobbed and sobbed and kept sobbing as her uncle pried her off her nanny and took her to his car.

After that, Lina went to live with Uncle Clark, Aunt Angela and her cousins, Chrissie and Beth. She hated it. She hated it for a lot of reasons, but mostly because her parents weren't there. It was the worst at night. She would remember lying between her mother and father. She would remember her mother's arm around her, and her body would feel ice cold in the place where her mother's arm used to rest. She felt sad and very, very alone. She cried every night – first because of sadness and then because of fear. Sometimes the fear was so bad that Lina wasn't able to see. It was as if a part of her shut down, unable to function under the weight of her terror. Her uncle and aunt didn't understand why she was so afraid. And they didn't really care. Her cousins made fun of her and called her a baby. She asked if she could go live with Ruth. Aunt Angela said no. She continued to cry. The crying lasted for a whole year, and then it stopped. Lina made it stop; she realized there was no use crying when there was no one who cared enough to wipe away the tears. Lina learned to hold her feelings in. She found a place deep inside to bury all the sadness and all the fear.

Chapter Two

New York 1946

Lina's parents had been dead for 13 years. This was a tragic and omnipresent fact in her life. She had been raised by Clark and Angela since that tragic night, and they had never bothered to love her. Lina could feel the stigma of her "lunatic" mother draped over her like a cloak, shielding her from the affection she wished her adoptive family would give her. Even as a little child, her aunt and uncle's prejudice had stopped them from offering her any real comfort. Never once had she been tucked into bed with a goodnight kiss. Instead, she had been left to put herself to bed every night while Angela read stories to her cousins in the other room.

As Lina grew older, she began to understand why her family was so cold to her, why they had never even thought of accepting her as their own. They had never come right out and said it, but their cold, watchful eyes and whispered conversations spoke volumes. Lina knew exactly what they thought about her: it was only a matter of time until she went insane, just like her mother.

Lina didn't remember her mother being crazy, but everyone said she was. More than once she had overheard her aunt criticizing her late father, calling him "foolish", "reckless" and "negligent" for not putting her mother in an asylum. Whenever Lina heard Angela say this, Lina's temper rose. She wanted to yell and defend her parents. She wanted to tell Angela that the 5 years she had spent with her "reckless" father and "lunatic" mother had been the best years of her life. She wanted to shout to her adopted family that if she did go insane it would be because of their coldness and cruelty, and certainly not because of her mother. But she knew if she did that, if she caused a scene, it would just strengthen everyone's suspicions about her. And so, Lina spent the majority of her life distant and removed, holding her tongue, and trying her best to convince everyone that she was sane.

It had been the same routine for the past 13 years; Lina would try to stay out of everyone's way, she was cautious and careful to never step out of line. It was never enough. No matter what she did or did not do, Clark, Angela, and her cousins constantly looked at her like she was diseased. But Lina kept trying, she kept up the act, hoping one day they would stop treating her with such disdain and mistrust, and then she would finally be able to breathe a sigh of relief.

That was what she was going to be doing tonight, putting on a show for her aunt and uncle to prove to them she was a regular, sane teenager. Her oldest cousin, Chrissie, was engaged to a man named Scott, and the last time Scott was over for dinner, he had suggested getting 2 of his pals together with Beth and Lina so they could all go dancing. There was no part of Lina that wanted to go to the dance, and there was no part of either Chrissie or Beth that wanted her to go, but no one wanted to call attention to these facts, and so they acquiesced to Scott's earnestness. Lina knew her aunt and uncle were sick of her hanging around the house every weekend. So, she forced a smile and told Scott that it was a wonderful idea and that she would love to go.

That was why, on Saturday afternoon at 4:25 pm, Lina put down her copy of *The Count of Monte Cristo* and went to her room to get ready for a dance she had no desire to attend. Lina looked in the mirror and felt the ache of her parents' absence. Maybe if her mother was helping her get ready and her father was waiting to answer the door for her date, she would feel excited. Maybe if she was getting ready because she actually wanted to look her best, and not just to prove that she wasn't a lunatic, then brushing out the tangles of her long auburn hair wouldn't feel like such a chore. Lina sighed as she secured her pins in her hair and then went to her closet.

"Don't wear the yellow dress. It looks awful with your hair," Chrissie said, standing in the doorway. "I don't even know why you have that dress."

Lina shot Chrissie a fake smile and pulled her blue dress from the closet. She showed it to Chrissie, who nodded approvingly, and then walked away. Lina changed into the dress, then grabbed her book and went into the living room to read while she waited for her date.

At ten minutes to 5:00, Beth and Chrissie walked into the living room, looking primped and perfectly polished.

"No makeup, Lina? Really?" Beth asked.

Lina looked up apologetically in an attempt to pretend that she cared about Beth's opinion.

Lina could tell Beth wanted to say more, but she was stopped by a knock on the door. Her uncle answered it. Scott and his friends stood smiling on the other side.

Lina had to admit that her date was handsome. His name was Peter, and he was 19. He had turned 18 right as the war ended, so he had not been drafted.

"I wish I was older," he told Lina. "I would have loved to kill some of those Nazis."

Lina smiled, as she was supposed to, at his patriotism.

"Are you going to school?" she asked.

"Yeah, I go to the university. That's where I met Scott." Peter said. "It's not much fun, but hey, I have to be successful so I can buy you girlies all the pretty things."

He laughed.

Lina forced a chuckle.

"What about you? What do you do for fun?" Peter asked.

"I'm planning on going to Columbia in the fall."

"That's a lot of money to spend on finding a husband," said Beth's date, James, who apparently had been eavesdropping. Peter slapped James on the back as the two of them laughed loudly at the "joke."

"I actually have a scholarship," Lina said softly, but they weren't listening. They had started talking about a party they had gone to the night before.

The dance was long. Lina kept wishing it was over. As Peter swung her around the dance floor, he chattered away, telling stories she pretended to care about. She didn't mind that there was little opportunity for her to contribute to the conversation, and was relieved when the dance ended. Lina let Peter open the car door for her and then slid in, anxiously awaiting her return home. Peter slid in next to her and rested his arm around her shoulders. Beth and Chrissie were laughing hard at something James had said. James grinned the grin of a man who knew how handsome he was. He put his arm around Beth and pulled her close to him. She giggled and twirled her hair around her finger.

Peter was saying something to Lina, but she didn't notice. She was lost in thought. He tugged on her hair teasingly. Lina turned to look at him.

"Hey Lina, are you in there?" he laughed.

"Sorry. What?"

"I was asking if you wanted to go see a movie some time, maybe next Friday?" Peter looked at her, waiting for an answer.

Lina knew what she was supposed to say. Peter was tall and handsome with thick brown hair and an infectious grin, and it wasn't like she had any other fellows vying for her attention. A normal girl would say yes to an invitation from a good-looking suitor.

"That would be lovely," she said, though she didn't mean it in the slightest.

As Lina lay in bed that night, she tried to think of something to make herself excited for her date with Peter. She couldn't think of anything. Peter bored her. She knew that wasn't a nice thing to think, but it was how she felt. She supposed, at the very least, having a friend of Scott's interested in her might ease some of the concerns her family had about her mental stability. Her family adored Scott, after all.

The next day was business as usual. In the morning Lina, finished reading her book. Later, Beth yelled at her for accidently dripping jam on the sleeve of her sweater. Her uncle and aunt ignored her. It was a completely normal Sunday for her. Soon enough she would be starting at Columbia, and there she could begin to shape her life into what she wanted it to be. She just had to get away from the family that never cared for her first. Once she no longer had to put on the same show she had been for the past 13 years, she would have the energy to pursue any number of dreams. She knew she needed to leave this all behind and find people who would see her as more than the daughter of a lunatic. Once on her own, she wouldn't have to worry about convincing everyone she was sane all the time. She wouldn't have to worry about her uncle and aunt watching her every move, just waiting for her to snap.

Lina felt incredibly restless. Her irritation at her family and her situation was eating at her and she needed an escape. She grabbed her coat from the closet and slipped out the front door before anyone could ask where she was going. She walked the quiet streets of her neighborhood and attempted to clear her head. Thoughts of Peter and her imminent date with him rolled around in her mind, combatting the peace she was attempting to feel. It irked her to no end that she felt obligated to go on a date for the sole purpose of proving to her family that she was sane. She walked aimlessly, fueled by indignation until the sun began to set. As she made her way home, she stopped in front of the Richardson's house. Lina didn't know Mr. and Mrs. Richardson very well but she had known their son, Stewart. Stewart had been Chrissie's age and a couple years ahead of her in school. Chrissie and Beth had done their best to turn all their classmates against Lina and most everyone had sided with her cousins because they were gorgeous and popular and Lina was bookish and shy, but not Stewart. Stewart had always been kind to Lina, her only source of friendship in school. When he graduated and Lina found out he had been drafted, she had locked herself in her room and cried silent tears.

Lina had been walking home from school when she heard Mrs. Richardson's wailing. Lina remembered watching from across the street as Mr. and Mrs. Richardson held each other sobbing on the doorstep. She knew what that meant, knew what the tears were for and her own came instantly. Stewart was dead. Kind, brave Stewart had died in the war.

Looking at their house again reminded Lina of that day and tears once stung at her eyes. Stewart had been a truly good person and Lina's only friend and the war had taken him away. The war had broken the Richardson's hearts and left them without a son. The war was over now, but that did nothing to lessen the pain for those who had lost loved ones. Lina thought again of Peter and his patriotic bravado and felt nothing but dread at the thought of seeing him again. She said a silent prayer for the Richardsons and then one for herself. She needed to get away from this life, she couldn't live it anymore. She couldn't stay with a family that hated her, a family that would continue to hate her no matter how hard she tried to show them she was worth caring about.

When she finally made it back to her house, she went straight to her bedroom and began to plan her escape from her miserable existence.

When Lina awoke on Monday morning she felt much better than she had the day before. She went to the kitchen and noticed the newspaper, lying discarded on the table by Uncle Clark. Lina wiped the crumbs from his toast off the front page and began to read. Something caught her eye. She stopped and read the paragraph once more. Then something else grabbed her attention. She didn't know why, but the words seemed off to her. She scanned the entire paper, her eyes darting up and down, looking to see if there was anything else strange. She was consumed with her task, unaware of anything happening around her.

"I'm taking your cousins shopping. Clean up breakfast while we are gone." her aunt said.

Lina didn't register the words until after Angela had closed the door, taking Chrisse and Beth with her.

Lina took the paper up to her room where she lay in bed scouring it. Over and over, she scrutinized it until finally exhausted, she stopped, rolled over on her back, and stared up at the ceiling. What was it that she was seeing? She didn't really understand. All she knew was that something was not right with these articles. She continued trying to figure out what it was until her aunt came home and yelled at her for not cleaning up after breakfast.

The next morning, Lina was eager for her uncle to finish the paper. She had hardly slept the night before. Her mind had been going nonstop trying to make sense of what she had read. She tapped her foot anxiously as she pushed her fruit back and forth on her plate. Her uncle coughed and stood up from the table. At last, Lina was able to grab the paper. She read quickly.

"I'm going for a walk," she said to her aunt as she opened the front door taking the paper with her.

She flipped through it four more times, her eyes wildly scanning the words.

Over the next few days, she stored the newspapers in her room and started circling the things that seemed off to her. A pattern was becoming evident.

Lina was reading Friday's paper when someone knocked on the door.

"What?" she called out without getting up.

"Peter is on the phone for you," Chrissie yelled through the door.

Peter? Lina had completely forgotten that he had invited her to a movie. Annoyed, she put down the paper and went to the phone. Lina kept the conversation as brief as possible. Peter was coming to pick her up at 6:00. They were going to the drive-in. The instant she got off the phone, she ran back upstairs and continued reading.

At 5:30, Lina forced herself to get ready. She hadn't showered in a few days, so she quickly washed herself and her hair. She threw on a clean skirt and blouse and tied a scarf around her hair. She looked in the mirror. She had bags under her eyes, and her face looked skinnier than she remembered.

Peter arrived promptly at 6:00, and Lina answered the door. She left quickly before either of her cousins could comment on how terrible she looked.

Lina struggled to pay attention to the movie. Her mind kept wandering. Her brain was frantically trying to comprehend the messages she had been seeing in the paper the last few days. She hadn't even noticed that Peter had his arm around her, or that he was sitting extremely close to her until he whispered in her ear. The feeling of his breath on her neck almost made her jump.

"You look amazing tonight," Peter said.

Lina knew that wasn't true. She looked pale and tired, and her clothes probably didn't match. It irritated her that Peter was lying.

"Lina," Peter said quietly.

She turned to look at him. He looked at her as if to ask a question. She didn't know what the question was, but she figured it out very quickly when Peter leaned in for a kiss. Lina quickly turned her head. She wasn't about to waste time kissing Peter. She had more important things to think about.

After that, they didn't talk at all. Peter drove her home, said a quick goodbye, and drove away before she was even through the door. Lina went straight upstairs and pulled out all the newspapers she had stored under her bed. She opened them up and spread them out over her bedroom floor. As she looked at them together, everything finally started to make sense.

As Lina lay in bed that night, she knew she could no longer stand waiting for her uncle to read the paper first. She felt an insatiable pull to keep putting the pieces of the puzzle together. Her body couldn't rest until she'd made more progress. She barely slept, and when she did, it was only in short spurts of fifteen minutes or so. She shifted around restlessly in her bed, angered that she could not study the newspapers in the dark room, but she worried that turning on the light would draw too much attention. So, when the first crack of light appeared in the sky, she snuck downstairs and retrieved the paper. She studied it furiously, making connections and ciphering codes, until she was called down for breakfast.

Every morning after that, Lina crept silently downstairs before everyone else. She had to. She desperately needed the newspaper if she expected to save everyone. The more she read, the clearer everything became. With each new front-page story, the plan became more obvious. Something big was coming – something only Lina could stop. Whoever was plotting this was clever, but Lina knew she could stay one step ahead. Lina thought briefly about telling someone what was going on, but she quickly pushed that thought aside. She obviously couldn't tell Clark and Angela about it because they would steal her glory. And her cousins were too daft to comprehend any of the secrets Lina had uncovered. No, the fate of the world was resting on Lina's shoulders. Lina felt chills as she considered that perhaps this was her purpose. It was as though everything she'd been through, every tragedy, every setback, every disappointment had made her tough enough to bear this load. The sleepless nights and constant decoding couldn't break her; she was too strong.

After a few days of missing his newspaper, Lina's uncle became irate. Lina mumbled lies or dodged the question when he asked if she had seen it. She couldn't risk him keeping the paper for himself; time was of the utmost importance. If Lina did not fully uncover the plan, the United States was going to be thrown into another war. They were just recovering from the last one, and the pain and loss was still fresh to so many people. The memory of Mr. and Mrs. Richardson holding each other as they cried clawed at Lina's mind and she knew she couldn't let anything like that happen again. She had to stop the evil plots . She had to save her country from what was coming.

Lina continued her routine of slipping outside to pick up the newspaper before everyone arose and tucking them neatly under her bed for review later. Every second that she did not have to spend out of her room she spent reading and decoding the papers.

On a Wednesday morning in mid-July, Lina's uncle announced that he, her aunt and her cousins were leaving tomorrow to vacation in the Hamptons for the rest of the summer. They were going with Scott and his family. As usual, Lina was not invited, but this time she was ecstatic. She couldn't wait to have the house to herself. Left alone with the code, Lina knew she might actually be able to connect the dots.

That night, Lina pulled all the papers out and organized them by date. They covered her floor and walls. With her family leaving, there was no longer a need for secrecy. Her eyes scanned them hungrily and wildly until finally it all came together. Lina laughed, and her body shook with excitement. All the sleepless nights, the early morning sneaking, and the frantic decoding had finally paid off. An attack was coming. She knew by whom and she knew when. This meant she could stop it. Her country was going to be safe. Her future was going to be saved. All Lina had to do was get the information to the President and everything would be okay.

In the morning, Lina forced herself to leave her room and say goodbye to her family before they left. She chuckled as she watched them drive away. She was going to be a hero when they returned. She couldn't wait to see the look on her cousins' faces. No one would be able to say she was crazy after she saved them.

As soon as they left, she ran back upstairs and burst into her room, ready to collect the papers and head out to find the mayor. Lina wasn't foolish enough to assume she could talk directly to President Truman, but as she'd scanned the papers, something inside her told her she could trust the Mayor O'Dwyer. Surely he could help her get in touch with President Truman. She folded the newspapers and her notes very carefully and put it all in a bag. For the next 6 hours, Lina roamed the streets, following the buzzing inside her that told her where to look for the mayor. A weaker person would surely have given up after the first 3 hours, but Lina was not weak; she was determined to fulfill her destiny. After another 6 hours of wandering, the sky was growing dark, and Lina had to face the fact that she wasn't going to find the mayor today. She went home feeling despondent. As Lina laid in her bed that night, she tossed and turned and tried to shake the feeling that something wasn't right. Eventually she succeeded and was able to sleep for a whole hour.

The next morning, Lina dressed quickly, grabbed her bag, and once again took to the streets in search of the mayor. The buzzing inside her told her she should visit the police station. Someone was expecting her there, someone that could take her to the mayor. When Lina arrived at the police station, she walked confidently through the front doors. She looked around eagerly. A young officer smiled at her; she smiled back. He must be the one that would take her to the mayor. She walked over to him.

"Hello, miss, is there something I can help you with?" he asked.

Lina's mouth opened but she didn't know what to say. She felt confused and jittery; wasn't he supposed to know why she was here? The universe had sent her to him.

"Ma'am, are you okay?" he asked, looking concerned.

"Oh, oh yes. Sorry. I'm fine." Lina responded.

"Are you looking for someone?"

"Yes, I was supposed to meet someone here, but I don't...I don't see him."

"What's his name? Maybe I can help you find him."

"Oh, no, that's okay," Lina said as she started backing away, "I must have misunderstood."

Lina hastily exited the building and made her way back home. When she finally made it to the house, she realized that she was crying. She felt confused and rattled. She took all the newspapers out of her bag and looked them over once more. *It's all still here,* she assured herself, *It's all still here and I still have time to save everyone.*

Lina took several deep breaths and decided that it may be best to call the mayor first. Clearly, he wasn't out on the street where he was supposed to be, so she would have to find him at his office instead.

"Hello, Mayor O'Dwyer's office." a woman answered the phone.

"Hi, can I please speak to the mayor?" Lina asked.

"What is this regarding? Is he expecting your call?"

"Yes, he should be."

There was a bit of a pause, "Can I please get your name and the reason for the call?"

Lina was rocking back and forth on the balls of her feet. She was irritated with this secretary, irritated that she was wasting time and acting stupidly.

"This is Lina Willis, and it's an urgent matter that I only feel comfortable discussing with Mayor O'Dwyer."

"One minute please," the woman said coldly.

The longer she waited, the more irritated Lina became. She was doing everything right. She had given up her life to solve this mystery. She had cracked an enemy code all by herself. She had searched for the mayor so she could get the information to the President. And now she was at the mercy of some idiot secretary who had no idea what was at stake. Lina knew the mayor was waiting to hear from her, she just knew it.

"Ma'am," the voice had returned, "Ma'am, I'm sorry but the mayor is not expecting your call. Can I please take a message?"

Lina's jaw clenched. "I really need to talk to him, only him."

"I'm sorry, Ma'am, Mayor O'Dwyer is a very busy man. I'm going to have to take a message, and someone will get back to you as soon as possible."

Lina felt tears of anger dripping down her cheeks. She hung up the phone and went upstairs to her room. She screamed into her pillow.

It's okay, she thought to herself once she had calmed down, *tomorrow I will go down there in person. I will go first thing in the morning.*

Lina slept for 37 minutes that night.

CHAPTER TWO

At 6:00 a.m. Lina was dressed and ready to head out the door, but something stopped her. Was it doubt? She pulled the papers out of her bag and looked at them again, and something stirred inside her. She wasn't sure what she was feeling, but she did her best to push it aside because she didn't like what it was trying to say.

Instead of heading out, Lina paced around the house all day. She was restless. She was worried. She needed to do something, but she couldn't bring herself to go down to the office in person. She called the mayor's office again instead, but she quickly hung up when she heard the same woman answer the phone.

The next day, she woke up feeling confident and determined. She gathered up the newspapers, put on her best dress and took the bus to the city offices. She walked up to the front door. She slowly entered the building and made her way to the mayor's quarters.

There was a blonde-haired woman sitting at the reception desk. It had to be the same woman Lina had spoken to on the phone.

"Hello, I'm here to see Mayor O'Dwyer." Lina said firmly.

"Do you have an appointment?" it was definitely the same voice.

Lina nodded.

"Okay, can I get your name?"

"It's Lina Willis."

The woman looked up at her in alarm.

"Ma'am, I'm going to have to ask you to leave."

Lina watched as the woman picked up the phone and dialed someone.

"I promise he wants to see me. I really need to talk to him, please." Lina begged, her desperation rising.

"Security is on their way. If you don't leave now, they will escort you out." The woman wouldn't look her in the eye.

Lina heard footsteps and ran out the door. She ran down the sidewalk and as far away as she could get before she ran out of breath. She clutched her bag tightly to her chest and looked around nervously. No one appeared to be following her, so she wiped the sweat from her brow and made her way home.

When she walked through the front door, she took off her shoes and threw them angrily across the room. She didn't understand what was going on, why weren't people doing what they were supposed to do? Confusion, frustration, and doubt swirled around in her mind with reckless disregard for any other thought or feeling in their path. Eventually, the confusion and frustration faded away, and Lina was left with only the feeling of doubt. It clung to her for the rest of the day, and for the next three days. Lina tried as hard as she could to pretend it wasn't there. She tried to focus on her feelings of victory and grandeur. She tried to deny what was becoming increasingly apparent because she was too afraid to admit it. But she couldn't deny it forever: everyone had been right about her. They had all been so horribly right. As the haze of the last few weeks faded away, Lina could see that none of it was real. Of course the secretary had sent her away; of course the mayor hadn't wanted to see her. There was no secret code in the newspaper, no plot that only Lina could stop. When she finally admitted it to herself, her heart broke. It splintered into a thousand pieces and the pain was too much for Lina to bear.

The crash had come.

Lina spent the rest of the week in her bed. She let the shame slowly gnaw at her insides. It started with her stomach and worked towards her heart. The gnawing was unbearable, but she knew she deserved it. She was shattered; she was so ashamed of herself. She felt sick to her stomach as she thought about the delusions that had controlled her for the past six weeks. As she replayed her thoughts and action over and over again in her mind, she sank further and further into the bed. By the time the shame had finished devouring her, there was nothing left of her but skin and tears. She wanted to die. She lay in her bed and waited for death to come and take her away from the awful reality of what she had done and who she was.

Lina didn't know if it was day or night when she finally heard her family come home; but she knew her fate was inevitable. She heard her aunt call her name and Lina wished desperately that she could disappear. Her aunt opened Lina's bedroom door. The look on her aunt's face was one Lina would never forget. She turned her head toward the wall as her aunt, looking horrified yet smug, yelled for her uncle.

Lina was gone within a week.

Chapter Three

Lina arrived at the asylum sobbing and screaming. She had heard stories, stories whispered by the adults as they waited for her to break just like her mother had. She could only imagine the horrors that awaited her. She knew no hope lay behind those thick, metal doors. She knew that, at just 18 years of age, her life was over. Lina was broken and shattered, yes, but she was still sane enough to know that her uncle and aunt never intended to see her again. They were going to let her rot to death in the nuthouse. Lina could still see the look of disgust in their eyes as they took in the newspapers, complete with manic scribbling, that covered the floor of her room . Those looks haunted her. She had hoped desperately that her tears of shame would rinse away the work of a lunatic, but they had not, and her uncle and aunt had wasted no time getting rid of her. They couldn't wait to be free of her. They rushed her to asylum as she slowly slipped out of mania and back into sanity.

It was too bad they didn't wait around to see it.

She had been there for a month, and she refused to speak to anyone beside Dr. Carrow. Even then, she did it grudgingly. Dr. Carrow was Lina's assigned doctor. His hair was gray, but you could tell it used to be dark. He was very tall and looked to be about 50. His skin had the sallow look of someone who spent too much time inside, and his pants were always just slightly too short for his legs. He had a large nose, dark eyes tucked below a heavy brow, and a formidably square jaw.

She hated that jaw. She hated everything about her doctor. And, even though he never said it, she knew he hated her as well. There was something so cold in the way he looked at her. Something in the set of his mouth that allowed his distaste for her to flood out of him and pool around his ankles as they sat in session. She couldn't really blame him; Lina hated herself, too.

For five months, Lina sat silently and watched the other lunatics. She spent most of her time in a corner of the recreation room, though the only item in there for recreation was a checkerboard with no checkers, watching and wishing she could leave. When it was time to eat, she would do it quickly, wishing only to return to her corner. Lina was fairly certain she would one day die in that corner. She was certainly never going to leave this place. People did not leave the asylum, even the ones who weren't truly crazy. They came and they stayed. People only got out if someone took the time to care. The people that worked here did not care. They were not paid enough to do so, and most of the people sent here did not have anyone outside of the asylum that cared about them. It was a miserable place full of miserable people. That was why Lina did not speak to anyone; there was no one worth talking to. Lina sometimes worried that she would forget how to speak in between her sessions with Dr. Carrow. But, despite the limited use of her vocal cords, they always remembered what to do when the time came, and she would hear her voice dangle in the air as Dr. Carrow's hateful ears chose which words to listen to. It was a thoroughly depressing existence, her only solace being the hope that she would die young.

The air in the asylum was heavy; it was filled with loneliness, shame and lunacy. The air clung to her skin and tried to push its way deep into her mind and heart. She tried to resist, but it was hard and it wore her out. The more days she spent here, the crazier she felt. At night, she dreamed of death, and after those nights, waking up in the morning was a disappointment. Everything was dark in the asylum. Slumped in her corner day after day, Lina found it increasingly hard to keep the darkness at bay. She found it harder and harder to hold herself together. Her sense of self was slipping away, and she didn't know what to do.

One hundred and fifty-seven days into her life sentence, something changed. A new girl was brought to the institution. She looked to be about 14, and everything about her was pitiful. She was nothing but skin and bones, with cheekbones so sharp Lina was afraid she would cut her fingers on them. The girl sat trembling in the corner opposite Lina's, watching everyone with wary eyes. Lina watched her back. There was something about the girl that drew Lina to her. For the next few days, Lina watched the girl. The girl did not seem crazy, only scared. Lina had been alone with lunatics for a long time, and this girl did not fit the mold. She reminded Lina of a bird that had fallen out of its nest, broken and scared, dropped into some place new, hoping desperately that someone would save her.

About two weeks after the girl's arrival, they were both sitting in the recreation room. Lina still had not said anything to the girl. She didn't know how. One of the loonies noticed the girl and began to shuffle toward her. His eyes were wild, and he was muttering excitedly. Lina saw the girl's entire body tighten in fear. The man grabbed the girl's hair, and she broke into tears, unable to control her terror. Lina's heart ached for her, and before she realized what she was doing, Lina rushed forward and pushed the man into the wall. Startled, the man walked away, and Lina slunk back to her corner. The girl watched Lina leave; Lina could feel her eyes on her back.

The next day, during breakfast, Lina saw the girl again. The girl recognized her, and for a moment they studied each other cautiously. The girl's skin was translucent, and her hair was so blonde it was almost white. The combination gave her a ghostly effect. Her lips were chapped, and there was a scar that extended from her left brow down to her jaw. Lina looked into her gray eyes and saw that she was right. They were not the eyes of a lunatic; they were full of sorrow and fear, but they were not crazy, not like so many of the other eyes that she had seen these past months. Looking into the girl's eyes, Lina began to feel slightly less miserable. Part of her misery was replaced by a desire to take care of the girl – a desire to take away some of the sorrow from those sad, gray eyes.

"My name is Lina," she said simply.

"Thank you. For yesterday." The girl's voice was very high. She was nervous.

"You're welcome."

They sat together, neither of them touching their food.

"What's your name?" Lina asked

"I don't know…or I don't remember," the girl whispered. "No one has used it in so long."

There was silence for a moment while Lina thought. The girl's words pierced her heart. What kind of life must she have lived to not even know her own name? Lina couldn't let the girl remain nameless; it wasn't right.

"Can I call you Bird?" Lina questioned.

The girl looked surprised but nodded, and Lina thought perhaps she saw the premonition of a smile on Bird's lips.

For a long while, Lina and Bird sat together. Lina hadn't had much of a chance at making real friends before she came to the asylum, and she had no idea how to make one now. So, the girls sat quietly, neither one having any idea how to be friends with someone you met in an insane asylum.

After breakfast, the girls walked together.

"Do you want to go outside?" Bird asked timidly.

"Outside?" Lina asked. The patients were allowed to go outside, but Lina never had. They were allowed to go anywhere within the confines of the monstrous brick wall that surrounded the grounds of the asylum.

They walked outside. There was actually quite a bit of space around the building itself. The ground was mostly dirt with a few patches of dry grass, and a handful of trees grew haphazardly around the perimeter. The green of the trees contrasted strongly with the dull, gray bricks of the asylum. Looking at the asylum from the outside, Lina was reminded of how terrifying it looked. It looked the way it felt inside – dark and hopeless. Not even the blaring sun could counteract the bleakness of the building. All the windows were barred, and Lina couldn't help but imagine hundreds of lunatic eyes peering hungrily out through the metal rods. There were a few orderlies walking around outside. They were supposed to be supervising the loonies, but Lina knew they didn't much care what the patients did, as long as it wasn't too violent. Lina and Bird walked past a small vegetable garden. Lina was surprised. The garden was not very grand. In fact, it seemed to grow only potatoes, but it drew Lina in. She was fascinated by the potato's will to live in this terrible place. Bird seemed entranced by the garden as well. The two girls sat just outside of the fence that surrounded the pitiful, yet proud, potatoes.

Lina and Bird picked awkwardly at invisible specks on their drab asylum garb. Lina knew she needed to say something. She fiddled with the ends of her hair.

"It could be worse," Lina said. The thought escaped her lips before she had time to decide if she wanted to share it.

"What could?" asked Bird.

It was too late now, no turning back. "Um…the asylum. There are some… in other places where the patients kill each other. I've heard that at least. They send lots of criminals there and no one really cares." She scratched her arm nervously before continuing, "I mean this place is terrible and miserable and the doctors don't care about us, but at least no one is trying to murder us."

"Yeah. It could be worse," Bird agreed.

Chapter Four

Lina's mind kept drifting to Bird as she attempted to fall asleep on her uncomfortable mat. She listened to the sound of the other loonies breathing around her. The mats were so close that she could have easily reached out and touched the ones on either side of her. Lina wondered where Bird was sleeping, and she wondered if Bird too felt locked in by the lunatics around her. There were several different rooms they herded the loonies into at night for sleeping, so Bird could be in any one of them. Tomorrow night, Lina would make sure that she and Bird were in the same room. She didn't know why she hadn't thought to do so tonight. Lina was sure they would both feel safer at night having the other nearby. She thought that would be nice, having someone she trusted close at hand.

It was then that she remembered.

She wondered how she could possibly have forgotten.

Lina remembered she was broken. She could have another episode. She could have one at any time. That's what Carrow said.

The delusions will take hold, she remembered Carrow saying. *Your mind is weak, and the delusions will consume you whenever they want.*

Lina hoped that, for Bird's sake and hers as well, she did not have an episode soon. Lina did not want to scare Bird away by breaking right in front of her. Lina needed Bird – she needed a friend – and Bird needed her as well. Lina tried to convince herself that if she and Bird became close enough friends, Bird would not cast her aside after her inevitable episode. She hated that she had no idea when she would go crazy again; she laid awake for a long time worrying. She worried about going crazy. She worried about

Bird. She worried about her future. She worried about everything.

The next morning, Lina got pulled in to help prepare breakfast. Loonies were put to work quite often in the asylum, due to both the laziness of the staff and a shortage of people working there. Under the direction of a bitter nurse, Lina and a few of her fellow lunatics prepared the tasteless mush they would be eating for breakfast. One of the patients kept trying to stick her hand in the flame that was cooking a pot of something gray, and another was shaking so badly that Lina feared his bones would break inside of him. Once the breakfast was prepared, she was required to help serve it. She watched each face that came through the food line, trying her best to gauge its sanity. There were a few people who did not look insane at all, but they were foreigners and spoke no English; they were just people with bad luck who had ended up in the asylum, and now had no way to communicate that they weren't crazy. They certainly didn't belong in this place. She pitied them, but not for too long because soon she saw Bird. Bird looked terrified and tired, but when she came through the line, Lina smiled at her, and Bird's eyes lost some of their fear.

Once she was done cleaning up breakfast, Lina went to find Bird, which was not an easy thing in an asylum filled with hundreds of lunatics. Bird could be anywhere. Lina wandered through the halls, doing her best to avoid the hungry, maniacal eyes of the other patients. Looking into their eyes reminded her of the shame that had torn her apart before she was sent here, the shame of knowing that she was broken. That shame was accompanied by the fear that Bird would find out her secret too soon, the fear that breaking right now would ruin the only thing that was giving her hope, the only thing that made her not want to die. Her shame and fear were beginning to claw at her, and Lina worried they would consume her again. She felt the panic rising up inside her. It caught in her throat and made it hard to breathe. She cast her eyes around wildly, hoping to find something to push the worry and shame away, and luckily she found it near the potato garden staring up at the sun.

"Hello Bird." Lina imagined that her words soared through the air and landed on Bird's shoulder.

"Hello."

Lina sat on the ground next to her.

Silence. Too much silence.

"I'm not really sure how to make a friend, especially here," Bird admitted.

"Neither am I."

"Are we friends?"

"Yes. I want to be."

"Me too."

The words felt good.

The two girls sat together, feeling the warmth of the sun. Lina looked down at the part of her arm that stuck out from her sleeve. Her skin shone very pale under the bright sun.

"Lina, is it wrong to ask how long you've been here?" Bird asked.

"No, it's okay. I have been here for about five months."

"Were you afraid too when you came here?"

Lina answered quickly, "Yes, I cried the whole first week. I'm still afraid. Less now that I met you, though."

"Do you think the fear will ever go all the way away?" Bird was looking at her intently.

Lina thought for a moment before she answered. "I don't know. This place is so dark."

"Dark?"

"I think it's because of the air. Have you noticed the air? It's heavier here than in other places. It weighs down on us. It's almost too heavy for light to break through."

"I never thought about the air, but you're right. It is heavy." Bird hunched over as if the air were pushing her down.

"I never talked to anyone besides my doctor until you came here," Lina said.

"Why did you talk to me?"

"I wanted to keep you safe, and also, I wanted a friend. Five months is a long time to be alone, surrounded by lunatics. And well, Bird, you're not crazy and it's nice to be near you." Lina was a little shocked by her honesty.

"You don't think I'm crazy?" asked Bird.

"I've had five months to study lunatics, and when someone is crazy you can see it in their eyes. It might be something small, but the eyes aren't right. They are either too dark or too bright, or they burn when they look at you. Your eyes aren't like that, Bird."

Bird closed her eyes and lifted her face toward the sky. "I'm glad you're my friend, Lina."

Lina agreed.

The pair grew close quickly over the next two months. Lina asked Bird about her life before the asylum and found that Bird had endured unimaginable horrors. Bird had no idea who her parents were. She vaguely remembered a woman from when she was little, who was probably her mother, but she could not remember what had happened to her. When she was little, there was a poor woman who took pity on her. She had found Bird asleep on a park bench. Bird thought she must have been about five at the time. The woman took care of her as best she could. She was very old, and she didn't speak any English, but she was kind and she let Bird live with her in what was, essentially, a one room shack. They slept on the floor at night and begged for food during the day. The woman kept her safe for a few years, but one morning Bird woke up to find the woman cold and unmoving. She had died in her sleep. Bird told Lina that she had found the first adult she could and told them about the dead woman, but when they started asking her questions, she became scared and ran away.

"I was too afraid to go back to the house," Bird told Lina, "I was just so confused and scared."

It was shortly after that incident that Bird had the misfortune of meeting Simon and Julie. She had met Julie first; she had been digging through some trash when a well-dressed woman approached her. Julie had seemed so kind and concerned. She had called Bird "Sweet Girl" and said she could take care of Bird. Half starving to death and terrified from a month of living on the streets, Bird had gone with her. Julie took her home to a small apartment. Julie let Bird bathe and then took her to get a new dress. After that, Julie introduced Bird to her husband, Simon. He was a "businessman" she had said. Julie and Simon let Bird sleep on their couch. They fed her, and in return all they asked was that she clean the apartment. And so, she did. Eventually, when she was probably nine or ten years old, they started asking her to sneak small items into her pockets when they went to stores. She was so scrawny and underfed that most people assumed she was much younger and didn't really pay her any notice.

"It's not really stealing," they had told her, "Not when it's something that small taken by someone so small."

Bird had known it was wrong, but she didn't want to upset them and risk being back on the streets. Eventually, she asked them if she could go to school.

"Aw, Sweet Girl," Julie had crooned, "whatcha need school for? We'll teach ya everything you need to know."

As she grew even older and entered her teen years, Simon and Julie began asking more of her. She would be the distraction while they pick pocketed, they would send her door to door claiming she was raising money for her sick mother, and they would send her to deliver packages to some of the scariest people she had ever seen. About six months before being sent to the asylum, Bird had started sneaking money from them, only a little bit at a time. She was trying to save up enough money to get a bus ticket and get far away from them. Julie had found her stash of coins and smashed a beer bottle on Bird's face, resulting in her scar.

Simon had slapped Julie when he came home and saw Bird's face. He had helped Bird clean off the blood. Bird thought it was because he had grown to care about her, but unfortunately she ended up being so very, very wrong.

Once her face had healed, aside from the scar, Simon had given Bird some money and told her to go buy herself a new dress.

"Make it something real nice," he had said.

When Bird returned home, Simon and Julie told Bird to put on her new dress because they were taking her out to dinner. Bird had just finished getting dressed when there was a knock at the door. She heard Simon open it and greet someone. She heard a man's voice respond.

"Let's see the girl," the voice had said.

"Let's see the cash," Simon had responded.

Bird started shaking from head to toe as she told this part to Lina. Unsure of what to do, Lina landed on putting her arm, somewhat awkwardly, around Bird's shoulder.

"No one's gonna come looking for her, right?" the man had asked.

"Nah, she ain't got no family, she ain't in school. Julie and me's the only ones who know about her." Simon had chuckled.

"Good, good," the man had responded, "As long as the scar you mentioned isn't too bad, there shouldn't be any problems then."

Tears started streaming down Bird's face as she told Lina about how terrified she had been.

"I knew he was selling me; he was selling me to that man." Bird had said as she hid her face in Lina's shoulder, "I couldn't let him."

Bird told Lina that Julie had knocked on the door.

"You bout done in there? There's someone we want you to meet."

Bird had grabbed Simon's razor and walked out with it hidden behind her back. She had let Julie lead her over to the man. The man was handsome, looked to be about thirty years old, and wore an expensive looking suit. He smiled at Bird.

"Well aren't you lovely," he had said to her.

"We told ya she was," Julie had said.

The man had then shifted his gaze to Simon and his smile turned sinister, "I actually like the scar, gives her a little something."

Julie had turned to her, "Sweet Girl, this here's James. You're going to be a good girl and go with him."

Bird had been too afraid to speak.

"You're his now, you understand?" Simon had chimed in, "You do what he tells you."

James had walked over to her and caressed her face, "If you listen and do the things I want without causing trouble, I promise I'm going to take real, real good care of you."

"Do you want me to grab her clothes?" Julie had asked.

"Oh no, that's okay. I have plenty of lovely things for her back at the house."

James had said with a chuckle, "Let's just take her to the car."

Bird had let them lead her outside, still clutching the razor in her hand. James and Simon had laughed and talked about how obedient she was and how happy they both were with the deal.

"We were almost to his car, it was a real fancy one." Bird told Lina, "That's when I did it."

Bird had screamed as she began slicing James with the razor. She had yelled and cried and then sliced Simon, too, when he tried to grab her.

"It ended up causing such a commotion that people came running." Bird had told Lina, "I heard people screaming as they watched me attack them. A policeman came and Simon, Julie, and James all started lying. They said they didn't know me, they said they had never seen me. I tried to tell the truth, but no one would listen. James was wealthy and Simon was a professional liar, and I was just a girl with no name and a razor. They called me a lunatic. The policeman believed them, and I ended up here."

Abused, mistreated, and lonely- Those were the three words that summed up Bird's life before coming to the asylum. Lina's heart ached for her. The more Lina learned about Bird, the more she felt the need to protect her. They slept by each other every night now and were together as often as possible. Lina often heard Bird having nightmares; she wished she could take them away from her. Lina did her best to make Bird as happy as she could, but it was not an easy thing to do in an institution full of darkness and lunatics.

Lunatics. The thought constantly scratched at the corner of Lina's mind. She had still not told Bird the complete truth about herself. They talked about many things, and Lina had told her that her aunt and uncle had sent her here, but she was vague about the details and knew she needed to come clean. But every time she thought about doing it, she would remember the shame that had torn her apart, the shame that plummeted her into a darkness that had resulted in her being sent to the institution in the first place, and she would become too scared to confess. Lina knew she needed to tell Bird, and soon. There was no way to know when she would break again, and she wanted Bird to be prepared. She knew she was being selfish and unfair, but she was so afraid of losing Bird. The stress ate at her for weeks, but still she put it off.

Chapter Five

With each passing day, life was falling into a routine. Lina liked the consistency. It made her feel strong and secure. Her mind felt alert and steady. Her episode must have been a fluke; there was nothing wrong with her. There couldn't be. She did not belong in the asylum. Lina was sane right now. Truly. Her previous episode had merely been a bit of bad luck; no more were going to come. She didn't need to tell Bird about one misfortunate incident, an incident that, if disclosed, could ruin their friendship. A friendship that Bird so desperately needed after the bleak life she had lived. Both she and Bird had been seriously wronged when they were thrown in here. Neither belonged in the asylum. It was as simple as that.

Lina pitied her uncle and aunt for the mistake they had made. She wished she could talk to them and tell them what they had done wrong, but they never visited. Lina supposed that should have made her sad, but it was probably for the best. Lina had never been close to them. Her aunt and uncle had been dull and distant, and her cousins a pair of daft day-dreamers. It had been draining to spend so much time with them.

Chapter Six

Lina couldn't recall quite when she first noticed the nurse acting strange, but it was on a Thursday that the nurse's behavior finally made an impact. Lina had been pulled in to help prepare lunch. As usual, they were having over-baked bread and something reminiscent of stew. Every time the nurse came close, Lina felt an alarm go off in her mind. She was being warned. This woman was not to be trusted. She watched the tight-lipped, pale-skinned nurse out of the corner of her eye. Lina just knew she was up to something. She also knew that she had been chosen to stop her.

Lina did not eat the stew that day; she wasn't hungry. She was too focused on the nurse and what was off about her. She allowed her eyes to follow the suspicious woman around the dining hall. She listened to the nurse reprimand a lunatic who was trying to steal another patient's bread. She watched her with heavy, focused eyes. She didn't know what it was, but what she did know was that something was wrong with this nurse.

The next week, Lina made sure she was near the kitchen every day as lunchtime approached. She wanted to get pulled in to help again. She wanted more time with the nurse. Eight days later, her wish came true. She nonchalantly shuffled her way next to the suspicious nurse while in the kitchen. She watched the nurse as best she could without drawing attention to what she was doing. Another pale-skinned nurse pulled the suspicious nurse to the side and Lina strained to hear them. They kept their voices hushed, but their eyes were dark. Lina was focusing so hard on trying to hear them that she did not notice her sleeve had caught fire until one of the cooks rushed forward and swatted it with a towel.

"Get this one out of here," the cook called out. "She's going to burn the place down."

One of the nurses grabbed Lina's arm. "Come with me," she spat her rancid breath filling Lina's nostrils. Lina swallowed down vomit. The nurse deposited her in the hallway and then headed back to the kitchen. Dejected, Lina went to the cafeteria and found Bird sitting and waiting for her.

Lina sat silently next to Bird, pushing her food around on her plate. She was deep in thought for quite some time before she realized that Bird was talking to her.

"Lina, are you okay?" Bird's voice was high and it hurt Lina's ears.

"Oh, um, yes, I'm fine. I just..." she trailed off, distracted by the thoughts running through her mind.

Bird looked at her confused, "Do you want to go to the garden today?"

"Yes...that would...If there's time."

"Okay." Bird sounded smaller than usual.

The following week, Lina was able to help with lunch three different times. She hadn't eaten hardly anything over the past three weeks. There was far too much going on to waste her time eating. Her mind was racing constantly, and she often found herself growing irritated at Bird. Talking to Bird was a distraction. She was too simple to understand what was going on, and spending time with her meant she could not spend her time watching the nurses. Lina began to distance herself from Bird. She needed to be away from Bird to follow the two suspicious nurses, to see what they did, who they interacted with.

"Lina, what's going on?" Bird stared at her intently one evening during dinner.

Lina tried to quiet her thoughts long enough to answer, "Nothing."

"Something's going on," Bird almost sounded worried.

Lina looked at her friend and knew that at least for now she needed to cut ties. She was wasting too much time having pointless conversations with Bird. She cared for her Bird and wanted to protect her, but she couldn't do that if she was distracted. She had more important things to do.

"I just...I can't...I need to be alone," Lina said quickly as she stood up from the table and walked away...

* * *

After weeks of observation, she was fairly certain there were five nurses plotting something together. Five nurses doing something wrong. Five nurses hiding something.

Lina also noted a change in the lunatics. They were worse off than usual. Lina couldn't help but notice the ultra-paleness of their skin and the constant speckling of sweat on every patient's forehead. They moved more slowly. Lina watched them shuffle through the asylum like corpses. Even Bird was showing signs of weariness. Lina continued to keep an eye on her friend, even though she didn't have any time to spend with her. Lina was fairly certain she was the only one not suffering from this newfound sluggishness. She needed to figure out what was going on, and she needed to figure it out soon. The alarms in her mind were sounding more frequently, and she knew time was running out.

Lina was in the kitchen helping with lunch. She was stirring the stew and watching. Three of the five suspicious nurses were in the kitchen that day, and Lina's head was buzzing. She dropped more potatoes into the stew, sending a splash of broth onto Lina's left hand.. The hot liquid burned worse than it should have, yet Lina stood frozen. She stared at the red mark beginning to appear on her hand. Every nerve in her body began to pulse. The stew. Whatever was going on had to do with the stew. She stepped away from the pot and tried to blend in with the other loonies. After a few moments, one of the nurses made her way over to the stew. The nurse's eyes were shifty. She grabbed the spoon and began stirring. She leaned over the pot as if to check it, and Lina saw her drop a handful of white powder into the broth. The nurse stirred the pot a few more times and then made her way back over to the two other nurses. Lina slowly inched towards them to better hear what they were saying. Lina wished she could get closer, but she didn't want to draw attention to herself. Fortunately, or perhaps unfortunately really, Lina heard one word; one word left the mouth of a nurse and landed hard in Lina's ear. "Poison."

With a sharp intake of breath Lina ran from the kitchen. She needed to act now. It was all coming together. The nurses were trying to kill them all. They were poisoning the food. She needed to save Bird and all the other lunatics. She berated herself for taking so long to figure out what was going on. The universe had trusted her, and she had almost let it down. Rushing into the dining hall, Lina saw that the first batch of stew was being served. With no time to waste, Lina ran forward, grabbed the pot of stew, and, with all her might, threw it to the floor.

"It's poisoned!" she shouted "The nurses are trying to kill us!"

She looked around the room and into the eyes of hundreds of lunatics on the verge of their demise. She spotted Bird near the back of the dining hall. Her eyes were wide and afraid, but she didn't need to be afraid anymore. Lina had solved it. She and Bird could go back to the way they were before. She just needed to explain it to her.

"The pale ones! The ones with dark eyes! They are doing it!" She yelled, trying to make people understand, trying to make Bird understand.

Bird's eyes began to fill with tears, and Lina stared at her in confusion.

Just then, all five of the murderous nurses walked into the dining hall. Lina's entire body was burning. Her mind was buzzing, and she was filled with rage. She closed her eyes and asked the universe what to do. *Attack*, her body seemed to scream. Lina listened. She rushed at the nurses. Just before she got to them, an orderly grabbed her. Lina thrashed about, straining to reach the nurses. She struggled against the arms around her, but they held her tight. Another orderly came toward her; next to him was a nurse with a needle in her hand. He helped hold her steady as the nurse injected the needle into Lina's arm. This new orderly watched Lina as her head became fuzzy. Everything was beginning to spin, and her head felt heavy, but in a fleeting moment of lucidity, she couldn't help noticing the orderly's eyes. They were big and blue, but more importantly, they weren't cold like all the other workers. His eyes almost seemed sad, like he felt bad about what was happening. She focused on those eyes until the drugs finally took full effect and darkness consumed her.

Chapter Seven

When Lina awoke, she found herself locked away alone in a small room. She was fuming, awaiting the inevitable arrival of her doctor. She only hoped she could convince him she was telling the truth. She shifted uncomfortably in her straitjacket, waiting for him to arrive.

The door opened.

"Lina." He sounded apathetic.

"Dr. Carrow."

"Would you like to tell me what is going on? I heard there was a disturbance in the dining hall."

"I discovered something, Doctor. They want to..." Lina trailed off; her head was spinning. *I need to get him to believe me. If I can convince him, I can save everyone. I am the only one who can stop them. It is my duty. I need to get out of here and stop the nurses.* "They are trying to kill the patients. I don't know why, but you can't trust them."

"Trust who?" asked Carrow.

Lina could feel her heart pounding against the straightjacket. "The nurses. Five of them. I watched them. The universe, it warned me."

Dr. Carrow narrowed his eyes at her. Lina knew he was far too idiotic to understand what was going on, but she had to try. *I wish Dr. Carrow weren't so stupid. I wish the universe could speak to him, too. But I am the only one who hears the universe. I am the chosen one. It is my job to save everyone, but first I need to get him to believe me!*

"I can show the nurses to you. We need to stop them. They are going to kill everyone! You have to believe me!"

Dr. Carrow laughed coldly. "Why would I believe you, Lina? You are having an episode. Don't you remember the episode that got you sent here?"

"This isn't an episode! I'm not crazy!" Lina began jerking aggressively against her restraints. She felt the power of the universe pulsing through her. It was screaming at her. Lina wanted to scream too. She needed to get out of here. She needed to save everyone.

"Do not yell at me, Lina. This is an episode. You are wrong about the nurses, and you need to calm down."

"Please, PLEASE, you must listen. Everyone is going to die! PLEASE I need to save them!"

Dr. Carrow stared at her for quite some time before simply stating, "I'll come back when you are feeling cooperative," and he rose from his chair and left the room.

Lina's body was on fire. She was so angry at Dr. Carrow. Why was he so stupid? Why wouldn't he listen to her? She could feel herself shaking. She closed her eyes and called out to the universe. *I am so sorry. You chose me. I need to get out of here. I need him to come back. Send the doctor back. I will do better this time. I will convince him. Please. I want to save them all.* Her anger was beginning to turn liquid. She could feel the tears forming, and had she been looking in a mirror, she would have been able to watch her crazy eyes slowly fill with the tears of anger and failure.

For several days, Lina's anger only strengthened her determination. Even if no one believed her, she still had a responsibility to save them. She couldn't just let the enemy win. She fought against the restraints of her straight jacket. She fought and fought and fought until the fight started to leave and the doubt crept in. If she had been right, if the patients had really been poisoned, surely many would have died by now. But if patients were dying wouldn't they have realized Lina was right?

No one was dying.

No one was being poisoned.

It had all been in Lina's mind.

Her horrible, ugly, broken mind.

CHAPTER SEVEN

When the crash finally came, it was much worse than the first time. It engulfed her. Each cell in her body burned with the horror of what she had done. For three days, all she could see were Bird's eyes filled with tears and fear- poor Bird who had already endured years of horrors and disappointment. Lina didn't sleep. She didn't speak. Instead, she let the shame gnaw at her just as she had the last time the depression came. On the fourth day, she began to cry. She cried and cried and wished she could die. Never in her life had she felt so low. Bird had been her one and only friend, and she had let her down. She had pushed Bird away and then shown her what a lunatic she really was. Just like Simon and Julie, Lina had entered Bird's life only to increase her suffering. She wretched at the thought of it, but there was no food in her body, so nothing but a burning trickle of bile escaped.

Lina willed her body to shrink into itself; she refused to eat the food they brought her. When Dr. Carrow came to see her, she sat in silence, refusing to look at him. She made the mistake of glancing at him once, and the disdain in his eyes was like a slap in the face. She could feel the heat of his mental hand stinging her, and she knew she could never unfeel the imaginary remnants of Dr. Carrow's angry handprint on her face.

For two weeks, Lina did not say a single word to anyone. On the fourteenth day of her crash, she sat staring at the door. She had run out of tears. The door slowly creaked open. She knew it would be an orderly or nurse. It was lunchtime, and someone was here to try to make her eat. A week ago, she had finally accepted the water they offered. She was weak and desperate and ashamed of herself for taking it. She didn't deserve water. Water meant life, and she wasn't worthy enough to live. She hated herself for being so weak, but at least she would not be weak enough to eat. Not even the hollow desperation of her stomach could withstand the shame that consumed her – the shame that reminded her of her worthlessness.

Without thinking, Lina glanced up to see who was bringing her food. She recognized him immediately. It was the orderly with kind blue eyes. The one who had been there when they sedated her. Her shame squirmed uncomfortably at the kindness she still saw in his eyes.

"Hello," he said. His voice was gentle and soothing. "Would you like to eat today?"

She only stared at him.

"Would you like something to drink?"

She looked down but gave the slightest nod.

He gently raised the glass to her lips, and she drank swiftly.

"Are you sure you don't want to eat?"

She looked at the tray of food. The bread looked dry and the stew looked cold. She shook her head.

The orderly sat across from her in silence. He was watching her; she could feel it. She kept her head down.

"Your name is Lina, right?"

She made no response.

"Lina." He paused and she could feel his gaze intensify. "I really think you should eat."

She closed her eyes and shook her head. She wasn't going to eat. She didn't deserve to eat. She didn't deserve this man being nice to her. She bit her lip hard and tasted blood. She wanted him to leave. She was too ashamed to accept his decency. There was no room in her darkness for someone kind. She looked down at her gown with its urine stains all along the bottom. They still hadn't removed the straight jacket, so she couldn't lift up her gown to use the toilet, and for the first eleven days she hadn't even bothered to try using the toilet at all. For the first time, she became aware of how rancid she smelled and how revolting she must be. She bit her lip even harder.

"Lina?"

A drop of blood escaped from her lip. It slid down her chin and onto the floor. The orderly saw it. He reached forward and forced her head up. She strained to turn away. More blood was dripping down her chin.

"Lina, please stop. I won't make you eat. I'll leave. But please stop hurting yourself."

She stopped straining and looked at him. His eyes were worried. She turned her head and wiped her bloody chin on her shoulder.

"Thank you." He wiped a spot of blood from her chin, got up and left.

Lina sat in her chair for a long time. She focused on the shame that was burning a hole inside of her. For many hours, she focused only on that, but eventually thoughts about the orderly crept in. He knew her name. He had used her name. He had been nice to her. Why? Why didn't he hate her? He should, and yet he didn't seem to. She turned her head and looked at the dried specks of blood on her straitjacket. He had been worried about her. He didn't think she deserved to be in pain. She let her tongue slide across her wounded lip and felt the shame subside just a little.

At some point in time, Lina fell asleep. She became aware of this fact when the sound of the door opening woke her up. It was Dr. Carrow. His eyes took in the blood on her shoulder, and he pursed his lips.

"Come with me."

Carrow grabbed Lina's shoulder and led her down a hallway. They entered a room she had never been in before. In the room was a machine, a nurse, and an orderly. The orderly removed her straitjacket and strapped her into a chair. Lina was aware that something unpleasant was going to happen, but she didn't care. She didn't have the energy to care. The nurse connected Lina to the machine as Dr. Carrow watched. She thought she saw him and the orderly exchange a smile, but she wasn't sure. Lina closed her eyes and soon felt electricity filling her body. She began to shake and then she blacked out.

Lina woke up on the floor by her chair. She felt disoriented. She felt as though Dr. Carrow had been there, but she was exhausted and couldn't really remember. She drifted back to sleep, only mildly aware that she was no longer wearing her urine-soaked gown and was instead wearing a clean one. A while later, Lina woke up again. She felt much better than she had before. The painful, searing shame had subsided. She lay staring up at the ceiling. She no longer wanted to die. Without the constant shame and desire for death demanding her attention, Lina began to grow bored. It felt as if an entire week passed while she stared at the ceiling. She slept again, but only briefly, and then continued to lie there awake, waiting. Sometimes they missed a day of bringing her food, but she knew someone would come eventually.

Someone came. She heard the door opening. She turned her head. It was him. It was the kind orderly. Lina felt a flicker of emotion she didn't recognize.

"Hello, Lina." The orderly smiled.

She sat up in her bed. He brought the food over and sat next to her. He raised the cup to her and simply asked, "Drink?" She nodded. She drank quickly. She drank too fast; she began coughing. He raised his hand and patted her gently on the back for a moment until the coughing went away.

"Would you like to try again?" he asked.

Lina turned and looked at him. She looked at his face and at his hand holding the cup. She nodded again. She drank more slowly this time and finished the whole cup.

"Very good," he said, and Lina thought he sounded genuinely proud of her. "I don't suppose you want to eat?"

Lina was surprised that his offer actually appealed to her, but she was still unsure.

"Just one bite," he whispered. "I won't tell anyone."

She looked at the pile of potatoes on the tray in front of her. Betraying her, her stomach growled. The orderly heard it.

"Lina, if you eat just some of these potatoes I will go straight to Dr. Carrow and see if we can get that straitjacket removed." He smiled slightly as he said it.

Lina couldn't help but perk up at that, if only a little. She had spent too long in this straitjacket, too long struggling against these restraints. She took a deep breath. The orderly was staring at her. She looked at his eyes. They were so kind. He was so kind. She opened her mouth. He smiled and gently fed her a spoonful of potatoes. She swallowed it. She ate four more bites before she had to stop. Her stomach was not ready for much food.

"That was very good, Lina. Thank you." He rose from his chair. "I have to go now, but I will see about the jacket and try to come back tomorrow."

As he was opening the door, almost as an afterthought, he added, "By the way, my name is Anders," and the door closed behind him.

Lina let his words drift into her ears. She relished the taste of his name in her mouth, hesitating to say it out loud for fear she would lose the flavor. His name was kind; his name cared about her. After several moments, she whispered it softly, speaking for the first time in two weeks. She said it again, louder this time and the name swirled around in the air. She imagined the swirling name for the rest of the day, and when she went to sleep, she seemed to feel it rest gently against her cheek.

Anders did come back the next day. It made her feel something. She wasn't sure if happy was the right word, but she did feel less dark when he was around. Being around him reminded her of the feeling she had when she was with Bird.

Suddenly Lina's heart fell. Thinking of Bird filled her with shame again, and she felt darkness creep back into her. She dropped her eyes. A few seconds later, she felt Anders sit in the chair next to her.

"Lina?"

She continued to look at the ground.

"Are you okay? Would you like to eat?"

She shook her head and shifted uncomfortably against her restraints.

Anders sat silently beside her for a few moments. "Lina, I have some bad news. Dr. Carrow said we can't remove the jacket yet. Perhaps if you eat again today, he will reconsider."

Still looking at the ground, Lina shook her head again. She had thought her body was all dried up, but she felt tears coming. Slowly, one escaped and dropped to the floor.

"Oh, Lina, I am so sorry."

Four more tears followed.

"I can talk to Dr. Carrow again today."

Lina shook her head again. She did not care about the straitjacket anymore. Her only concern was Bird. She felt so ashamed for hurting her. She had lied to Bird, never telling her the truth about herself. She had scared Bird and then left her alone. Her sweet Bird who didn't belong in this wretched asylum. Who knew how the poor girl was doing? Lina began to cry harder. It was becoming harder to breathe. She had almost forgotten Anders was there until she felt his hand on her shoulder.

"What can I do?" He sounded so sincere, so truly invested in taking care of her.

She was afraid to speak, but perhaps Anders could help her. He could check on Bird for her, make sure she was okay. She needed to speak. Through the tears, Lina managed to croak out one word.

"Bird."

"What?" asked Anders.

The tears had lessened. "Bird. She's all alone. I frightened her and now she is alone."

"Who is Bird?" He asked.

"My friend…well she used to be my friend, I don't know about anymore. Can you make sure she is okay? Please?" Lina begged.

She knew it was a big request. She knew he would probably say no. He didn't have time to search for one small girl among hundreds of lunatics.

"Is she the girl you sit by the potato garden with?" Lina looked up at him, and he seemed almost as surprised as she was that he had said it.

Lina stared at him. She didn't know what to say, but she nodded.

"I've noticed you sitting there. It's kind of hard to miss. You two were there every day." Anders rubbed the back of his neck as he spoke.

She looked at him very closely now. She wondered how he had ended up working here. He was so different from everyone else.

"I'll look for her."

"Thank you," she said quietly.

Lina anxiously awaited Anders' return the next day. But when he walked in, she could tell by his eyes that he didn't have good news.

"I haven't found her yet. I'm sorry," he said, confirming what she already knew.

"It's a big asylum," Lina responded, and even though she knew it was true and that the chances of Anders finding Bird in one day were very slim, her heart ached at his news.

They were both very quiet as Anders fed her soup. When he was finished, the spoon slipped from his hand and fell onto Lina's lap.

"Sorry," he said as he retrieved it carefully.

He set the spoon back on the tray and then got up to leave. "I'll keep looking," he said as he walked out the door.

The next three days brought no Anders. Instead, all she saw was a tall, thin nurse and a cruel-eyed Dr. Carrow.

"The orderly says you seem better," said Carrow.

"Yes, sir," whispered Lina. Ever since she had seen the overwhelming hate in his eyes, she had grown afraid of him. A man filled with that much hatred could not be trusted.

"Well good," he said gruffly, "we need you out of this room."

Dr. Carrow stared at her coldly for a long time and then got up and left. He left a chill of disdain behind him, and Lina shivered.

Her room was getting darker, and Lina knew it was time to sleep. The room still felt cold as she laid down and closed her eyes.

When Lina opened her eyes it was snowing. At first, she was excited. She loved the snow, but then she realized how cold she was. She looked down. She was wearing only her asylum gown, and she didn't have any shoes. Her toes were already turning blue. She started walking, hoping to find help.

"Hello," she shouted. "Is anyone there?"

She walked further, and the pain of her freezing toes caused her to cry. The tears froze on her cheeks. As she tried wiping them away, blood came with them. More tears came now and they mixed with the blood, forming painful red diamonds of ice that clung to her face.

"Help," she cried out as loud as she could. "I need help."

She thought she saw people up ahead, so she sped up, trying to reach them. The snow was thick on the ground, and she kept falling as she ran, but she didn't give up. She ran and ran until she reached the spot where the people should be, but no one was there. The snow was coming down harder now. Huge mounds of snow fell onto Lina's back, pushing her down. No longer able to stand, Lina crawled on her hands and knees, leaving a trail of blood behind her. She knew she wasn't going to survive much longer. She wanted to keep fighting, to keep looking for help, but she was tired. She couldn't do it. She curled up with her knees pulled close to her chest. The snow pounded against her head, and as it fell, Lina closed her eyes, hoping her death would be quick.

"Hello?" A voice called out.

It was Bird.

"Lina, are you there?" she yelled.

Lina tried to call out to her, but her mouth was frozen shut. She hoped Bird would spot her lying on the ground, but when she opened her eyes, she realized she was buried deep beneath the snow.

She tried desperately to move. She mustered every ounce of her strength, but she was no match for her icy grave. She cried snowflakes as the darkness came.

Lina's eyes shot open. She took several gasping breaths. For a moment, she was a child again, and she looked around for her parents to comfort her, but of course no one was there.

Her parents were long dead and she was alone, locked up in an asylum.

She never fell back asleep.

When the sun started peeking through the windows, Lina was finally able to feel some relief. She was still shaken by her nightmare, but freed from the pitch black of the night, it was easier to push the fear aside.

Lina shifted anxiously in her straitjacket, hoping someone would come soon. She wanted it to be Anders. She was desperate for news about Bird. Time stretched on, and still no one came. The long hours of silence weighed on Lina, and she clicked her tongue against the roof of her mouth just to hear a sound.

Finally, she saw the door handle begin to turn. When she realized it was Anders coming through the door, her heart jumped. His lips curled into a smile as he said hello.

"I have good news. I found Bird. I talked to her for a long time yesterday. She's been very worried about you."

"Is she okay?"

"She's fine, but she misses you a lot. She wanted me to tell you that she misses her friend."

There were tears in Lina's eyes. "She doesn't hate me?"

"Of course not," he said gently as he rested a hand on her shoulder.

Lina was filled with several emotions at once. She stared at Anders, not sure what she wanted to say.

"Thank you." It was all she could manage.

Anders smiled. "I have more good news for you. I get to remove the jacket."

Lina's smile grew wider. Anders undid the restraints that had bound her for so long now. Her arms felt strange, and Lina was afraid the aching would never go away. Slowly she stretched one arm and then another.

"Better?"

Lina nodded and lifted her arms over her head. Anders watched her for a moment and then stood up quickly.

"I have to go now. Be good, Lina. I'll see you soon."

The rest of the day passed quickly. It was amazing what a difference it made being able to use one's arms. When night came, she fell asleep flat on her back with her arms spread out wide, as if she were trying to fly.

Lina awoke the next morning to the door opening. At first, she was hopeful, thinking of Anders, but there stood Dr. Carrow instead.

"Get up, Lina."

She quickly got up and stood in front of him with her head down.

"I'm going to let you out of the room today. Don't make me regret this."

Dr. Carrow escorted her out of the room and down to the dining hall.

"Breakfast is starting," he said as he walked away.

Lina tentatively entered the dining hall; she looked around hoping to find Bird, and also hoping to find Anders. Anders had said Bird missed her. Lina had not thought that was possible, and she wanted to see if it was true. After several moments, she spotted Bird sitting alone at a table in the corner. Lina headed that direction. When she was about four feet away, Bird noticed her.

"Bird, I am so sorry. I should have told you the truth. I should have told you why I was sent here. I swear to you, Bird, I am not crazy all the time. I don't know why it happens. I don't know why I have these episodes. I am so – I am just so so sorry." Lina said it very quickly.

Slowly, Bird stood up. She didn't say a word. She just came forward and gave Lina a hug. Lina hugged her back, and the last little bit of shame clinging inside of her disappeared.

"I missed you so much, Lina. You were gone for so long."

"I know, I know, but I am back now, and I will never leave you again, Bird. I promise." And she meant it.

Lina was glad to be back with Bird. She had missed her so much.

Chapter Eight

The next day, Bird had to go see her doctor, so Lina was left alone. She wandered the halls and did her best to avoid talking to any of the other asylum residents. The place was crawling with lunatics and there was very little supervision. Many had illnesses that were left untreated, and the asylum cemetery was where most of the patients ended up. It truly was a miserable place, a miserable place only made bearable by Bird, and if Lina was being honest, Anders. Lina wanted to see him again very badly. She missed him. She looked around to make sure no one was around and whispered his name again. It felt warm, and she caught it in her hands. After a moment she let the name go and slid down the wall to sit on the floor.

Lina continued to sit in the hallway for quite a while. She had probably missed lunch, but she didn't really care. Eventually, she figured it had been long enough for Bird to be finished with her doctor and headed to the garden. Bird and Lina always met there. She arrived to find Bird already there.

"I think I would like to paint." Bird spoke quickly and quietly.

"Paint?"

"I know there's no way to paint here. It's just a thing I hope to do someday." Bird was looking firmly at her feet.

"I bet you would be a wonderful painter." She lifted Bird's face gently up.

Bird smiled with half her mouth. "Yeah?"

"Yes." Lina smiled. "In fact, why don't we practice?"

"How?"

"Come with me."

After a few minutes, Lina found what she was looking for.

She picked up a twig, broke it in two and held a half out to Bird.

"Your brush."

Bird smiled with her entire mouth, and the two of them knelt in the dirt.

Lina began drawing in the dirt and Bird followed suit. With nothing else to do and nowhere else to be, the girls spent the rest of the day making art in the asylum ground. When the night came and it was too dark to see, they stood up and walked back inside.

"Thank you, Lina.'

"Thank *you*, Bird."

As they lay on their mats that night, dirt still covering their clothes, Lina was able to imagine, for just a moment, that they weren't trapped in the asylum. She was able to imagine a sliver of a life not filled with darkness and lunacy. She was able to feel hopeful for a few glorious moments as she drifted off to sleep.

The next day was too quiet. Lina and Bird were walking together around the asylum grounds. They weren't talking. Sometimes there was nothing to talk about. The day was feeling long. Lina did not like days like this. They made her sad. They made her anxious. She understood that these days were going to happen. She understood there would not always be days spent drawing in the dirt. She understood that she and Bird would not always have things to talk about because when you spend almost every waking moment with the same person in a place where it was rare to come by an event that broke up the mundane routine of asylum life, there were times when no words could be found. She knew there were going to be long days of silence, but when the silence lasted too long, Lina's thoughts took over. She did not like to be left alone with her thoughts. They were filled with fear, sorrow and darkness, a darkness she thought she had long ago buried away. She would remember the days before Bird, the days when all she wanted was to die. She would panic, worrying that those days would come back, worrying that Bird would leave her, or that she would become too crazy and hurt Bird again. She worried she would have another episode, only the episode would never end. Lina felt her chest getting tight. The darkness was attempting to claw its way out. She needed to end the silence.

"Bird, can I ask you a question?"

"Of course."

"How crazy do you think I am? Be honest." Lina said it quietly, afraid of the answer.

Bird looked slightly taken aback. She tilted her head to the side and was silent for a time. "Only a little bit," She finally answered.

"Are you sure?" Lina asked, feeling desperate.

"Yes, I'm sure. Remember what you told me about eyes? Well, I can see your eyes and they are perfectly calm. Just because you might do something crazy every now and then, well, that doesn't make you very crazy." Bird smiled at her.

The words felt good to Lina. She didn't know if she believed them, but they felt good.

"Bird, I am so glad I met you."

"Me too, Lina."

When the sun started to go down, Lina and Bird headed inside for dinner. Lina felt better. Her dark thoughts were being pushed out. Unfortunately, much of that good feeling was taken from her when the two girls walked past Dr. Carrow. Bird was talking excitedly about something and didn't notice him, but Lina did. She was acutely aware of the hatred that emanated from Carrow's eyes. He was standing next to an orderly, and he was looking at them as if they were filth. The mental slap Lina had received from him several weeks ago seemed to burn again. She felt certain Bird would notice the handprint on her face. She didn't understand how Bird could be unaware of the change in the air. It was as if Dr. Carrow had filled the entire hallway with a thick fog of loathing. Lina turned away from him as quickly as she could and breathed carefully, worried she would choke on all the fog.

Lina tried hard to focus on what Bird was saying, but only managed to catch the last few words.

"Oh look, it's Anders."

Lina turned to look. She had seen Anders around since she had been released from her confinement, but only in passing. He had smiled at her in the hallways, but they had not spoken, even though she very much wanted to.

Bird and Lina got their food and sat at a table in the corner. Anders was standing against the wall one table away from them. Lina tried not to watch him. She forced her eyes down so that they wouldn't stray and betray her.

"Hello." He was standing by their table.

"Hello," Bird responded.

Lina looked up, but didn't say anything.

"How have you been?" He was looking at her; she knew she needed to respond.

"Fine." She glanced up briefly as the word dropped blandly out of her mouth, and then quickly looked back at her plate.

"And how about you, Bird?"

"I've been okay."

Lina could feel Bird's eyes on her. She was no doubt confused by Lina's behavior.

"Has either of you ever been to the library?" Anders asked.

"There's a library?" Lina looked up. She couldn't help herself. She loved reading. Before being locked up in the asylum, she had spent most of her days with books. Her uncle had a spectacular library. It had been the only good thing about growing up there. She had not even looked at a book since she finished reading *The Count of Monte Cristo* all those months ago. She hadn't known she could.

Seeing how excited she was, Anders responded gently, "Well, it's not much of a library. I think there are about ten books total there, but we do have one."

"Can we see it?" Bird asked.

Anders nodded. "Follow me."

Lina and Bird walked behind Anders as he took them to a room they had never been in before. There were some torn and discolored pillows on the floor and a table with six books on it. There were a few more on the floor next to what appeared to be a urine stain.

Despite the bleak atmosphere, Lina still felt excited. Even the worst library in the world was still a library. She walked over to the table and ran her finger down the stack of books.

Brave New World

Teeftallow

The Scarlet Letter

Finch's Fortune

Macbeth

The Strange Case of Miss Annie Spragg

She didn't look at the ones on the floor. She grabbed *Brave New World* off the top of the pile.

"Can we take them out of the library?" Lina looked at Anders hopefully.

"I won't tell anyone if you do." Anders said.

It wasn't really an answer either way, but Lina didn't care.

"Bird, would you like to read one?" Lina asked.

"I don't know how to read." Bird sounded ashamed.

Lina tucked Bird's hair behind her ear. "We can read one together, okay?"

Bird nodded.

"Thank you, Anders," Lina said as she and Bird began walking out of the room.

"You're welcome." He smiled.

Anders stayed in the room as they walked away. Lina thought she felt him watching them, but she was too nervous to turn around and check.

For the next few weeks, Lina and Bird worked together reading the book. It was very slow going. They often stopped so that Lina could help Bird sound words out or Bird could learn the meaning of a word she had never heard before. Despite having had no education, Bird was very bright, and she began recognizing letters and words very quickly.

"You know, Bird, you're very smart," Lina said one day after they had stopped reading.

Bird blushed slightly.

"You really are. I promise."

"You really think so?"

"I do. I had many classmates who didn't pick up on things nearly as quickly as you do. Oh Bird, I wish you could go to school. You would love it."

"I wish I could too," Bird said quietly.

It was sad then because Bird would never go to school. It was sad because Lina was supposed to be at Columbia. and now that would never happen. Unless there was a miracle, Lina and Bird would live their whole lives in the asylum. They both knew how this worked. You came in and you never left, and if the sad, pathetic souls who were trapped here didn't die off fast enough, it would become overcrowded.

Overcrowded.

That was one of the things Lina remembered the adults talking about when she was younger, when they would whisper, thinking she couldn't hear. She remembered her aunt's sister once mentioning the asylums. Lina had been in the other room eavesdropping.

"Do you think she's going to be like her mom?" The sister had asked.

"I have no idea. No one else on Dave's side of the family is ..." her aunt dropped her voice, "a lunatic, so let's hope not."

"Those asylums are so overcrowded as it is," her sister said, also in low voice that Lina had strained to hear. "My friend Jill's brother works as an orderly at one in Virginia, and he told her that the patients sometimes kill each other just so they can have a place to sit at dinner."

Her aunt had gasped, and Lina had run away from her hiding spot, not wanting to hear anymore.

Now, here with Bird in their asylum, Lina remembered the conversation. She remembered the terror it had caused her as she waited to see if she would go crazy like her mother and get sent to her death in an asylum. She reached out and grabbed Bird's hand. She had never seen anyone get killed in the asylum. She had to remind herself of that. Yes, Bird would never get to go to school and, yes, they would never leave this place, but at least they weren't killing each other for a place at the dinner table. She forced herself to cling to that thought as they finished their day and went to bed.

The next day, Bird was put on lunch duty. Lina went to the recreation room. She hadn't been there alone since she and Bird became friends. Sitting there silently waiting for Bird to finish, Lina was reminded of her months before Bird arrived. She sat in the same corner and watched the same loonies. She was studying a man across the room from her. She remembered him from before. He sat by himself as he always had, but while he used to sit in complete and utter silence – Lina distinctly remembered being entranced by how calmly he sat as he stared at the window – now every ounce of calm was gone. Instead he sat muttering angrily to himself, rocking and jerking back and forth. He looked very upset. Lina couldn't explain why, but she felt an urgent need to know what he was saying. She slowly made her way across the room. She planted herself as close to him as she dared and strained to hear him.

"Don't go on the table. Don't go to the lab. It's all very, very bad. Don't do it. Don't, don't, don't."

The man was rocking faster now with his arms around his knees.

"Listen to the doctor. No. Do what he says. No. Don't go on the table."

Suddenly the man turned his head. His wild eyes focused on Lina. He stopped rocking. His hand shot forward and grabbed her arm.

"Don't trust the doctor!"

Lina felt a cold chill creep from her toes all the way to the top of her head. His eyes burned into hers. Her arm tensed in fear. Finally, he let go of Lina and resumed rocking. Within an instant, he seemed to have forgotten she was there. She wanted to move away from him. She didn't want to be near him, but the chill was heavy, and it was hard for her to move. It took her a moment, but she managed to unfreeze her legs and crawl away from the man. She slinked back to her corner of the room and avoided looking in his direction. Lina held her hands in fists and slowly slid her thumbs back and forth across fingers. Back and forth, back and forth, just like the man with the wild eyes. She focused on her thumbs and waited for the nurse to come in and tell everyone lunch was ready.

Lina followed behind several lunatics as they made their way to the dining hall. She wished they would walk faster. She wanted to be with Bird. She wanted someone sane. She waited in line. She got her food. She found a table and waited for Bird. Bird smiled as she approached the table, and Lina felt better. She didn't feel afraid of the man anymore. She didn't want to tell Bird what had happened. Lina wanted to be strong. She wanted to be brave and to take care of Bird. She wanted to keep the lunacy surrounding her as far away as possible from the young girl, so she kept it inside and let herself enjoy Bird's sanity. After lunch, Lina and Bird went for a walk. They walked all around inside the asylum and then they walked outside. They walked all the way to the big brick wall that kept everyone trapped inside.

"I wish we could leave." Bird sighed.

"I wish that too, Bird. You don't belong here. You should be on the other side of the wall."

"You don't belong here either, Lina...you know that, right?" Bird looked at her.

Lina shrugged. "I guess."

Bird moved so that she was standing in front of Lina and said, "You really don't. Don't let this place make you think you're crazier than you really are."

Lina shifted and nodded her head to appease Bird, but she didn't really believe her, or maybe she did. She wasn't really sure anymore how she felt about her sanity.

Chapter Nine

Lina wasn't certain, but she felt that today might be her birthday. If she was right, that meant she was nineteen. Nineteen-years-old. If she had been outside of the asylum, she supposed she would be excited. She would have walked to the bakery two streets over and bought a cookie for herself. She had been doing that since she was thirteen. Her aunt and uncle had acknowledged her birthday, but it had never been a reason for a celebration. At first, when she was very little, she had been so jealous of the attention her two cousins got on their birthdays. There were decorations and so many treats and songs filling the house. Lina would eat the treats and sing the songs, but the treats never tasted right to her; they were tainted with jealousy and the knowledge that there would be no songs and no treats on her birthday. When her thirteenth birthday arrived, Lina decided not to be jealous anymore. She decided to make her birthday special for herself. She had a tiny bit of money from the allowance she was given for doing chores, and she took that money with her as she set out to make her birthday special. She had seen the bakery before, but had never gone in. That day she did. It smelled heavenly. Just standing inside the gloriously scented shop, Lina felt excited. She looked at all the treats on display. Her eyes were immediately drawn to a stack of cookies. The cookies were big and golden.

"What are those?" she had asked the man standing behind the counter.

"Peanut butter cookies." His voice had been big.

"Can I have one?"

"Have you got money?"

Lina had held out the coins in her hand and the man had taken them and replaced them with a marvelous peanut butter cookie. She had taken the cookie outside and walked to a park where she had eaten it slowly underneath a tree. It had tasted like happiness. She had licked her fingertips when she was done to make sure she enjoyed every last speck.

Every year after that, Lina did the same thing. She walked to the shop, bought her cookie from the baker, walked to the park, and ate it. It had made her birthdays special.

On her last birthday, the cookies had been smaller; the baker was not there. A woman stood behind the counter.

"Are you here for a peanut butter cookie?" the woman had asked.

Lina looked startled. "Yes."

"My husband told me about you. He said to watch for the girl with the long red hair. He said you would probably come in and that if you did, you would want a peanut butter cookie. I'm not very good at making peanut butter cookies. I'm sorry."

"He remembers me? Where is he? Your husband I mean."

The woman smiled. "Yes, he remembers you. He is at home – with two broken legs."

Lina's hand went to her mouth. "What happened?"

"He shot a sick horse and it fell on him."

Lina remembered that she had wanted to laugh. She knew it wasn't right, but it was the most ridiculous thing she had ever heard. She remembered the baker's wife smiling. "He went the whole war without being drafted and then when I finally think we are in the clear, he goes and does the stupidest thing he's ever done."

Lina stood silently with a smile hidden behind her lips.

"Is it your birthday?" the woman had asked.

"Yes," Lina responded.

"That's what we thought. Someone doesn't come in on the same day every year if the day isn't special." The woman picked up a cookie and handed it to Lina. "Happy Birthday, dear."

"Thank you," Lina said, holding out her money.

"No, no." The woman waved her hands. "It's a present."

Lina had gripped the cookie as her eyes got misty.

"What's wrong dear?"

"Oh nothing," Lina had responded, wiping the rim of her eye, "I've just... this is my first birthday present in a very very long time."

The woman had looked sad then. "Well, that's not right," she said as she walked around the counter.

"What do you usually do after you get your birthday cookie?" she had asked.

"I go and eat it in the park."

"Can I come with you?" the woman asked as she took off her apron.

"Don't you have to stay here?" Lina had asked.

"I can do whatever I want." The woman then grabbed a few more cookies, put them in a bag, led Lina out the door, and locked it behind them.

"To the park then," the woman said firmly.

Lina led the woman to the park and then to her tree and together they sat and ate the whole bag of cookies. Lina told the woman about her life, about living with her aunt and uncle. The woman, whose name turned out to be Hilda, told Lina all about her husband and their daughter. Lina remembered that sitting in the park that day eating slightly dry and overcooked peanut butter cookies had been the best day she had had since her parents' death. It gave her a tiny glimpse into what life could have been like had she been raised by people who loved and cared for her.

After they finished the cookies, Hilda gave Lina a hug and said, "From now on, Lina, come celebrate your birthday with me. My husband will be back next year, and he'll make us some good peanut butter cookies, okay?"

"Okay," Lina had responded. "Thank you so much. This was my best birthday in a very, very long time." Hilda then gave Lina a kiss on the forehead and headed back to her bakery.

As Lina lay in her asylum bed remembering Hilda, she hoped she was wrong. She hoped it wasn't her birthday. She thought of the baker and his wife and the peanut butter cookies and cried silent, hard tears until Bird woke up.

Lina knew her sadness was showing. She tried to act normal so that Bird wouldn't notice, but she couldn't do it. She kept thinking about Hilda and the batch of peanut butter cookies her husband would have prepared. She wondered if they were both at the shop, if the wife had come in special just for her, if she had remembered her day with Lina.

"Lina, are you okay?" Bird interrupted her thoughts.

"I think it's my birthday."

"Oh," was all that Bird said, and Lina could tell she understood. Lina knew that if Bird had any idea when her own birthday was, she would not feel happy about it either, not in a place like this.

"Do you want to go read?" Bird asked.

"I do."

Lina went and retrieved *Brave New Word* from under her mat, and the two girls walked outside to read. They lay down in the brown grass and Lina began reading aloud as Bird followed along. They continued like this for quite a while until a shadow came over them. Lina turned her head and saw Anders just as he opened his mouth to greet them.

"Hello there," he said smiling.

"Hello," they responded.

"How is the reading coming?" he asked.

"I like the book a lot so far," Bird said.

"And you, Lina?" He looked at her.

"I've read it before. I like it better this time though."

"I never finished it," Anders admitted.

"Why not?" Bird asked.

"I left my copy on a train and never bought another one."

"That's very sad," Bird said.

"Yes, it is."

"Do you want to read with us?" Bird asked, and Lina felt nervous.

"You don't mind?"

"Not at all," Bird said with crinkled, smiling eyes.

"What about you, Lina? Do you mind if I read with you?"

Lina looked at him, at his blue eyes, and all she could do was shake her head.

"Wonderful," he said as he moved to sit down next to Lina.

Lina was almost too nervous to continue reading. She knew she was saying the words, but her mind was not registering anything her mouth said. Her body was extremely aware of Anders, and her nervous hands struggled to hold the book steady.

Lina read the same passage twice and almost began to read it a third time before she realized what she was doing.

"Oh sorry," she stammered, her cheeks burning.

"That's okay," Anders said reassuringly. "Would you like me to take a turn reading?"

Lina nodded and handed him the book. His voice was clear and steady as he read. Lina found herself studying Anders as she listened. He looked close to her age, only a few years older. He was tall and skinny but still looked strong. He had faint freckles up and down his forearms and even a few on his cheeks. His hair was dark brown, and she suspected that if he let it grow a little longer, it would be curly. She liked the way he looked. She also liked the way he read. He didn't read too fast for Bird, and he often stopped to make sure she wasn't falling behind. Anders continued reading with them until another orderly called his name.

He stood up quickly and handed Lina the book. "I have to get back to work. I'll see you around."

Lina watched Anders as he walked away, and when she turned back around, Bird was staring at her and she was smiling.

"You don't look as sad anymore," was all Bird said.

Lina felt her cheeks warm, so she lowered her head and continued reading, focusing intently. In fact, she was so focused on the book that she did not notice Dr. Carrow watching her and Bird until he turned to walk away. Once she saw him, she put the book down and told Bird they should probably go back inside. She wondered how long he had been there. She wondered about this until she fell asleep that night with her mat moved extra close to Bird's.

Lina had to visit Dr. Carrow the next day. There wasn't much of a schedule as to how often or when you needed to see the doctor. A nurse or an orderly would simply come and find you and let you know when it was your turn. All of the lunatics in the asylum had numbered tags on their wrists. It was how the asylum staff knew which patient belonged to which doctor. Lina walked slowly behind the nurse as she led her to Dr. Carrow's office. With each step, Lina grew colder and colder, and her feet grew heavier and heavier. She could barely lift them by the time they reached the door. Was he going to say something about yesterday? Had he seen Anders with them? Was he angry? Was Anders going to be in trouble? Was Bird in trouble? Lina stepped inside to find Dr. Carrow sitting in his chair glaring at her. She sat stiffly in the uncomfortable metal chair across from him. Lina wished desperately that she had been assigned to a different doctor. She curled her toes and sat silently waiting for him to speak.

"Have you noticed anything interesting lately?"

She shook her head.

"No spies? No poison? No one trying to kill us?" His tone was mocking.

She shook her head again.

"Did you forget how to talk?" he sneered.

"No, sir."

"Good. So Lina, do you think you're getting *better?*" He stumbled over the word better as though it were a piece of rancid meat he had had the misfortune of putting in his mouth.

Lina surprised herself by answering, "Yes."

"Really?" Dr. Carrow looked her up and down.

"Yes."

"Oh, I seriously doubt that." Carrow laughed a cold laugh.

Lina looked down at the floor.

"Are you feeling depressed?" Carrow asked.

"No," Lina mumbled.

"Lina, don't lie to me. I've been watching you lately, and you have the stink of depression all over you. I'm going to recommend some electroshock treatment. That should perk you up."

Dr. Carrow picked up the phone. She could see his mouth moving, so she knew he was talking, but the moment he had mentioned electroshock, her ears had started buzzing. Fear welled up inside her.

"Good news, Lina. The room is available. Let's head over now, shall we?"

Dr. Carrow took her by the arm and led her out the door and down the hallway. Lina started crying. Something about this felt familiar, but she wasn't sure why.

"I knew you were depressed," he whispered in her ear.

They arrived at the room. Lina looked into Dr. Carrow's eyes and knew better than to resist. He was going to get his way. She sat very still while a nurse connected her to the machine. Lina looked at the doctor one more time. He was talking to the orderly in the room. She had seen them together before, but she couldn't remember when. Carrow turned and smiled a cruel smile as the nurse turned on the machine and Lina began convulsing.

Lina woke up alone on a mat. There were a few other loonies asleep in the room as well. She couldn't remember getting here, but she was very tired, so she closed her eyes and fell back asleep.

"Lina." Bird was shaking her arm. "Lina, wake up."

"Bird?" Lina asked sleepily.

"Where have you been?

"Huh?" Lina rubbed her eyes.

"I haven't seen you since this morning. Since you had to see your doctor. I was looking for you everywhere. We need to go have dinner."

"I'm not hungry. And besides, dinner's not for hours. I'm going to go back to sleep." Lina felt groggy.

"Lina, dinner is almost over." Bird started to sound worried.

"Oh." Lina pushed herself up so that she was sitting.

"Why are you so tired? Have you been in here all day?" Bird asked.

"Um, I don't know." When she stood up from her mat, she felt dizzy and quickly sat back down.

"Lina, are you okay?" Bird was looking at her with worry in her eyes.

Lina put her hand on her head to hold it steady, and as she did so she noticed a strange bruise spreading out around one of the veins on her forearm.

"Lina?" Bird's worry was filling the air around them.

"Sorry. I…I must be getting sick." She didn't know what was happening, and the strange bruise had her worried. She knew that if she told Bird that a mysterious bruise had appeared on her arm and that she had lost track of a whole day, Bird would undoubtedly think she was having an episode, so she lied. "I came in to take a nap after meeting with Dr. Carrow, and I must have slept for a lot longer than I thought I would. Sorry."

Lina felt Bird's worry lessen, though it didn't dissipate entirely.

"Should I get a nurse?" Bird asked.

"No, that's okay. I'm just going to rest a little longer. If I don't feel better tomorrow, I will go see a nurse." Lina forced a smile.

"Okay. Do you want me to stay with you?" Bird asked.

"I'll be fine. Go have dinner. I'll be here when you get back." Lina held Bird's gaze to assure her of her sanity. After a moment, Bird seemed satisfied and left for dinner.

Lina waited until Bird was out of the room before she got to the bathroom as quickly as possible and threw up. Why couldn't she remember an entire day? Where did this bruise come from? Now that she had been awake longer, she was aware of a brutal ache that consumed her entire bruised arm. Her face felt clammy, but her neck felt as if it were on fire. Lina had no idea what was going on, and it terrified her. She threw up again. She sat on the floor in front of the toilet until her terror subsided, and then she wiped her mouth and shuffled back to her mat. She laid down and curled up in a ball with her knees pressed tightly to her chest. She knew she needed to pull herself together before Bird came back, so she gently rocked her knees back and forth as she tried to focus on something far away from whatever had happened that day. It didn't work. She just kept trying to piece together any memory of the day she could find. When she heard footsteps coming toward her, she closed her eyes and pretended to sleep. She didn't think she would be able to face Bird without worrying her all over again.

At some point, Lina really did fall asleep. She woke up, and for the tiniest moment forgot about the previous day. Then reality set in and she felt sick again. She rolled over and saw Bird sleeping on the mat next to her. This helped her feel better. Once Bird woke up, they could find a way to distract Lina. They would eat, take a walk, read and find simple ways to pass the day like they always did. A routine was something to cling to; a routine would help her not to think about the bruise and the vomiting. A routine would keep her sane.

Clinging to this thought, Lina waited patiently for Bird to wake up. She counted cracks on the ceiling and listened to Bird's breathing until she opened her eyes.

"Good morning," Lina said.

"Good morning," Bird replied.

Lina did not want to eat anything for breakfast, but she forced herself to. She moved the cold mush around with her spoon, occasionally forcing down a bite. She lied and told Bird she felt better, and Bird believed her. She walked side by side with Bird around the asylum and pretended that she couldn't feel the throbbing in her arm. She kept her sleeve pulled down so that Bird wouldn't see the bruise. She played the role she needed to play to stick to the routine. She only allowed herself one break from the routine – she allowed her eyes to search for Dr. Carrow, although she had no idea what she would do if she saw him. Perhaps she hoped seeing him would trigger some sort of memory from the day before. There were times she could have sworn she was feeling his icy stare, but when she turned to look, the only people around were the other loonies, oblivious to her presence.

Amid this inner turmoil, she made sure she carried on a conversation with Bird. Bird told her about a lunatic man she had heard singing the day before.

"I haven't heard much singing, but I think it was good. It was in a language I didn't know, but I liked it just the same."

"I wish I had heard it," Lina said, which was true. She wished dreadfully that she had spent the day with Bird yesterday, that she had been with her to hear the foreigner singing.

"I really hope we can find him again," Bird said.

"That would be wonderful."

After they grew tired of walking, Lina and Bird sat down to read. They read until it was time for dinner, and then went for another walk. This walk was more silent, but that was ok. It still fit into the routine, and Lina was grateful for that. This silence was normal. This silence was expected. This silence didn't make her anxious.

Bird broke the silence.

"I talked to Anders at dinner yesterday."

Lina listened intently.

"He told me about an aunt of his who runs a school for girls." The way Bird said it made Lina wonder why Bird had waited all day to tell her this.

"Oh really?" Lina asked, unable to explain the extreme panic bubbling up inside her.

"Yeah," Bird answered while chewing on her lip.

"Why do you…." Lina began. "I mean, do you have any idea why he was telling you about his aunt and her school?"

"I don't really know. He had to leave before he could say much more." Bird shrugged, but the shrug seemed forced. Lina felt that she was hiding something.

"Did you talk about anything else?"

"Not really."

"He just stopped by to tell you about his aunt and then left? That's very odd. Don't you think so?" Lina asked.

"I don't know," Bird said the words quietly.

Their silence resumed, only this time it wasn't normal. Lina didn't like it.

The silence, broken only a few times with clumsy words, lasted until they went to sleep.

When the girls woke up the next day, it didn't feel awkward to Lina anymore. The strange conversation from the night before was left in the past, and they went about their day as usual. They walked and they sat down to read. They were almost finished with *Brave New World*. There was only one chapter left. They were sitting against the wall surrounding the asylum grounds.

"May I join you ladies?"

The girls looked up, not a little surprised to see Anders standing in front of them. Lina stared up at him, seeming not to remember that a reply was in order. Fortunately, Bird had more presence of mind.

"Of course you can," she said.

Bird was reading that day. Lina had to help with a lot of words, so the reading was much slower, but Anders didn't seem to mind. Lina could not help letting her eyes wander over to him. Her hands were sweaty, and she couldn't stop playing with the hem of her sleeve. She was glad Bird was sitting in between them so that she didn't have to sit too close to him. She liked having him around, but he made her incredibly nervous. Lina was so focused on her unpleasant nerves that she realized too late that Bird had asked her a question. Bird turned to ask Anders. His eyes were closed. They had been since he sat down.

"Anders?" Bird said softly.

He opened his eyes. "Yeah?"

Bird asked him the meaning of a word.

Anders explained it to her and she continued reading.

After that, Lina tried very hard to focus on the book and not on her proximity to Anders, or the nerves he induced in her.

Eventually, it began to grow dark, so Bird closed the book, and the three of them headed back inside. Bird was walking slightly ahead of Lina and Anders.

"Hey you," an orderly called to Bird. He looked familiar to Lina, and she tried to remember why. He was tall, with broad shoulders, and there was an overwhelming boorishness to him. His blonde hair was cut extremely short, and his nose looked as if it had been broken more than once.

Bird stopped and looked at him, pointing to herself questioningly.

"Yeah, you. We need one more to help with dinner." His voice was hard, and Lina suddenly remembered where she had seen him. He had been with Dr. Carrow, though she couldn't quite think of when.

"I'll come too," said Lina. She wanted to stay with Bird.

"Not this time," the orderly said, and the look in his eyes made her feel uncomfortable.

"Please," Lina asked.

"No. There isn't enough room for both of you."

Lina began to pull nervously on her hair. She was filled with an urgent need to stay with Bird.

Anders looked over at Lina reassuringly and spoke up. "These two are friends. Are you sure they can't stick together?"

"Friends? You think they know what those are?" the orderly laughed.

Anders didn't.

"Come on, Sam. Let them both go." Anders knew the other orderly.

"Okay, okay. Anders, you're too soft. Come on tics. Let's put you to work."

Lina and Bird followed behind Sam. Anders watched them and then followed them from a distance. Once Sam dropped them off at the kitchen, Anders left and went down a different hallway.

Lina and Bird stepped inside the kitchen.

Dinner was almost finished.

"What are you doing here?" an angry looking cook asked them.

"We were told to come and help," said Lina.

"We don't need any help. Go wait for your food with everyone else." The cook shooed them out.

Lina and Bird left the kitchen. Lina felt something heavy inside her chest. She looked at Bird. Bird looked confused.

"What now?" Bird asked.

"I don't know. I guess we just go to the dining hall." Lina tried to hide her nerves.

Lina walked behind Bird and pulled up her sleeve to look at her bruise. She couldn't shake the feeling that Sam had been a part of her lost day. She knew for certain she had seen him with Carrow more than once. Did he give her the bruise? Lina didn't think Sam had really planned on taking Bird to the kitchen. Why had he wanted her alone? Lina was feeling sick again. Something was going on, and she needed to find out what it was.

Chapter Ten

Lina hardly slept that night. Every time she started to fall asleep, she would think of Sam trying to trick Bird into going with him, and she would open her eyes to make sure Bird was still on her mat. When morning finally came, Lina was certain that she hadn't slept for more than ten minutes at a stretch. Her eyelids felt heavy, and her head was pounding.

After they finished eating breakfast, Lina said, "Let's go to the rec room today."

Bird scrunched her nose but complied.

Lina was nervous as they navigated – afraid someone would try to separate them – but they made it safely to the room. Once in the room, Lina felt safe. The room was crowded with lunatics and various nurses and orderlies. Lina knew no one could take Bird away from her in here. This room was not pleasant, but it was secure.

Lina convinced Bird to spend their days in the rec room for the rest of the week, but after that, Bird refused.

"I want to go outside, Lina."

Lina didn't like this. There were too many hallways to pass through on the way outside, too many chances for something bad to happen, but she didn't know what else to do. She didn't want Bird to think she was crazy, and she didn't want to drive her away. They went outside.

They walked around outside for a while with Lina's eyes constantly searching for any threats. Her heart sped up when she saw someone approaching them from far away. Was it Sam? Was it Dr. Carrow?

"Bird, let's go back inside," Lina said quickly.

"Why?" Bird stood still.

"I feel kind of dizzy," Lina lied.

"Why don't we go sit down in the shade?" Bird turned and looked at one of the trees on the asylum grounds.

"I...um...." Lina hurried to think of another lie.

"Lina, Bird!" Anders called out to them. He was the figure Lina had seen. The relief washed over her like a sudden downpour of much needed rain.

"I have something for the two of you," he said standing in front of them. He held out a book.

"Mary Poppins." Lina let Bird sound the title out.

"Have you read it, Lina?" Bird asked.

"I have. Thank you, Anders."

"You're welcome...I know it's more of a children's story, but I thought you might enjoy it." He handed it to Bird.

"Do you want to stay and read with us?" Lina felt uncomfortable asking this, but she felt safer with Anders around.

Anders smiled. "I would love to."

"Bird, do you want to try reading?" Lina asked.

Bird nodded and sat down. Lina let Anders sit down first, and then Lina sat on the other side of Bird.

Lina didn't know how it happened, but she had fallen asleep. She heard Bird and Anders talking quietly beside her.

"I think we should talk to your doctor about it," Anders was saying. "I can talk to my aunt, too."

Lina kept her eyes closed and her breathing steady. She felt Bird shift beside her.

"Do you really think...I mean, could it actually happen?" Bird asked.

"I honestly think it could."

There was a moment of silence, and then Anders spoke again, "Do you want me to talk to your doctor, to see if he wants to meet with you about it?"

Lina didn't hear anything, so she opened her eyes just barely and saw Bird give the slightest nod. She wondered what they were talking about.

She wondered if Bird would tell her about it after Anders left. Lina shifted, pretending she was waking up. She coughed and then pushed herself up. She could feel dirt on her cheek; she used the back of her hand to wipe it off.

"Sorry," Lina murmured.

"It's okay," Bird said with her eyes down.

"I probably need to get back to work," Anders said. He didn't look at Lina as he stood up and walked away.

Lina watched Bird, wondering if she was going to say anything about the conversation she had just overheard. Based on the way Bird was avoiding looking up, Lina didn't think so.

"We should probably get inside," Lina said.

Bird nodded, and the two of them walked back into the large, dark asylum and waited for the day to end.

That night, as Lina lay in bed, she replayed the conversation she'd overheard in her mind. She replayed it repeatedly as she worked out in her mind what it could mean. As realization dawned on her, she felt angry inside. Bird was going to leave. That's what it meant. Anders was going to take her away. She knew she should be excited for Bird; she knew Bird wasn't crazy and that she didn't belong here, but an unpleasant side of Lina still felt bitter and angry about the whole thing. It was an ugly side of her, and she didn't like it. Lina fought against herself, trying to shove the anger aside, until morning finally came.

Bird said nothing about the conversation. They ate breakfast in uncomfortable silence until Anders appeared.

"Bird, your doctor wants to see you. I'll take you."

"Okay," Bird said and stood up. Then she turned to Lina and opened her mouth to say something.

Lina cut her off. "I will be in the rec room when you're done."

"Are you sure?" Bird asked. "I don't know how long I'll be."

"I'm sure."

"Okay. I'll see you later."

Lina watched her leave. She hated herself for feeling angry at Bird and being so petty. Lina didn't want to be alone with herself, so she stood up and walked toward the rec room.

"Stop."

It was Sam.

"Come over here."

Lina obeyed.

"Where's your little friend?" His voice dripped with sarcasm.

Lina shrugged.

"I have a job for you. Follow me."

Lina didn't want to follow him. She knew she shouldn't. She stood still.

Sam took a couple steps before he noticed she wasn't coming.

"Get over here."

She shook her head and took a step backward.

"Don't you dare," he said, and he rushed toward her and grabbed her arm. He gripped it tight. "Come with me."

Sam dragged Lina behind him and led her into a dark room. There were two buckets in the middle of the floor.

"Clean the floors, tic." Sam said as he shoved her towards the buckets. One was filled with water. The other one, she didn't know what it was, but it smelled terrible. There were no rags or sponges, only buckets. She glanced at Sam. He was leering at her, blocking the door. She dipped her sleeve into the bucket of water and began scrubbing the floor. She moved around the floor on her hands and knees, hoping that Sam would stay where he was, hoping he would leave her alone as long as she kept working. She felt something wet hit her face. She was sure it was spit.

"Get over here," Sam ordered.

Lina wasn't finished cleaning the floor. Her chest felt tight as she stood up and walked over to Sam.

"There's something on my shoe. Get it off."

Lina knew it was pointless to resist his command, so she knelt down and used her sleeve to wipe Sam's shoe. Her whole body was shaking. Suddenly Sam yanked her up by her hair. He put his mouth close to her ear and hissed, "I could kill you, tic, and no one would care."

Lina didn't say anything. What could she say? Sam was still gripping her hair. He lifted his other hand and slapped her as hard as he could right across her face.

"Don't get in my way ever again," he said as he walked out of the room.

Lina slumped to the floor. Her body was shaking even harder now, and she felt tears dripping down her face. She bit her fist so that the crying would make no sound. She didn't know if Sam was still on the other side of the door, and she didn't want him to hear her. She bit her fist so hard she tasted blood. The pain distracted her from her fear. She stood up, wiped her fist on her gown and then ran a sleeve across her face to get rid of the tears. She opened the door just a crack. No one was around. She left the room and began walking.

Only one thought consumed her mind: Bird had to leave. Any betrayal she felt about Bird leaving was gone now. She needed to get Bird out of the asylum and away from Sam. She needed to do it as soon as possible. Lina wouldn't be able to keep her safe here; she couldn't even keep herself safe.

Lina knew who she was looking for. She just didn't know where to look. She checked the dining room. She walked down every hallway she saw. Finally, she went outside. There he was.

"Anders," she shouted.

He didn't hear her. She ran toward him.

"Anders!" This time he heard.

"Lina…hi." He stopped and looked at her. "What happened to your face? Are you okay?"

"It's nothing. Anders I…"

He cut her off. "It's not nothing. You have a bruise covering your face. What happened?"

She ignored him. "You need to get Bird out of here. That school – the one you told her about – you want her to go there, right? That's why she's talking to her doctor, right? You set it up."

"How do you know about that?"

"Anders, you need to make sure she goes to that school, okay?"

"Lina, what's going on? Are you okay?" Anders asked again, his eyes wide.

"Don't worry about me. The only thing I need is for Bird to go to that school." Lina felt tears welling up. She fought to keep them from escaping. "You can get her there, can't you? She's not crazy. She can go. She doesn't belong here."

"It's not that easy, Lina. First Dr. Ferrell needs to okay it, and then all of the other doctors need to okay it, and then I need to work it out with my aunt."

"But I heard you. You told Bird you thought it could work."

"When...? Oh, you heard that?" Anders seemed surprised.

"Yes."

"I thought you were sleeping."

"I woke up. Anders, please. You need to make it happen. Bird isn't crazy. You know that. I'm sure her doctor knows that. Get her out of here. She has been unlucky her whole life and she deserves something good. This place will ruin her if she stays." Lina was desperate.

Anders looked at her, his eyes focused on the bruise. She wondered if it looked like a hand.

"Lina, will you tell me what happened to your face?" Anders asked.

"Will you get Bird out of here?" Lina asked in return.

"I'll try."

"You get her out, and then I'll tell you."

Lina didn't want to tell Anders about Sam. It would only make things worse. Anders would be upset, he would talk to Sam, and Sam would surely take it out on Lina, or worse he would take it out on Bird. Lina knew, even if Anders didn't, that no one else in the asylum would care if an orderly were roughing up a loony. Sam had been right; he probably could kill her without anyone caring. They would find Lina lying dead in some forgotten room and no one would do anything to investigate.

Anders looked at her for a long time. She could tell he wanted to say something, to ask more questions, but thankfully he didn't.

"Please," Lina pleaded.

"I'll do my best," Anders finally said.

Lina started to leave.

Anders grabbed her arm. "Lina, be careful."

Lina looked into Anders' blue eyes. They were full of worry. It made her sad. She felt bad for making Anders worry. She felt bad for making anyone worry, but she knew she needed help. She couldn't keep Bird safe all on her own. She needed Anders. She hoped desperately that he could help Bird escape the nightmare that Lina saw coming to life. Bird had lived through enough nightmares already.

"I will," Lina lied.

Lina left quickly before Anders could stop her again. She headed straight to the rec room. She didn't know if Bird would still be there, but it was her best guess. She walked quickly to the room. Her eyes flew across the faces crowded together until she found the one she wanted.

"Bird, hi," Lina said.

"Lina! What happened to you? Where were you? Are you okay?"

Seeing Bird so full of concern pained Lina's heart, "I'm fine," she lied again.

"Your face. Who did that?" Bird asked.

Lina reached up and touched her cheek. It was tender, "I fell down." Another lie, and not a very good one.

"You fell down?" Bird's voice was filled with disbelief.

"Yes." Lina had to stick to the lie now.

"No you didn't. What happened?"

"I was running outside, trying to get back here to meet you, and I tripped over a rock. I landed really hard."

Bird continued to stare at her. "You landed on your face?"

Lina shifted. She looked down at her fist. It was red and still had specks of blood from when she had bitten it earlier.

"I hurt my hand too. In the fall," Lina said, holding it out for Bird to see.

Bird looked at Lina's hand and then back at her face. Lina knew she still didn't believe her, but that was the best she could do.

"Why weren't you in here? Where did you go? You said you would be here." Bird was upset. Lina could tell Bird had been scared.

"I..." Lina paused, she didn't have a lie ready. Fortunately she was saved from having to find one.

"My arm!!!!!!!!!!!" screamed a lunatic. He was running around the room.

"Save my arm!!!!!!" He was waving his right arm all around "He's going to steal it!"

The man started sobbing as two orderlies rushed into the room and grabbed him, "Please....don't let him steal it. Please, please, please, please, please...."

The man continued to sob and plead as he was carried out of the room. Lina didn't want to watch, but she didn't want to look away either. The whole scene had lasted barely a minute, but Lina was shaken. He had sounded so scared, so sincere in his belief. Lina remembered how that felt. She remembered the orderlies grabbing her. She remembered the fear and anger she felt thinking no one believed her. She remembered "knowing" that what she thought was real, "knowing" the worst was coming because no one believed her. Watching the man, remembering this and understanding his fear, Lina couldn't help herself. She started to cry. When Bird noticed, she reached out and held Lina's hand. Bird held onto her tightly to let her know she was there, and even though Bird had never experienced it, and even though Bird wasn't even the least bit crazy, Lina knew that Bird understood. Bird understood why Lina was crying, and right now Bird was taking care of her. Bird was protecting Lina. This thought made her cry more. She wished she could make herself stop, but she had no control. She just had to wait until the tears ran out, until they all escaped and the last one dropped off her chin and onto the floor.

After that, Bird didn't ask Lina about her face anymore or about where she had been. They ate dinner in near silence and went to sleep shortly after. What else could they do? How else did you end a day like the one Lina had just had?

Lina didn't know what was going to happen tomorrow. She was nervous for the new day, and the nerves made her feel sick. Her bruised face felt warm against her mat and her thoughts were racing. Her heart still ached from watching the lunatic. The fear of having another episode weighed heavily on her chest. She didn't want to be like that man. That thought terrified her. She was also terrified of running into Sam again. Terrified of what he might do. She wondered if Anders had done anything that might help Bird get out of the asylum. She couldn't get her mind off it. Her legs felt restless. She needed to move. She couldn't stay in bed. She listened to see if Bird was asleep. Her breathing sounded steady. Lina sat up as quietly as she could and silently put her feet on the floor. She walked out of the room.

Lina walked through the dark asylum hallways. As she walked, she occasionally crossed paths with other loonies – ones who, like her, could not sleep. She tried not to look at them. Sometimes it was hard. Sometimes they yelled at her, sometimes they ran into her and sometimes she heard them crying. Lina had never been in the hallways at night. She had not had any idea that it was like this. She had thought the asylum was depressing during the days, but it was so much worse at night. She had yet to see an orderly, nurse or any other sort of asylum worker in any hallway. She wondered where they were. She knew they were around, knew there were people assigned to work every second of every day, but she could not find any of them.

These night time lunatics were left unsupervised as they roamed the halls, their desperation, anger, and madness filling up every inch of the asylum. The longer Lina stayed among them the emptier she felt. She was losing herself in their madness. She wrapped her arms around herself and walked outside. She couldn't stay trapped in the maze of hallways with them any longer, and she knew she wouldn't be able to sleep. The instant she walked outside, she took a deep breath. She hadn't noticed it was hard to breathe inside until she got outside. She filled her lungs with the cold night-time air. It burned her throat as she swallowed it down, but she didn't mind. It took Lina a moment to realize there was snow on the ground. She had nothing on her feet, and her toes felt like ice. She walked faster, hoping the movement would keep her warm. She walked until she came to a tree. There was not as much snow under the tree, so she curled her toes and stood there shivering.

She didn't know why, but for a brief second, huddled beneath the branches of the tree, she felt completely safe, but she knew that in reality she wasn't safe at all. The list of horrible things that could happen to her in this moment alone ranged from frostbitten toes to the appearance of Sam. She knew all of this, but still she felt safe, so for right now she was going to let herself feel that, even if it wasn't true. She would have time to worry and panic as soon as she moved. She would spend the rest of the night awake, filled with fear about what could happen. She would spend every second obsessing over Bird until Anders got her out, if he was able get her out at all. Lina had no idea whether he would succeed, but Lina pushed those thoughts away and stood breathing slowly underneath the tree. The wind picked up, and some snow fell from the tree branches onto Lina. It slid from the top of her head and down the side of her cheek and then dropped to the ground. Lina watched it fall. She knew that her false sense of security would soon be gone. She took one last worry-free breath, and then took a step out from under the tree.

Lina began walking back toward the asylum. The snow was falling again, so she started walking faster. As she realized how dark it was, panic began to overtake her. She found herself longing for the company of the lunatics she had fled from just a few moments ago. Her fears and worries pounded inside her head. They clawed at her, demanding to be heard. They seemed to feed off the thick darkness of the night. Lina squeezed her head tightly as she made her way back to the asylum, trying to keep the fears under control. She shoved open the doors to the asylum and quickly stepped inside. She must have been moving too fast because she tripped over the threshold. Her hands were still on her head and she landed hard on the asylum floors. She heard someone shuffling toward her. She peeked up and saw that it was the lunatic from the rec room – the one with the wild eyes, the one with the eerie warning. She suddenly felt colder than she had outside. She curled herself into a ball, hoping that if she could wrap herself up tight enough he would ignore her and go away. It didn't work. She felt him nudge her with his foot.

"Girlie," he whispered. "Girlie, hide. Don't walk alone where the Doctor can find you."

Lina shivered, but not because of his words, but because of his voice. He sounded calm. He sounded sane. Lina turned her head and looked at him. His eyes met hers and she gasped. They weren't the wild eyes she remembered from before. They looked tired and a little cloudy, but they were not the eyes of a mad man.

"Get back to bed," the man urged. "Don't let him find you. He wants to find you."

"Don't let who find me?" Lina asked, sitting up.

"The doctor." His hands started shaking.

Lina reached forward to take one of his hands in her own, "Which doctor? What will he do?"

The man opened his mouth to answer, but stopped. His head twitched to the side and he closed his eyes. He pulled his hand away from Lina and entwined it with his other. Lina watched and waited, not sure what to do. The man reopened his eyes slowly. They were once again wild and unhinged.

"Don't trust the doctor," the man croaked, and then ran away.

Lina quickly stood up and hurried back to her room. She lay down on her mat next to Bird and breathed deeply. She tried to calm her mind and sleep, but sleep never came. She spent the remainder of the night lying wide eyed in the suffocating darkness of the asylum.

When morning came, Lina felt drained. She couldn't remember the last time she had felt so tired. She had gone without sleep before. During her first episode she had hardly slept at all and she hadn't felt the least bit tired. But now she was exhausted. Her body and soul were worn ragged with worry. She had never been as concerned about someone as she was for Bird. She couldn't bear the feeling of powerlessness that consumed her. As she and Bird went about their day, Lina was constantly checking over her shoulder, watching and waiting for Sam to appear. She knew he had something horrible planned, and the thought made her sick.

Lina did not sleep for the next four nights. She lay on her mat paralyzed with worry. She was trying to hold herself together, trying to keep Bird from realizing that anything was wrong. She was worried about frightening Bird over Sam when there was nothing she could do about it, and she was also worried that Bird would just think she was going crazy again. It would be nearly impossible to trust a known lunatic when she spouted off a crazy idea to you. Lina needed to keep Bird close. She couldn't scare her away with her fears about Sam and Dr. Carrow. She had to keep those to herself. She had to keep her thoughts under control and keep Bird safe until Anders got her out. Anders had to get her out. He had to get Bird away from this place. He simply had to. There was no other option.

On the sixth day after Lina's encounter with Sam, Bird was summoned to her doctor once again. This made Lina hopeful. She could only assume Anders had arranged another meeting. Lina followed Bird to the office. She wanted to make sure she got there safely. She told Bird she was going to go for a walk and that she would find her later, but in reality she sat a few feet from the door watching and waiting. She chewed on her lip and stared at the door. She wondered what was happening on the other side. She hoped Bird would be leaving soon. She would miss her terribly, but it would be better to miss her knowing she was safe than to miss her because something awful had happened to her – in the heartbreaking way that she still missed her parents. That thought was unbearable, and she tried to shove it back down into the furthermost corner of her mind, back into the darkness it had crawled from. But it refused to go back, and instead Lina felt tears slipping down her cheeks.

Lina saw the door open slightly. She hurried around the corner so that Bird wouldn't see her crying and quickly wiped away her tears. She started walking slowly, knowing Bird would soon see her.

"Lina!"

Lina turned around and forced a smile. "There you are little Bird – just in time for lunch, and I'm starving!"

Bird smiled back and the two girls headed toward the dining hall.

"We should start another book," Bird said. "I like reading with you."

"I like it too."

After they finished eating, they went to get another book from the pitiful asylum library. Bird selected *The Scarlet Letter*, and they spent the rest of the day reading it.

That night as they lay on their mats, Bird rolled onto her side to face Lina. "It's nice having a best friend, or really any friend."

"I agree completely."

"Do you think we would still have become friends if we had met outside the asylum?" Bird asked.

"I would have wanted to be your friend no matter where we met."

"Do you think that if we had met outside of the asylum and become friends, well, do you think we would have stayed friends even if we didn't see each other for a very long time, like if one of us went on a trip and..." Bird stopped. Lina could tell she was starting to cry.

"Bird, you will forever be my friend, no matter what."

"Thank you for being my friend." Bird spoke softly.

"Of course, and thank you for being mine," Lina whispered back.

"Goodnight, Lina."

"Goodnight, Bird."

Lina listened to Bird as she fell asleep. She let herself grasp at a small sliver of hope. Bird seemed to think she was going to leave. That meant Anders really was keeping his promise. He was trying to get her out. Lina had to believe he would succeed. No honest doctor could deny Bird's sanity. All Bird needed was an advocate, and Anders was that advocate. He was the one thing none of the other loonies here had – someone trying to save them.

Lina's excitement over Bird's potential release and her anxiety over what would happen if Bird stayed swirled around inside her. The emotions clashed against each other. She couldn't stay on this mat any longer. Her body wouldn't let her. She lifted herself quietly off her mat and once again joined the nighttime lunatics. Despite her exhaustion, she moved aimlessly around the hallways, knowing she wouldn't be able to sleep if she made her way back to the sleeping quarters. She couldn't even hold still. As she walked through the asylum, she imagined her life without Bird here. She knew it was for the best, that it had to be done, but the thought of being without Bird still pained her. Without Bird, her life would return to endless hours spent in loneliness, a string of purposeless days. The panic rose up inside her. She had been so focused on taking care of Bird and keeping her safe that she hadn't let herself feel these things. Once again, she found herself outside in the frigid night. She walked quickly to the wall that surrounded the asylum. She rested her hand on it. If all went as she hoped, Bird would soon be on the other side of that wall. Bird would be safe, and that was what was most important. Lina would have to deal with the rest the best she could. The most important thing was to keep Bird safe. Lina's life would be hopeless no matter what, but Bird deserved more than that. Bird deserved an escape. Bird deserved happiness.

Lina took a deep breath and let cool air fill her body. Centering her thoughts solely on Bird's safety allowed the clashing to stop, and she turned to go back to her bed. Perhaps tonight she would actually be able to sleep. She desperately needed to. She quickened her pace so that she could lie down next to her friend. She wanted to soak up any time she had left with her. She would need good memories of Bird to look back on while she rotted away in the asylum.

Lina wondered if they would be able to finish reading *The Scarlet Letter* before Bird left. They were nearly half way through. The best part was the ending, and she wanted to be with Bird when she read it for the first time.

A little ahead of her, Lina saw something lying on the ground. She couldn't tell what it was. It hadn't been there before. Her heart started to beat more quickly. She wondered what it could be, so she approached the form. It was a person. Lina's heart was now pounding violently against her chest. She knelt down and turned the small body over. She screamed. She screamed as loud as she could.

"HELP!"

She tried to lift Bird's unconscious body off the ground, but her arms were shaking too much.

"HELP!!!"

Her eyes were burning. She began dragging Bird toward the asylum. She looked down at her beautiful, unconscious friend, and her heart broke. Right before the tears spilled out and blurred her vision entirely, Lina saw the bruise on Bird's scrawny arm. A bruise just like Lina had found on her own arm. It was big and angry and contrasted terribly against Bird's translucent skin. Choking back bile, she got Bird inside and screamed loudly and wildly until three orderlies appeared.

Chapter Eleven

Lina was inconsolable.

"She's still breathing," one of the orderlies said as he picked up Bird while another ran to make a call.

Lina couldn't stop screaming. A nurse came with a needle. Lina screamed louder.

"NO! NO! NO!" She pushed the nurse's hand away.

"A little help, please," the nurse said through gritted teeth.

Lina took off running. She ran after the orderly who was carrying Bird. She heard heavy footsteps behind her.

"SAVE HER!" Lina shouted, right as a big arm grabbed her from behind. She fought against it. Another smaller arm gripped Lina's wrist tightly.

"Hold her still, John," the nurse ordered.

Lina felt the orderly's hold on her tighten. She felt the needle go in.

"Please save her," Lina pleaded one more time before the darkness consumed her.

Line woke up surrounded by other lunatics. She was on a mat. She rolled over and looked at the spot where Bird usually should be. She wasn't there. Last night was real, not a nightmare. Lina jumped out of bed and ran out into the hallway. She stopped the first person she saw. It was a nurse.

"The girl from last night, where is she?" Lina asked.

"Go eat breakfast," the nurse snapped.

The nurse didn't even register Lina's question. Lina was sure the nurse saw her as nothing more than a rambling lunatic. Lina felt like a lunatic. She needed to find out what had happened to Bird. She needed someone who would know, someone who would tell her, someone who would actually listen to her. Every cell in her body hoped that Anders was on duty today, that Anders would be standing in the dining hall.

He wasn't there.

Lina's heart fell to the floor.

She stopped another orderly.

"A girl was unconscious last night." She tried to sound as sane as she could, "They took her somewhere. Do you know where?"

The orderly stared at her. He scratched his chin. "They sometimes send the really sick ones to the hospital."

The orderly walked away.

The hospital. Lina knew that was the best she was going to get for now. She wasn't going to get any more information until she found Anders. All she could do was wait for Anders, and so she did. For a day and a half Lina waited for Anders. She spent her time going to every place she usually saw him. She didn't talk to anyone. She was outside when she finally saw him. He waved and smiled. Lina was sure he didn't know what had happened.

Before he could even open his mouth to speak, the stored-up words came pouring out of Lina.

"I found Bird unconscious two nights ago. The orderlies took her somewhere. I don't know where. A nurse gave me something that knocked me out. Anders, I need to know where she is. I need to know what happened. I need to know if she's…." Lina couldn't say it, she couldn't say what she feared the most.

"Wait right here." That was all Anders said before he ran back into the asylum.

Lina sat down. She must have been sitting there for over an hour before Anders came back.

"She's at the hospital. She's still unconscious. The doctors don't know what's wrong, but she's stable." Anders said it quickly.

"Stable?" Lina looked at him questioningly.

"She's not getting any worse. She's not dying. The doctors will fix her." Anders said gently.

"Will they?" Lina felt tired and sad.

"They will." Anders was firm.

Lina let her head fall forward and rest in her hands.

Anders sat down beside her.

"She's going to be okay, Lina."

Lina turned and looked at Anders. She could feel her eyes growing desperate. "Anders, if she wakes up…if the doctors save her…she can't come back here. Can you make sure she doesn't come back?"

"Lina… " Anders sighed. He reached out to touch her hand, but she pulled it away.

"Don't let them bring her back here. Please? Do whatever you have to do, but DO NOT let Bird come back to the asylum." Lina's heart was pounding.

"I told you I would try."

Lina held up her hand. "Trying isn't enough. You can't let it happen. She can't come back here. She's been seeing her doctor, right? So he can let her out? Do whatever you must to convince him to send her to that school."

"I don't understand your urgency, Lina. What are you not telling me? You need to tell me what's going on." Anders said firmly.

Lina stood up. "If Bird comes back here, she will die."

With that, Lina took off running. She ran towards the asylum without thinking or looking. She didn't want to have to talk or think or explain herself because she knew Anders didn't understand what it meant to be stuck in here without any hope for the future. Nor did he understand the feeling Lina had deep in her bones that Bird was in real danger here. The running eased some of the tension in her body. As she relaxed, she closed her eyes briefly. Which is how she ran right into Dr. Carrow.

Grabbing her wrist, he said coldly, "I think it's time we had another visit."

Dr. Carrow grabbed Lina's wrist and led her to his office. He shoved her toward the cold metal chair in the middle of the room. He sat down behind his desk and stared at her. The seconds ticked by in agony as Lina waited for whatever was coming.

Dr. Carrow began speaking. His voice was cold and monotone.

"When I was a boy, I had a pet bird. It was a songbird; my aunt gave it to me. I was very fond of the bird. I used to sit and stroke its feathers every night after dinner. It was all very nice."

He paused. Lina had no idea what was going on, and she was too terrified of him to say anything.

"Most of the time, my parents ignored the bird. My father was usually at work and my mother was busy with the house. My sister, on the other hand, did not like the bird. I was never very fond of my sister; she was odd. No one else seemed to notice it, but I knew something was wrong with her."

Carrow lowered his voice and whispered. "Even then I knew how to spot a lunatic."

He returned to his tale.

"It was early in the morning and my bird was singing a lovely song. I went into the living room to feed it and saw my sister standing by the cage watching my bird. I said her name, but she didn't respond. She continued to watch my bird. She began to open the cage. I rushed forward to stop her. I did not trust her with my bird. She pushed me to the ground, took my bird out of the cage and twisted its neck. My sister dropped the bird back in its cage and then walked back to her room. I was left alone with my now dead bird."

Dr. Carrow stopped talking and for several moments stared at Lina, his face expressionless. The room felt cold. Lina felt like ice.

"Naturally, I told my parents what happened, and soon after that my sister was sent to an asylum. My parents got me a new bird and I never had to deal with that nasty sister of mine again."

He coughed. "That's why I work here now, to keep you lunatics in check. Because as I just told you, when lunatics step out of line something, like my beautiful bird...or that horrible, disgusting Bird of yours, will always get hurt."

He stared at Lina with dark, evil eyes, and the ice inside of her hardened and then shattered, and she was left filled with complete fear and utter hatred.

Dr. Carrow stood up from his chair and stood in front of Lina, looking down at her.

"Can I trust you to behave, Lina?"

She nodded stiffly, her throat filling with acid rage.

"Good. We are done for the day. You can leave."

Lina jumped out of her chair and left the room as fast as she could. She turned the corner. No one was around. She threw up. With no food in her stomach, all that came out was painful bile that set her throat on fire. When she was done, Lina wiped off her mouth and ran away before someone caught her sitting by the mess.

Whatever had happened to Bird had happened because of Dr. Carrow. Lina had been so worried about Sam that she had forgotten about what Dr. Carrow could do. He had done it to punish Lina, to keep her in check. He had done it simply because he could, simply because there was no one to stop him. Sam was terrifying, but Dr. Carrow was even worse. Lina felt completely powerless over Carrow. She was losing pieces of herself as she ran away. She could feel it, and she knew that's what Dr. Carrow wanted. He wanted to break her.

Lina ran outside. She ran until something hit her toe. The pain stopped her. It was a rock. She picked it up and anger welled up inside her. She drew her arm back to throw the rock at the building. She aimed for a window. She knew it was stupid and pointless, but she wanted to break something. She wanted to hurt the asylum the way Dr. Carrow was hurting her, but just as she was about to release the rock, she stopped. She let her arm fall to her side and slipped the rock into her pocket instead.

Chapter Twelve

The rock was heavy in Lina's pocket, and she fell asleep with it pressing against her leg. When Lina woke up the next morning she felt better than she had in a long time. She didn't feel afraid, and she didn't feel anxious. Instead, she felt that everything was going to be fine. Fine. Very fine. Bird was going to wake up, Anders was going to get her sent to the school, and nothing else bad was going to happen.

Lina spent the day watching lunatics in the rec room. She felt peaceful. She felt good. Nothing unusual happened that day. She didn't talk to anyone; she went to bed early and fell asleep easily.

Lina woke up the next morning feeling even better than the day before. She still had the rock in her pocket. She took it out. She held the rock in her hands and it seemed to vibrate. It was the rock; the rock had healed her. Lina looked around to make sure no one was watching and gently slipped the rock back into her pocket. She felt invincible. Lina knew it was only a matter of time until the doctors saw that she was healed. Soon she would get to leave. Bird would wake up, Lina would join her, and everything would be all right.

Lina was leaving the dining hall after breakfast when she saw Anders. He came and stood in front of her.

"I've been looking for you. Bird is still unconscious, but she hasn't gotten any worse. But Lina, I need to know what happened."

"It doesn't matter. She is going to wake up soon."

It was a fact. The rock rested against her leg, and Lina could feel its warmth through the thin fabric of her pocket. She knew she was right.

Lina was thinking about the rock and thinking about all the things she and Bird would do once they were both out of the asylum. The first thing they would do would be to get peanut butter cookies. Bird would like those. Bird would go to the school, and Lina would get a job. Anders would visit them when he wasn't working. It was going to be a very good life. Lina couldn't wait. She wondered if she should tell Anders about it. Not yet, she decided.

"Lina?" Anders was staring at her.

"Huh?" Lina looked back at him.

"Did you hear what I said?" Anders asked.

"No." Lina wanted to go outside. She was sick of the dark hallway. "I have to go." She walked away. She would have plenty of time to talk to Anders later.

Lina spent the next week waiting, waiting for the doctor to see that she was better. Dr. Carrow was mean, but once he saw how well she was doing, even he would have to say she could leave. She finished reading *The Scarlet Letter*. She couldn't wait to read it again with Bird. She spent a lot of time outside. It was easier to look at her rock out there. It wasn't as crowded as the hallways, so she didn't have to worry about wandering eyes and greedy lunatics who might try to steal it. She was holding it in her hand. It was soft and smooth. She liked that.

"Hi, Lina." It was Anders.

Lina quickly slipped the rock back into her pocket before he could see it.

"How are you doing?"

"I'm very well," she responded with a smile.

Anders looked at her differently than he normally did. Could he tell she was better? Did he like her the way she was starting to like him? The prospect thrilled her, and she reached into her pocket to check and make sure the rock was still there. It was, and it buzzed happily in her hand.

"That's...good," he said, looking slightly confused.

"Isn't it though? I have to go to dinner. Take care of yourself, Anders. I'll see you soon." She winked at him as she turned to walk away.

Lina noticed Anders watching her the next couple of days. He didn't approach her, but that was fine. Lina was simply biding her time until the doctors said she could leave; then she would explain everything to Anders.

A few days later, Anders approached her again. She was out in the garden reading a book.

"Lina, can I talk to you?"

"Oh, of course," Lina replied.

He sat next to her and she inhaled his scent. It was glorious.

"I'm not quite sure how to say this, I..." He trailed off.

Lina rested her hand on his. "Just say it, Anders." She put her other hand in her pocket and cupped the rock.

Anders looked down at her hand and swallowed. He gently slid his hand away, and Lina couldn't help but feel somewhat slighted. "Lina, I feel that I need to tell you this because I am hoping it might help. I believe you are having another episode."

"An episode?" she asked.

What is he talking about? Can't he tell I'm better. What a stupid thing to say.

"Yes...like with the nurses."

"No. I'm not."

Has he always been this dim? How could he possibly think I'm crazy? He doesn't understand anything.

"Lina, I'm not trying to make you angry."

"Then stop talking this way. I'm not crazy, I've been healed."

"What are you talking about?"

"It's not your..." Lina reached into her pocket and allowed her fingers to cling to the magic rock. "Not your business. I'm healed."

"Lina I'm trying to help," Anders said, and his voice grated on Lina.

"Stop. I don't need your....There is nothing wrong with me."

Lina could feel the anger bubbling up inside her and she wanted Anders to leave.

"Go away."

"Why don't we just go talk to Dr. Carrow?"

"No."

"Please, let's just go see him. He can help."

"Dr. Carrow is an idiot himself... He wouldn't...nobody would. I've been chosen. I've been healed. I am the lucky one and you just don't..."

Lina's mind was racing so fast her words could not keep up with her.

"I don't what?" Anders asked.

"Anders, you wouldn't understand. No one would understand."

The rock felt like fire in her hand. She needed to get away from Anders; the rock didn't like him. It was letting her know she needed to leave. Lina stood up quickly and began walking away.

"Lina!" Anders shouted at her.

She began running. The rock was burning her hand and she needed it to stop. She needed to get away from Anders. Then the rock would cool down. She needed to heed the rock. The rock was powerful, and it had chosen her. She didn't want to let it down.

She ran and ran and ran and finally the rock stopped burning. She was near the asylum cemetery. She didn't usually come here. Anders wouldn't look for her here. She was safe. Slowly she took the rock out of her pocket, careful that no one was watching, and rested it against her cheek. Its happy buzzing played a warm and peaceful melody against her skin.

After that, Lina tried as hard as she could to avoid Anders. The next morning she saw him standing near the garden, so she quickly ran back inside and went to the library. The library was nearly empty except for a surly looking nurse. Lina wished the nurse were not there. She desperately wanted to take the rock out of her pocket, but she was worried that if the nurse saw it, she would get jealous and want the rock for herself.

For over a month, Lina absorbed power from the rock. The rock was her best friend. At night she would cup it in her hands and let its cool surface rest on her lips as she fell asleep, although with the power of the rock she only needed to sleep for a few minutes at a time. She didn't talk to anyone unless she absolutely had to. Other people annoyed her; they were so simple, so stupid. She held onto the rock all the time. She would let its energy direct her. Sometimes the rock would burn, and she knew she needed to leave. When it burned, she would run and run until it stopped. She ate little. She didn't feel hungry with the rock around. She knew it was only a matter of time until she got to leave the asylum. She couldn't wait to see Bird again. Bird was the only person Lina felt that she could show the rock to. She trusted Bird; she knew Bird would not steal the rock because Bird was a good friend. She held the rock between her two hands and let her palms glide over it. The rock buzzed happily when she thought of Bird.

One night, Lina was assigned to help with dinner. Annoyance oozed from her pores. There was no way she could risk touching the rock in the tiny kitchen. Someone was bound to see – someone with crazy eyes and greedy hands. She worked quickly and sneaked out as soon as she could. She walked down the hallway. Almost everyone was waiting for dinner, and the halls were nearly empty. Her body ached to touch the rock again. She reached into her pocket to retrieve her mineral salvation. She couldn't feel it. Panic began to fill her lungs. She felt her other pocket, the rock was not there either. Her head was pounding. Her hands were sweaty. Where could it have gone? Lina felt sick. She began retracing her steps; her feverish eyes scanned the floor for her beloved rock. She stumbled into the kitchen, her eyes wide and searching. She didn't see it. Panic coursed through her veins. She went back out into the hallway to look for her rock. The longer she walked without finding the rock the more forced her breathing became. Her eyes were on the floor, and she shoved aside anyone who got in the way of her search. She didn't care about them. The only thing she cared about was the rock.

For a week Lina searched for her rock. She examined every inch of the hallway and every corner of every room. She combed the asylum grounds. The rock was gone, and so was Lina's confidence. She tried to cling to the power of the rock, but if the rock was so powerful, why was it not calling to her? She tried to pretend that what she had felt was real, but deep inside she knew it wasn't. She didn't want to admit it. She couldn't admit it. Admitting that the rock was nothing more than an ordinary rock meant admitting that not only was she not healed, she was insane. Anders had been right. She'd had another episode. She tried to push away the shame that was grasping at her, but it reached up from the ground and scratched at her ankles hoping to pull her down into despair. She picked up her pace hoping to outrun the shame.

Suddenly Lina collided with something. It was a person. It was two people.

"What are you doing?" an angry voice asked.

Simultaneously she heard a kinder, although startled voice.

"Lina?"

Dazed, Lina lifted her gaze to see Anders and a nurse staring at her. The nurse looked at her angrily, and Anders' eyes were filled with pity. The combination of Anders' pitiful eyes and the shame that was threatening to consume her was more than she could bear. Lina rested her hand on her chest. It was hurting. Her whole body was hurting. She felt sick.

"What's wrong with her?" the nurse asked Anders.

Anders ignored the nurse and reached forward to touch Lina's arm. She jerked away. She began to move away from them.

"Lina," Anders said again, "are you okay?"

Lina couldn't answer. There was too much pain in the hallway. She turned around and began to run. She felt tears on her face. She ran out of the building. She ran toward the cemetery.

Lina felt as if she couldn't breathe. All the shame and sadness and self-loathing were suffocating her. Lina collapsed to the ground. All she wanted in the whole world was to die right at that moment. She didn't want to move. She didn't want to get up. She didn't want to do anything. It was so hard to breathe that she decided to stop trying. She rolled over so that her face was buried in the ground. Dirt filled her nose. She closed her eyes and held her breath.

"LINA! LINA! WAKE UP!"

Someone was shouting at her. Her head felt light, but the rest of her body still hurt. She didn't want to open her eyes. She didn't care who was there trying to make her live again.

Hands began to shake her. They gripped her shoulders. The hands let go. They came back, but this time they were lifting her up. She was being held.

"Lina." The voice was desperate. She recognized the voice.

For a brief moment Lina opened her eyes and looked into Anders' blue ones. She closed her eyes and held her breath again. She wrapped her hands around her throat hoping to speed up the process. She didn't want to look at Anders; she didn't want to be near him. It hurt. Everything about him hurt her. She felt nothing but sorrow when Anders pried her hands off her throat. He looked at her with sad eyes.

"Lina, please stop." There was hurt in his voice.

Why did he care whether or not she lived? He shouldn't care. Lina didn't deserve to live. She was stupid and broken. Bird was lying unconscious in a hospital because of her. She missed Bird. She didn't even know what was happening with Bird. Was she still alive? Had Anders tried to tell her all those times she had hid from him?

She closed her eyes tight as hot tears leaked out and ran down her cheeks.

"Bird?" she asked. She didn't know if he heard her through all the tears.

"Bird is fine. She's at my aunt's school, Lina. Everything is going to be okay. I promise." Anders continued to hold her as she sobbed, and she was too tired to stop him. She cried all through the night. For hours Anders sat with her. He whispered soft words she couldn't understand. Lina knew the sun would be coming up soon. She feared the morning. She uttered one desperate sentence.

"Don't take me to Dr. Carrow."

Anders didn't say anything. Still holding her, he stood up and began walking. Lina didn't know where they were going. Anders carried her into the small shed near the edge of the asylum grounds. Lina had never been there before. He set her down and sat beside her.

"Leave," was all Lina said.

"I'm not leaving."

Lina was finished crying, and all she could focus on now was the shame she felt and the pain Anders caused by being near. She wanted him to go away. She didn't want him to see her so broken and pitiful. She didn't want him to feel sorry for her. She didn't want anyone to feel sorry for her. Lina shifted away from Anders.

"You have to go to work," she said.

"I'm not leaving, Lina."

"Please leave. Please.".

"No."

"LEAVE."

"Lina, I'm not leaving you here to kill yourself." Anders' voice was firm.

Amid all her shame and sorrow, this made her angry. What right did Anders have to stop her from doing whatever she wanted? It was no business of his whether she wished to live or die.

She narrowed her eyes at him. "Leave."

"No." He held her gaze.

Lina turned away from him. She wrapped her arms around her legs and rested her head on her knees. She dug her fingers into her legs. Her fingernails were long and they cut her. She dug them in deeper.

Anders pulled her hands into his and told her to stop.

She yanked her hands away, but she kept them in fists. Anders used his shirt sleeve to wipe away the blood that was dripping down her legs. After he was finished, he began to talk. Lina did not listen at first, but he kept talking. He told her about his family. His mother was from Norway and his father was from Minnesota. They had met when his father went to Norway for the summer with his friends. His mother baked him a chocolate cake every year for his birthday. He had an older sister. She had a son. He was four. She had a daughter. She was two. He talked about religion and faith. He whispered a prayer for her. Lina didn't want to let his words in, but she couldn't help it. His words were good. She still felt shame, but she didn't want to die as much anymore. Anders told her a story about his dog. He told her he wasn't very good at swimming, but he was all right at dancing. He talked for what seemed like hours without stopping. When Lina finally lifted her head up and looked at him, he stopped. He looked back at her.

"No more trying to die?" He asked.

She shook her head.

He stood up and offered her his hands to pull her up. She accepted. Before she could start to walk away, Anders pulled her into a hug. She kept her hands at her side. She still hated herself and Anders still hurt her. She didn't want to feel his hug.

Before releasing her he whispered, "I'm going to take care of you, Lina. I promise."

He let her go and she walked away.

Lina walked back into the asylum. She walked slowly. She felt heavy. She made her way to her bed. She didn't know what time of day it was. She didn't care. She collapsed heavily onto the mat and fell asleep.

When Lina finally woke up, she felt as if she had been asleep for a week. Her body felt stiff as if she hadn't used it in a long time. She didn't feel hungry, and she had no idea if it was time for a meal, so she made her way to the recreation room. Her insides hurt and she hated herself. She wanted to be around people crazier than herself. She reached the rec room and planted herself against the wall. Her eyes scanned the room looking for someone worse off than she was. It didn't take long. She saw several loonies mumbling angrily to themselves. She saw a man repeatedly smacking himself in the face. She saw an abundance of insanity. She allowed herself to wrap the insanity of the other lunatics around her like a safety blanket so that no one could see that she, too, was insane. She sat in the room all day until finally a nurse came and made them all go to bed.

Lina continued her pattern for the next few days. She woke up, went to the recreation room, and went to sleep. Often Anders would come to the room. He would stand by the wall and watch her. She knew if she left the room he would talk to her, and she didn't want that, so she did her best to ignore him. One day. he came forward and put a piece of bread in her hands.

"Eat it."

She waited until he was back on the other side of the room and then took a bite.

Lina's routine was finally interrupted when she was forced to help prepare lunch. She chopped carrots with hunched shoulders as she tried her best to keep the safety blanket of others' insanity wrapped around her. Once she finished her work, she left the kitchen and began heading back to her regular spot in the rec room. She didn't make it.

"Lina. I haven't seen you in a while."

Lina had no idea how she had missed the hatred emanating from this man and filling the hallway, but her heart turned to ice as she recognized Dr. Carrow's voice.

"Why don't we have a little chat?"

Lina hunched over even more and wished she could wither away. She didn't move.

"Lina." Dr. Carrow's voice grew darker.

She turned slightly to look at him. His eyes were burning with hatred and disgust. He gripped her shoulder and began leading her forward. Lina wasn't sure where they were going, but she knew it wasn't his office. Inside, Lina cried out for help. The words "Don't trust the doctor" ran through her head. They passed a few lunatics in the hall, but Lina knew they couldn't help her. She looked desperately around for a source of safety when suddenly, she saw Anders

"Hello, Doctor," he said, nodding to Dr. Carrow.

"Hello," Dr. Carrow said as he barely glanced Anders's way.

"Do you need help with this patient?"

"It's all right. I found her mumbling in the hallway. She seemed very confused. I'm just escorting her to the rec room," Carrow lied.

Lina lifted her eyes to Anders. She knew they were filled with fear, and she hoped Anders would notice.

"I can take her the rest of the way for you," Anders said.

"No, thank you. I can do it."

"Of course, Doctor, but surely you have more important things to do? Escorting a patient is generally left to an orderly."

Dr. Carrow shoved his thumb into the back of Lina's shoulder where Anders couldn't see. It hurt. Lina could tell Dr. Carrow was frustrated by Anders' persistence, and he was taking it out on her. She was grateful Anders knew she was afraid of Dr. Carrow, and recognized that at least today, Dr. Carrow wouldn't have the chance to hurt her any further.

"Don't cause any problems for the orderly," he said and shoved her forcefully towards Anders.

Anders took her hand and led her away from Dr. Carrow. Once they'd turned the corner, Anders took her into what seemed to be a broom closet.

"You're shaking," he said.

She was. She hadn't noticed.

"Lina, why are you so afraid of him?"

She didn't answer. She knew that listening to Anders was the price she had to pay for his saving her from Dr. Carrow, but that didn't mean she had to respond.

"Why won't you talk to me?" Anders asked. "Did he do something to you?"

She shook her head. Even if she had wanted to talk to Anders, she couldn't tell him why she was afraid of Dr. Carrow. Dr. Carrow could do horrible things. He could hurt the people Lina cared about.

Anders was silent for a long time.

"Bird is at my aunt's school," he finally said.

"I know. You told me," Lina responded.

Anders stared at her.

"Thank you," said Lina, and even though it didn't sound as if she meant it, she did.

"It's probationary," Anders said. "Dr. Ferrell said she could try it out, but if anything goes wrong, he's going to have her brought back."

"She can't come back here."

"You keep saying that. Why, Lina? What will happen if she comes back? Why was she unconscious in the first place? Why won't you tell me what's going on? You promised you would tell me what was going on if I got her into my aunt's school." Anders sounded upset. "I'm trying to take care of you, Lina, but you won't let me."

Anders was still holding her hand. She pulled it free.

Anders stepped in front of the door and slid to sit down. Lina knew this placement was intentional. He wasn't going to let her leave until she talked to him.

"I can't tell you Anders. It will make things worse. If you want to take care of me...if you want to help me, you will keep Bird away from this horrible place," Lina said.

"Lina..." Anders' voice was gentle again. "Are you...are you sure that whatever it is....I mean that it's real?"

On the last word Anders looked down. He seemed ashamed of his question, of having to ask the question.

"Real?" Lina felt as if she had been punched.

Did Anders just think this was all another delusion? How could he? Well, why wouldn't he? It's not as if Lina was a very reliable source. He had been there to pick up the pieces of two complete breakdowns. He had seen Lina at her worst. And he hadn't tried to get Lina out of the asylum, only Bird. Why hadn't she realized this before? Anders was nice, yes. Anders said he wanted to take care of Lina, but that didn't mean he thought she was different from everyone else here; she was just another loon with wild eyes and frantic ramblings to him.

Lina didn't know what else to say. She reached over Anders, opened the door, and stumbled out of the closet.

That night, for the first time in a long time, Lina was afraid of the dark. She hadn't been afraid since she was five or six. Her fear had begun after her parents died. She would lie in bed at night and cry quietly into her pillow as the terror of the night consumed her tiny frame. She never knew why the night frightened her so much. Her aunt and uncle would ask, and she could never give them an answer. Now, nearly 14 years later, as she lay in a room full of lunatics, she still could not explain why she was afraid. She supposed this time around it stemmed from Dr. Carrow, but when she closed her eyes, it was not his menacing eyes that haunted her. It was simply darkness – a darkness so heavy it crushed her and made her sink deeper into her mat. Tears slid down her cheeks and onto the mat as she waited for the sun to rise and her fear to subside.

Lina was trapped in a clear box, her hands and feet tied. Outside of the box was Bird, lying motionless on a table. Lina screamed and banged her bound hands against the box until they bled. She was trying to wake Bird up, trying to see if she was alive. Nothing. Lina exhausted all of her strength, and fell down, drained and too tired to pound anymore against the walls of her prison. Dr. Carrow and Anders came into the room. Anders looked at her and then whispered something to Dr. Carrow, which caused them both to laugh. Lina yelled out Anders' name, but he didn't seem to hear her. He lifted Bird off the table and carried her away.

Lina was left all alone with Dr. Carrow. Without wasting any time, Dr. Carrow opened the clear box and strapped Lina to the table.

"Time to see what's so broken in that disgusting brain of yours," he said as he began to saw right into her skull.

Lina shot up covered with sweat, her head on fire. She hadn't realized she'd fallen asleep, and she didn't sleep at all after that. She lay shivering on her mat, afraid of breathing too loud, afraid of stirring, afraid of disrupting the darkness.

Lina felt immediate relief when the faint rays of sunlight began to make their way through the barred windows. She still felt terrible, but not terrified. She stayed on her mat until the last loony woke up and left the room. She stood up, walked to the door, and peered carefully down the hallway before she quickly headed outside. Making sure she wasn't being followed, Lina snuck into the shed Anders had taken her to. She spent her day there, hidden in a broken down shed waiting for the day to end, but also fearing the arrival of night.

When night finally came, Lina did not sleep once again. Not even for a minute. Every sound terrified her. Anytime a loony turned over, she was sure it was Dr. Carrow or Sam coming to finish her off.

This pattern continued for three more days. She knew she needed to sleep. She knew that if she didn't sleep she was likely to slip into another episode.But she couldn't. Not at night, not in the dark. On the fifth day of hiding in the shed, Lina closed her eyes. She needed to nap; she couldn't stay awake any longer. She didn't know what was going to happen with Bird, but she knew that if Bird did come back, Lina would be no use if she were a rambling, sleepless mess.

So, she slept.

Lina woke up to someone kicking her in the stomach. It was Sam. Lina quickly tried to stand up, but Sam shoved her back down.

"You stand up when I say so," he yelled and he spit on her.

Lina ignored him; she tried to stand up again. Sam slapped her hard in the face and shoved her down once more. He kicked her again in the stomach and rested his foot on top of her throat.

"You thought you could hide, but you can't escape from me, tic. There's nowhere you can go that I can't find you, and there's no one that can save you from what's coming." Sam laughed.

Lina felt tears stinging her eyes. It was hard to breathe. She felt herself spiraling into darkness.

Sam crouched down so his face was close to Lina's, "There's no way you can keep yourself safe or that little friend of yours. The doctor will make sure of that."

Sam stood back up; he spit on Lina again before removing his foot from her throat.

"If you step out of line, I will kill you. That's a promise."

Sam walked to the door laughing.

"I'll see you at dinner," he sneered as he slammed the door behind him.

Lina curled into a ball and stayed on the ground. She didn't know what to do. She was filled with fear and hate and loneliness. Lina had no one to turn to, no one to take away any of the pain. Bird was gone, and if she came back, she would soon be dead. Anders thought she was delusional. There was no one to save Lina from the horror she was living in. No one. The loneliness, fear, and hate made it impossible for Lina to stand up. She was trapped on the floor. If Sam came back now, he could kill her, and she wouldn't even fight back. There was no fight left in her.

She needed to get off the floor, but she couldn't. She could feel her body giving up, feel her soul giving up. She was tired. The asylum was killing her. Carrow and Sam wouldn't have to do it. Simply staying here was going to kill Lina all on its own. She could feel it being sucked right out of her with each passing day, and right now, she felt that she had barely any life left. If not for her concern for Bird, she would die right here on the shed floor. Bird was the only reason Lina would try to live. Lina needed to be alive to take care of Bird in case she came back. Lina pushed herself up so that she was sitting. She paused, looking deep inside for more strength. Taking a deep, painful breath, she found just enough to stand up and walk out of the shed.

Lina knew she had to go to dinner. Sam was expecting her to be there.

It was a test. A test that, if failed, would surely result in more pain for her. She slowly walked toward the asylum. The sun was starting to set. It was cold. She looked down at her gown. It had once been white. She couldn't remember the last time she had put on a new one. She couldn't remember the last time she had washed. Her filth clung to her and weighed heavily on her as she pushed open the asylum door and stepped inside.

Somehow it felt even colder inside the asylum. She heard maniacal laughter echoing through the hallways. The echoes froze in the chill and fell to the ground, shattering as they landed. Lina wrapped her arms around herself and shivered. She walked past a pair of nurses. They looked at her with indifference. They felt no concern for the dirty loony shuffling through the halls. No concern for the bruise on her face or the sorrow in her eyes. Nobody cared what happened to Lina. It hurt, but not as much as it should have. She was used to it.

Lina stepped into the dining hall. Dinner had already begun. It had been several days since Lina had eaten anything, and the smell of the food made her feel sick. She looked around the room. Sam was leaning against the wall flirting with a couple of nurses. When he saw that Lina had walked in, he shot her a smirk. It wasn't a smile she ever wanted to see again. Lina turned away quickly. She could feel Sam watching her. She got into line. She waited. She held out her plate as it was filled with food. Sam was still watching. She sat at a table as far away from him as possible. She stared at her plate where two piles of gray and brown mush ran together. She had never felt less hungry. Lina glanced over at where she had last seen Sam, and was startled to see he wasn't there anymore.

"Eat it all, tic," Sam suddenly hissed as he walked behind her before moving to a nearby spot against the wall.

Lina loaded her spoon and took her first bite. It was hard to swallow. She took five more bites. Her stomach was full. Unfortunately, the plate was too. She kept eating. Lina could feel the mush clinging to her insides, coating them, desperate for somewhere to go. She finished her last bite. It slid down her throat and landed heavily inside her. Lina knew she was going to be sick. She also knew Sam would be watching her. She knew he would be expecting it, and she knew he was hoping for it.

She closed her eyes and stayed at the table. She felt someone sit across from her. Nervous, she opened her eyes. It wasn't whom she expected.

"Lina, where have you been?" Anders' eyes burned her.

Lina didn't speak. It was taking all of her strength to not throw up everything she had just eaten.

"About what I said...I wanted to talk to you...."

Lina stopped listening to Anders. She had felt Sam's glare harden on her. She turned and looked at him. He was watching her, and his eyes were dark. Very dark. He glanced at Anders and then back at Lina. He shook his head. It was a subtle movement, a movement no one else would have noticed, but Lina had. Lina pushed herself up from the table. She felt Sam's glare lessen. This was what he wanted; he wanted her to leave. He didn't want her to be with Anders, and she wasn't about to ignore him. She quickly walked out of the room, leaving Anders confused and alone.

Lina walked straight to her mat and lay down. She did not move until lunch the next day.

When Lina finally got out of bed, she headed to the rec room. The room was crowded. It was more crowded than Lina remembered. Were there more loonies in the asylum? There wasn't enough room for more. Lina felt her anxiety rise. Was Bird back? Was she here in the packed asylum looking for Lina? Lina felt sweat drip down her forehead. She tried to take a breath. She couldn't get all the air she needed. Half of it got stuck in her throat and wouldn't go any further. Desperate, she tried again. Every time she took a breath, she got less air. She looked frantically around the room. Was somebody stopping the air? Dr. Carrow would love to take the air away from them. She could imagine him watching, smiling, as the lunatics fell to the floor one by one, no longer able to breathe. Lina made her way toward the door. She prayed it was open. Prayed they weren't all trapped. She had to get out of here.

It was open.

She slipped out and took a deep breath and filled her desperate lungs with air from the hallway.

Lina didn't know where to go. She didn't want to go anywhere Sam could get her alone. She didn't want to go anywhere Carrow could get her alone. She slid down against the wall and sat just outside the doorway to the rec room. She closed her eyes and leaned her head back. The sounds of lunacy seeped through the thin wall and into her ears. The sound was somehow both comforting and terrifying. Lina imagined Bird sitting beside her. She rested her hand on the ground, palm up, and Bird's imaginary hand took hers.

I miss you, Bird, Lina thought, *but I hope I never see you again. I never want you to come back to this horrible place. Please don't come back.*

Lina felt a few tears escape and slip down her cheek. The salt stung a cut she hadn't even known she had. Her imaginary Bird was gone. Lina moved her hand and let it cling to the collar of her gown. Her eyes were still closed. She counted to 857 and then fell asleep in the hallway.

Chapter Thirteen

Lina woke up scared. There were no more sounds coming through the hallway. She peered through the doorway of the rec room. It was empty. She heard quick footsteps coming from a different hallway. She jumped up. She hadn't meant to fall asleep. She quickly made her way toward the dining hall, hoping to find all the lunatics eating, hoping to find a place to hide among them. The room was empty. Lina felt sick. Lina felt terrified. She ran toward the room where she normally slept. She threw the door open. It was full. She heard several lunatics snoring. Some of her terror subsided. All of the mats were in use, so Lina lay down on the cold floor and tried to steady her breathing.

It wasn't until the morning came that she noticed the huge bruise covering her arm, a bruise that stemmed from a tiny hole on top of her vein. Voices in her head screamed as she bit down hard on her hand to keep the cries from escaping her lips.

Lina did not sleep for three days. The voices never quieted down long enough for her to be able to accomplish such a task. Day and night they screamed loudly in her head. No words, just high-pitched screams. Screams which plagued and horrified her. Screams that made her wish she were dead. She could feel her sanity slipping away. She wanted to reach out and grab it, but she didn't have the strength. The screams were sucking the life out of her. They carved holes in her skull and laughed when she asked them to leave.

On the fourth day, Anders tried to talk to her, but she couldn't hear him over the screaming. She stared at him, unable to say anything, unable to think. She saw his mouth moving and she shook her head bewilderedly. He reached forward to touch her arm, but she ran away. She ran as fast and as far as she could. She ran until she reached the wall that kept them all trapped. She collapsed before it and held her hands over her ears and screamed along with the voices in her head.

She felt hands on her shoulders. She jumped up quickly. Anders.

"Lina." She could see him mouthing her name even if she couldn't hear it.

He was saying more things that she couldn't hear. The voices were screaming louder. She imagined blood spilling from her ears.

"THEY NEED TO STOP," she cried desperately, her screams only a whisper to her own ears.

"THEY NEED TO STOP! PLEASE MAKE THEM STOP"

Anders stepped toward her. He reached out for her. Confused and scared, Lina shoved him away.

As he tried to restrain her, Lina flung her head to the side and it collided with the wall. Everything went black.

Lina may have woken up for a moment. Someone was carrying her. Probably Anders. She reached up and touched his face; his cheek was wet. The screams were growing faint. She fell back into darkness.

Lina opened her eyes, but everything was blurry. The voices were gone. No more screaming. She sensed someone sitting beside her.

"They stopped," she whispered as she turned her head, expecting to see Anders.

"Who stopped?"

It was not Anders.

As Lina's vision cleared, she saw Dr. Carrow's cold eyes looking down at her. Lina tried to shift her body. She couldn't. She was strapped to a table. She began thrashing against the restraints.

"Calm down, Lina," Carrow said. "You're safe now."

Why was he being nice?

Lina looked all around the room. They weren't alone. There was a nurse in the room and another man she didn't recognize. He wasn't wearing an orderly uniform. Perhaps he was another doctor.

"Now what did you mean when you said 'they stopped?'" Carrow asked evenly.

Lina didn't like this. She didn't like this pretend Carrow. The real Carrow was evil. That Carrow was probably the one who put the voices in her head. She didn't answer. She wouldn't answer.

"The orderly said you were shouting about something and then you hit your head on the wall. Do you remember that?" Carrow studied her, waiting for a response.

She gave none.

Lina knew Carrow was getting angry. She could see it in his eyes. She knew he would punish her for this later. She didn't care. Here in this room with the nurse, the unknown doctor, and the pretend Carrow, she didn't have to do what he wanted.

"Lina." Carrow's voice sounded so strange. It sounded sympathetic, "I can't help you if you don't tell me what happened."

Lina locked eyes with Carrow. She stared deep into the darkness. She saw something there. A flash so quick she almost missed it. She saw mania in those eyes. It burned brightly for only a moment before he hid it away. There was more to Carrow than evil, more to him than hatred. Somewhere inside, Carrow was a lunatic. This realization made him so much more terrifying. Evil was calculating. Evil, however skewed, had logic. Lunacy was wild; lunacy had no rules.

Carrow continued to stare at her, but he asked no further questions.

"I'm done…for now," Carrow said to the others in the room.

The nurse came over; she undid the straps on Lina's arms but left the ones on her legs. She helped Lina to sit up.

"Drink this," the nurse said, handing Lina a cup of water.

Lina obeyed.

The doctor she didn't recognize came over and examined the side of her head. He wore round glasses and looked just how someone would expect a grandfather to look. He was balding and he wore a colorful sweater under his coat. He smiled kindly at Lina and his eyes crinkled beneath his glasses. Lina was taken off guard by his comforting demeanor. It was completely out of place in this life-draining asylum.

"I'll remove the stitches in a few weeks," he said. "My name is Doctor Stevens. I work over at the hospital."

Lina lifted her hand to feel stitches, and as she did she discovered that a large portion of her hair was missing.

"We had to shave it for the stitches," Doctor Stevens said, clearly aware of what she was thinking. "How does your head feel?" he asked.

"Okay," Lina lied. Her head was pounding, but she wanted to get out of there.

"Do you feel any dizziness?" he asked.

"No." That too was a lie.

"It doesn't look like you did any serious damage." He paused. "I'm going to keep you here over night though, just to be sure."

Lina nodded.

"Do you feel like eating?" Dr. Stevens asked.

"Not right now."

Lina reached up and touched the stitches again; they covered a large portion of her head. She felt Dr. Carrow watching her. It made her self-conscious. She dropped her hand back down to her side. She lay back down and turned her face away from Dr. Carrow. The nurse came over and strapped her arms to the table.

"For your own safety," the nurse muttered as she tightened the straps.

There was nothing else to do, so Lina closed her eyes. The pounding in her head echoed loudly throughout her skull. She wondered where Anders was. Had he waited around to see if she was okay? Was he even the one that brought her here? She thought she remembered him carrying her. She thought she remembered touching his face, remembered feeling tears, but maybe that had been a dream. It was hard to remember what was real. She could still feel Dr. Carrow's eyes. They burned holes in the back of her head. Would he ever leave or would he stay here the whole time? When they let her leave, would he follow her? Once they were out of this room, the real Carrow would return. Maybe she shouldn't have lied about her head. Maybe it was better to stay here longer. She didn't want to think about it right now. Her head already hurt too much. She tried to think of different things, of better things.

Her mind drifted to her cousins. She hadn't thought about them since coming to the asylum. She wondered if they ever thought about her. She was sure Chrissie was married by now. She wondered what Beth was doing. Thinking about her cousins made Lina miss them. This surprised her. She tried to picture their faces. The difficulty of the task made her sad. Was she forgetting her life outside the asylum? How could she not recall what the girls she had grown up with looked like? Thirteen years they had lived together. They hadn't been close, but she had seen them every day. They had gone to school together. Lina strained and strained until a clearer image of her cousins popped into her head. It wasn't perfect, but it was better. She clung to the image and closed her eyes. She forced herself to keep remembering their faces as she fell asleep.

Lina was lying on the table. She was strapped down. She tried to speak, but she couldn't. Her mouth was sewn shut. She panicked. Screams echoed inside of her, screams that couldn't get out. Dr. Carrow leaned over her.

"You're going to need stitches, stitches everywhere. We'll start with your head." Dr. Carrow forced her head to the side.

Sam came forward and held her head steady. Sam winked at her and flicked her mouth as a horrible pain exploded on the back of her head. She writhed against her restraints.

"We've got to get this nasty hair out of the way," Carrow said as he showed her the knife covered with blood and hair.

"Your crazy is coming out, Lina. We have to get it back inside."

Her father appeared in the room. He was in his party clothes, the ones he had been wearing the night of the accident. He looked at her with tears in his eyes. He tried to come forward, to reach her, but orderlies came in and took him away. He fought against them, but he wasn't strong enough.

Lina's eyes filled with tears, blood dripped onto her face and the two mixed together and fell onto the table in an angry red puddle.

Dr. Carrow began stitching up the back of her head. She felt the needle pierce her skin. She tried to cry out in pain, but no sound could escape.

Lina heard a scream. She looked past Sam. Her mother was standing by the door. Her mother too was in her party clothes, her white gloves shining brightly in the dark room. Her mother looked at her. She looked heart broken.

"I'm sorry, I'm sorry, I'm sorry," her mother sobbed as she collapsed to the floor.

Lina fought to speak. She wanted to tell her mother it wasn't her fault, to tell her she didn't blame her...but she couldn't. All Lina could do was watch as more orderlies came in and picked up her mother.

"I'll take care of that one next," she heard Dr. Carrow say.

Sam started laughing. He put his face right next to Lina's and forced her to watch his horrible, hateful laughter.

Dr. Carrow finished stitching up the back of her head.

"Now for the heart," he said as he lowered the knife.

Lina's eyes flew open. She felt sweat dripping down her forehead. She felt the straps on her arms and legs. Disoriented, she tried to remember where she was. She turned her head. That was a mistake. Dr. Carrow sat in the darkness. He was awake, he was watching. He smiled and leaned close to her.

"Bad dream?" he whispered. After that, he stood up from his chair and left the room.

Lina watched him leave. Once he was gone, she looked around. No one else was in the room. They had been alone. She felt an ache in her neck, an ache she was sure would be accompanied by a bruise. All she could do was wait and see what horrors had been injected into her. She began counting to pass the time. She counted to 2,748 before she began throwing up. It was wretched and violent and forced tears from her eyes. Her head pounded and she felt dizzy. She was still alone in the room, so with her head turned to the side, she spent the rest of the night sobbing and retching. With nowhere else for it to go, the vomit clung to her gown and to her skin. She called out for help but nobody came. She was forced to wait, covered in her own sickness, until the morning arrived and someone finally came to check on her.

"Oh my word!" the nurse cried when she came into the room.

She picked up the phone and called for help. Two orderlies came rushing in. One was Anders. Lina turned away. She could feel her face burning.

"Help me get her to the showers," the nurse ordered.

Anders was already undoing the straps.

"I've got her," he said to the other orderly as he picked her up. He followed the nurse out of the room and down the hall. He held her close.

"I'm so sorry," he whispered to her. "I wanted to stay. They made me leave."

Lina was too embarrassed to speak. Her vomit was covering his shirt and arms. She cried hot tears of shame.

She felt Anders kiss the top of her head. This made her cry harder. She remembered when she was a little girl and her father would hold her just like this and kiss her on the top of her head just as Anders had. She wondered what her father would think if he could see her now: a broken-down lunatic covered in her own vomit and doomed to die in an asylum.

When they arrived at the showers, the nurse asked Anders to help her get Lina's gown off.

"I can do it," Lina said, her voice shaky.

"Are you sure?" the nurse asked.

Lina nodded.

"I'll wait outside," Anders said to the nurse, but his eyes looked at Lina.

He left the room.

With a little help from the nurse, Lina removed her puke-stained gown and stepped under the water. It was painfully cold but Lina didn't care. She scrubbed herself until she was raw.

The nurse handed her a towel. Lina wrapped it around herself and stood awkwardly in front of the nurse. She had nothing clean to put on.

The nurse realized this. "I'll tell the orderly to get you a gown."

She opened the door. Anders handed in a gown, obviously one step ahead of the nurse.

Lina put it on and then ran her fingers through her hair, trying to undo all the tangles.

"Are you okay to walk back to the room?" The nurse asked.

"Yes," Lina said.

"Let's go," the nurse said as she headed toward the door.

Lina followed her.

"We are going to be fine," the nurse said to Anders who was waiting patiently just outside the door. She eyed the mess Lina had left on him, "Why don't you go clean yourself off."

"Are you sure?" Anders looked at Lina, so she nodded reassuringly.

"Okay," he said to the nurse.

Lina followed the nurse down the hallway. When they got back to the room, the table was clean and Dr. Stevens was waiting for them. She sat on the table and Dr. Stevens stood in front of her.

"What happened?" he asked Lina.

"I woke up and I felt sick and then I started to throw up," she said, leaving out the parts of her night she was too afraid to tell.

"No one was around?" he asked.

"No."

"How do you feel now? Any nausea?"

She shook her head.

He began examining Lina. He checked her eyes. He checked her stitches. He stopped when he saw her neck.

"Where did these bruises come from?" Stevens asked.

"What?" Lina asked, despite knowing exactly what he meant.

"The right side of your neck is covered in bruises," he said. "You don't know where they came from?"

Lina shook her head and tried to look confused. "They weren't there before?"

"No," he said, furrowing his brow.

Lina sat silently.

"Does your neck hurt? Any stiffness?"

"No," Lina said, "Could it be from when I hit the wall?"

Dr. Stevens shook his head, not really looking at her.

"Please get something for her to eat," he said, turning to the nurse.

Once she was gone, he looked directly into Lina's eyes, "Was there anyone in here last night?"

Lina stared back at him. She wanted to tell him the truth. She wanted to tell him about all the mysterious bruises and the missing days and about what happened to Bird, but she was terrified. Terrified he would think she was lying, terrified Dr. Carrow would find out. As long as she was in the asylum, Dr. Carrow owned her. He was the doctor. She was a lunatic. She had no doubt he could kill her in an instant. All these thoughts jumbled around in her head as she looked into Dr. Stevens' eyes. She wanted to tell the truth, but she couldn't. "No. I was awake most of the night. No one was here."

"Are you sure?" he asked again. He looked uncertain.

"I'm sure," Lina said and she pitied herself. She pitied her situation and the fear that ruled over her. She pitied how distrustful she was of everyone in the asylum. She had no way to know what words of hers would find their way to Carrow. She hated Dr. Carrow more than she thought she could ever hate a person. She hated him more than she hated Sam. She hated him and feared him to her very core.

Dr. Stevens continued to watch her curiously until the nurse returned.

"I want you to eat something," he told Lina.

She took a small bite of bread.

"We are going to keep you here another night, and we are keeping someone in the room." He looked hard at Lina one last time before dropping his head and writing on his clipboard.

Lina ate a few more bites of bread before her stomach protested. She jumped off the table and ran to the waste basket where she proceeded to retch violently. She felt the doctor stand beside her. When she was finished, he helped her stand up. He handed her a cup of water.

"Only drink a little," he said.

She obeyed.

He helped her back onto the table. He took her temperature. It was very high. He told the nurse to bring a cold towel for her head and had Lina lie down. The towel felt cool on her forehead. Lina had not realized how hot she'd felt. Lina spent the next few hours lying on the table, while the nurse made sure the towel was always cool. Dr. Stevens gave Lina medicine and water. They checked her temperature periodically. She fell asleep.

When Lina finally awoke, it was the next afternoon and Dr. Stevens was there.

When he took her temperature, her fever was gone, and he seemed relieved. The nurse gave her more water, and she drank it greedily before the cup was taken away. For the first time in two days, Lina realized how hungry she was.

"Can I try eating again?" she asked Dr. Stevens.

"Do you think you can keep it down?"

"Yes."

The nurse left and returned a short while later with some soup. It was cold and tasted terrible, but Lina ate half of it, and she did not throw any of it up. Dr. Stevens kept her there for a few more hours.

"Be mindful of the stitches when you leave," he told Lina.

"Okay."

"I'll be back to remove them in about two and a half weeks."

"Okay," she said once more.

"Please be careful," the doctor said, and he looked at Lina strangely.

She looked back at him, at the concern on his face, and wondered what thoughts were running through his head. Did he suspect what was really going on? How could he possibly? Lina wasn't even entirely sure what was happening, and she was the one living it. Once again, she ached to tell him the truth, but she didn't. She couldn't. Instead she said nothing and left the room.

Chapter Fourteen

Anders found her moments after she left the room. She jumped when he called her name.

As he walked towards her, he stared at her intently. His brow was furrowed in obvious concern, and he stood silently for a moment as though trying to think of what to say.

"Can you forgive me?" he asked.

Lina was confused. "Forgive you? For what?"

"For everything," Anders said as he ran his fingers through his hair. "For not being there and for not taking care of you as I promised I would."

Lina studied him carefully, she just didn't understand why Anders was so nice to her. He knew she was a lunatic. He had seen her at her very worst. Why did he care so much about taking care of her? It didn't make sense. And now here he was asking for forgiveness when it was Lina who owed him a debt of gratitude that she could never pay.

"You don't need to be forgiven," she finally said. "You've already done more than enough for me – you got Bird into your aunt's school."

Bird. Saying her name pushed hundreds of questions and thoughts into Lina's mind. For the first time since Bird left, Lina was lucid enough to ask all about her. How long had she been gone? Lina had lost track of time.

Anders began to say something, but Lina quickly cut him off. "Have you talked to her at all? Is she doing okay? Is she still on probation? How long will the probation be? Does your aunt like her? Is she fitting in? Please tell me she's fitting in. She has to fit in there because she cannot end up back here."

Anders watched Lina carefully as she spoke, and when she paused to take a breath, he cut in.

"I haven't seen Bird myself, but my aunt says she seems to be doing very well. Dr. Ferrell has met with her a few times, and so far he has no reason for concern. I don't know how long the probation will be, but I think it's going to end soon. I have no reason to doubt that Bird will be able to stay at the school."

Lina felt her legs begin to give out. Her escape from deep lunacy had allowed all her fears for Bird to come bursting forward. Anders' report was such a relief that Lina's body seemed to have no idea how to respond.

Anders must have noticed her shakiness because he grabbed her shoulders to steady her.

"Are you okay?"

Lina smiled. "Yes, yes I'm okay. Thank you so much, Anders. I'll never be able to repay you for this, for saving Bird."

Lina rested her hand against her heart and whispered, "Bird is safe." The reality of it was finally setting in.

"Yes, she is," Anders replied and then took a deep breath.

"Lina, I, um...can you please tell me what you're so afraid of?"

There was a hint of desperation and pleading in his voice.

Lina's smile disappeared.

She was suddenly hit with a memory of the embarrassment and shame she felt last time they talked about this.

She didn't want to talk about this with Anders. She wanted to savor this feeling of relief, but instead his words had summoned a dark cloud of anxiety.

"Why?" Her voice sounded so small. "You won't even believe me."

There. She had said it. She hated how petty it sounded, especially when she owed Anders everything, but she had said it and there was no taking it back.

Anders' hands were still on her shoulders, and Lina couldn't avoid seeing the hurt in his eyes with his face so close to hers.

"Lina," he began.

She cut him off. "Please just forget about it. You kept your promise. You took care of Bird, and now whatever sense of duty you felt to take care of me is fulfilled. I really am so grateful. I mean it. I'm sorry if I'm not showing it very well."

Lina attempted to move away from Anders, but he held firmly onto her shoulders.

"I am not through taking care of you, and it's not just because of some sense of duty. I care about you, Lina. That's why I want to take care of you." He looked her straight in the eyes, "And I do believe you. I'm sorry for before. I believe your fears are real, and I want to help you, so can you please tell me what's going on."

Lina stared back at him, and she could see that he really meant it. She wanted to tell him everything. Maybe he really could help? People trusted Anders. Maybe if he knew what was going on he could stop it.

"I…" she began, but a vivid memory of Dr. Carrow's hateful glare and cruel words made her stop. People trusted Dr. Carrow too, even though they shouldn't. He was a doctor, and people respected doctors. Even if Anders did believe her, why would anyone believe him over Carrow? Plus, Carrow had Sam, and Sam was dangerous. What if Anders confronted Carrow or Sam? Would they kill him? She believed they could and they would. It didn't matter if Anders believed her or not. Telling him would only put him in danger, too. She couldn't do that to him.

"I can't tell you," she said firmly.

"Please tell me. Tell me and it will all be okay, I promise," Anders pleaded.

"No, I can't."

"Please, Lina, I want to help you. What are you so afraid of?"

Lina felt panicked. She needed to get away from Anders. What if someone saw them together? She began to back away, but Anders reached out for one of her hands. He held it in his and looked at her imploringly.

Just then, Sam appeared. He was behind Anders at the end of the hallway. He smiled his devil smile at her. Lina tensed up. Sam shook his head at her and motioned for her to walk away.

"I, I," she said, backing away from Anders, trying to find something to say to keep him from following.

Anders could see the fear in her eyes and he turned his head.

He made eye contact with Sam.

"It's him," he whispered as realization dawned on his face.

Lina was too afraid to speak.

"He's the reason you're afraid, isn't he?"

Anders could see terror filling her eyes, and he walked over to Sam. Sam stayed where he was.

"Having fun with your tic?"

"Stay away from her."

"Oh don't worry, I'll wait until you're done with her, and then I can have my fun too," Sam sneered as he winked at Lina.

Before Lina realized what was happening, Anders had punched Sam in the stomach. Sam struggled to catch his breath.

"Don't you dare," said Anders, "You're done hurting her. I'll make sure of that."

Sam had recovered enough to punch Anders in the jaw, hard.

"You're a lunatic too if you think that piece of smut is worth anything" Sam said and started to walk away.

Lina was afraid Anders was going to follow him.

"Anders!"

Anders turned and looked at Lina.

"Please don't. Please!" she said.

Anders took a deep breath and walked back over to her. She had never seen him so upset.

"He's the one who bruised your face." It wasn't a question.

"What else has he done?" Anders asked.

"That's all it was. He slapped me," Lina said quietly.

"That's not all. What else? What else, Lina?"

"He threatened Bird. He said to stay out of his way."

"There's more." Anders wasn't backing down.

Lina squirmed uncomfortably. She didn't want to tell him everything, but there was no point in hiding it now, Sam was already angry, and she needed to let Anders know what he was capable of.

"He choked me and kicked me and threatened to kill me. Anders, he's going to do it. Now that I told you, he's going to do it." Lina's eyes started to burn, and she struggled to breathe.

Anders pulled her into him, wrapping his arms around her as if to protect her. "I won't let him," he said gently.

She stayed in Anders's hug. She breathed him in. He felt safe. She wished the hug could last forever. She liked feeling protected. She liked being close to Anders.

They heard footsteps, and Anders released her and stepped back.

"I'm going to find Sam and turn him in. He will be gone, and he will never hurt you again."

Anders walked Lina to the rec room and told her to stay close to other people. "Don't let yourself be alone," he said firmly.

He left Lina there and went to get rid of Sam.

Lina tried to stay safe. She really did. She stayed in the crowded room and surrounded herself with lunatics and nurses. But she was anxious. She knocked over a tray in the corner of the room. It held a glass pitcher filled with water. A nurse yelled at her. She told Lina she was going to have to clean it up. She told everyone else it was time for dinner. She threw a towel at Lina. Lina knelt down and frantically started picking up glass. The room was emptying quickly. As Lina's anxiety grew, she accidentally cut her hand on a large piece of glass. She wiped the blood on her gown and hurried to finish cleaning. The nurse stood by the door, watching her until every last piece of glass was picked up and every speck of water was dry.

"Now get to dinner," the nurse ordered.

"Can you show me the way there?" Lina asked. She was desperate to keep the nurse with her.

"Figure it out yourself," the nurse said as she walked away.

Lina hurried so that she could follow her. She walked quickly around the corner, hoping to catch up with the nurse or the rest of the loonies. She saw the nurse turning another corner just ahead and felt relief, but suddenly hands grabbed her and pulled her into a room. She yelled out, but the door was closed before the scream could escape—her cry of fear stayed trapped in the room with her.

Sam shoved her against a wall. "I thought we had an understanding, tic."

He spat in her face. "You were going to behave. You weren't going to cause any problems." He cracked his neck, "But you must be more stupid than I thought. You went and whined to your little boyfriend."

"No! I didn't . . ." Lina started to reply, but her words were cut off when Sam slapped her hard across the face, and the sting made her start to cry.

"You know, I'm just going to kill you now, and Carrow will just have to find a new tic to amuse himself with," Sam said as he punched her hard in the stomach.

It dropped Lina to her knees. When Sam moved to push her to the floor, her instincts and adrenaline took over. She grabbed his hand and bit it hard. She could taste blood. Sam yelled and yanked it back while Lina made a run for the door. Sam grabbed her leg to trip her, but Lina pulled him to the floor with her. They got back up at the same time.

Sam laughed. "You aren't going to win."

He grabbed her by the throat and started to choke her.

Lina thrashed out with all her limbs. She dug her nails into his arms, but he didn't loosen his grip. She kicked him in the legs. Nothing. Mustering all of her strength, she kicked him in the groin as she simultaneously scratched his face. Finally, he was in enough pain that Lina was able to make a final run for the door and open it. She screamed as loud as she could. By now, Sam had recovered enough to grab her, and he began to pull her back into the room. As she clung to the doorway, he hit Lina hard where her stitches were. She choked back her sobs as she screamed even louder. Sam wrapped one arm around her waist and used the other to punch her arms off the doorway. He picked her up and threw her on the floor. Gasping for breath, she looked at his eyes and saw nothing but hate and murder and evil. She wasn't going to survive this. She wasn't strong enough to win this fight, but she thrashed and clawed at his arms as he wrapped his hands around her neck. She continued to claw at his arms. She was going to die trying. She wouldn't give Sam the satisfaction of giving up. He would have to work for her murder, and she would leave her mark on his devil body. She could feel herself dying. The life inside her was dimming. She hoped someone would at least find her body soon. She wished she had had a chance to say goodbye to Bird.

Just as the darkness was about to consume her, the door swung open, and Lina could see a large form hit Sam hard in the back of the head and he fell to the floor.

"I found him," an orderly shouted through the now open door.

Lina tried to sit up, but she couldn't. Instead, she rolled to her side and pulled her knees to her chest, and rocked gently back and forth. She used one hand to wipe the blood that was dripping from her mouth.

Another orderly ran into the room. It was Anders.

"Go get help," Anders said to the other man as he knelt beside Lina.

Lina stared at Anders, her heart beating in her ears.

She had almost died. Sam had almost killed her. As she looked at his unconscious body on the floor, her terror and fury took control.

"Get him out of here!" she yelled at Anders

"James is bringing help. They're going to take him away." Anders spoke smoothly, trying to calm Lina. She didn't want that.

"GET HIM OUT!" She cried, her body shaking with tears and rage, "HE'S GOING TO KILL ME, GET HIM OUT."

"Lina, it's okay. It's over. They are going to take him away and he is never going to come back here."

He tried to hold her, but Lina pushed him away.

"No!" she said and punched his chest.

Anders let Lina sob and pound until several men came into the room. They picked Sam up and carried him away. After that, Lina lay back on the floor. Her tears had stopped.

Anders stayed kneeling beside her.

She didn't know how long he would have let her lie there had several nurses and orderlies not arrived to help.

"Let's get her to a doctor," one of the nurses said.

Lina grabbed Anders' arm. "Don't leave me," she pleaded.

"I won't," he said, and he picked her up.

"Where are we taking her?" He asked the nurse.

"Room 13."

Lina held weakly onto Anders' shirt, desperate to keep him close.

When they got to Room 13, Anders laid her gently on the bed. There were two doctors she didn't recognize.

"Does she need to be sedated?" they asked Anders. "Is she dangerous?"

"No," Anders said loud enough so that Lina would hear. "She's the victim."

"These lunatics are always causing trouble," one of the doctors said as he examined her injuries.

"It wasn't a patient. An orderly attacked her." Anders spoke firmly.

"An orderly?" The doctors sounded shocked.

"Was he provoked?" they asked in a whisper.

"No, she did nothing wrong." Lina could tell that Anders was upset.

"Can I take her now? Is she okay to leave?" Anders stared hard at the doctors.

"Sure, there doesn't seem to be any serious damage," one of them said while making notes on a clipboard. They seemed to have lost interest in Lina already.

Anders walked over to her, and the doctors left the room.

"I want to go to bed," she said, her eyes dry and tired.

"We should get you something to eat."

"I'm not hungry."

"Okay," he said, helping her up.

He stopped by the kitchen on their way back and grabbed her a few rolls.

"For later," he mumbled.

He helped her walk to the room. There were a few other loonies already asleep in there. He helped her onto her mat and set the rolls next to her. She could feel him watching her as she fell asleep.

Physically and mentally drained, Lina slept restlessly as anxiety ate at her. When she awoke, she was starving. She reached for the rolls Anders left for her, but they were gone. One of the loonies must have taken them. She walked to the dining hall hoping it was time to eat something. The hall was empty. She must have slept through breakfast. She headed to the rec room to wait for someone to come and tell them it was time for lunch. She curled into the corner.

Lina noticed a woman standing near the center of the room. The woman swayed from side to side, and Lina found herself mesmerized. As Lina watched, she realized the woman was dancing. Her eyes were closed, her head bending towards her shoulder and a faint smile playing on her lips. Lina found herself feeling jealous of the woman. This woman was happy. No one had tried to kill this woman the day before. She was not tired to her very core as Lina was. The woman didn't even know she was crazy. She had no idea anything was wrong with her. She was dancing peacefully, completely unaware of her surroundings. Lina wanted that. She needed that. She stood up and walked over to the woman. She wanted to be near her. She wanted her serenity. When she got closer, she realized the woman was humming very softly. Lina closed her eyes and opened her ears and let the woman share her music. As she listened to the soft, sweet melody, Lina began to sway along to the tune. She didn't know how long she danced alongside the woman, but the longer she danced, the more she was able to forget where she was. She pushed away the horror of the day before. She pushed away thoughts of Sam's devil eyes. She forgot those awful things and instead thought of Bird. She allowed her happiness for Bird to join in the dancing, and then she simply listened to the music and imagined she was somewhere else.

All too soon, Lina's serenity was interrupted with a tap on the shoulder. She opened her eyes and saw Anders. He looked as though he felt bad for stopping the dance.

"Dr. Carrow wants to meet with you," he said, his cheeks wet. Lina wondered if he had been crying.

It was strange for Lina to hear such harrowing words from someone who, to her, represented safety. She could only look at him.

"I think it's a good idea, after what happened yesterday. You need to talk to someone."

"I'm so hungry," she said pitifully.

"Okay. I'll get you something to eat first."

Lina followed Anders out of the room. He led her to the kitchen. He stepped inside and came out a few moments later with an apple.

"It's all I could get," Anders said as he handed it to her.

It was bruised and very sour, but Lina ate it quickly.

They continued on to Dr. Carrow's office. She was scared. She wished she could reach out and hold Anders' hand for comfort. Instead, she clutched her hands into fists and tried to prepare herself for Carrow.

When they reached the door, Anders rested his hand on her shoulder. "I'll come find you when you're done, okay?"

She nodded. She wanted to tell Anders the truth about Dr. Carrow, but after what had happened with Sam, she knew she couldn't. Dr. Carrow was far more powerful and evil than Sam. Besides, she couldn't provide any evidence of what Carrow was doing. She wasn't even sure herself what was happening. But she was certain that if she told Anders anything, Carrow would waste no time trying to kill her and probably Anders as well and that he, unlike Sam, would succeed.

She stepped through the door.

"Sit," Dr. Carrow said as soon as she entered.

She looked around. The chair she normally sat in was not in there. The only chair in the room was occupied by Carrow himself.

"Sit," he said again.

Lina sat on the cold floor.

Carrow smiled. "Bad day yesterday?"

Lina said nothing.

"Actually, it seems that you've had a string of bad days. It's a wonder you're holding up under all the stress, all the pain," he said.

Still, she said nothing.

"But you're not really holding up are you?" His eyes darkened. "You're dying inside. Your mind, already weak and pathetic to begin with, is deteriorating even more. Frankly I'm surprised you haven't dropped dead."

He got out of his chair and knelt before Lina. "Your body is giving up on you, I don't know how much longer you expect to survive. Just look at yourself. It's sickening." He shoved a small mirror in her face.

She made herself look. She didn't even recognize herself. Her eyes were dull and lifeless, surrounded by dark purple smudges. Her pale skin was stretched tightly over her face. The chunk of hair missing on the side of her head revealed the bumpy, zig-zag of stitches made by Dr. Stevens. Her cheekbones were sharper than Bird's had been the first time she saw her. She was hardly more than a skeleton.

Her eyes shifted away from the mirror and met with Carrow's. He ripped the mirror away.

"Hideous, isn't it?"

He stood back up and walked over to his chair.

His loathing of Lina made the air in the room thick. She could see it curling against the walls. The room could barely contain it.

Lina could no longer bear the hatred and the power he held over her. In an unexplainable moment of bravery and strength, she stood up.

"Sam is gone now," she said. "He's gone. There's no one now to help you with whatever sick game you're playing."

Carrow laughed. "No one left to help me? There are plenty of people that can help me. Plenty of people who want to fight the good fight. It's not a game, Lina. It's a war. A war against lunacy that I'm going to win."

"I could stop you."

"We both know that's not true. You think Bird is safe from me just because she's not here anymore? You think I can't get to her in that little school? You think you're so clever for getting her there? I could pay her a visit anytime I want. Do you think that if you confide in that idiot orderly, he will save you? He can't save you. Only I can save you. I make the rules, and I decide who lives and dies."

He stood up from his chair, walked up to Lina, and stared deep into her eyes. "But you already knew that."

He paused.

"Maybe your mind is not as gone as I thought. There's just enough reason in there left for you to know what will happen if you try to break the rules."

Lina's fleeting bravery was gone. She had never been so terrified of Dr.

Carrow before. His dark eyes filled with murder and lunacy, and she knew every word he said was true. She couldn't stop him.

"I want you to remember all of this. I want your tiny, pathetic brain to remember every word I just said," Carrow snarled. "We are done for today. Get out."

Lina left the room and walked down the hall as her skeletal body shook with terror.

Chapter Fifteen

She had added more fuel to the fire of Dr. Carrow's hatred. She regretted ever opening her mouth. She *was* a lunatic. She had to be. Only a lunatic would try to fight back against that man. He would continue playing with her until he got bored, and then he would kill her. Her only hope was that if she played along, the only two people in the world that she cared about would be okay. If she followed the rules, he would leave them alone.

Darkness seeped inside of her and Lina was powerless against it. It weighed her down and filled her with sorrow and self-loathing. It was too heavy for her. She lay down, right in the middle of the hallway. What did it matter if it was strange? She was in an asylum. She was insane. She had every right to lie down on the cold, dirty floor. She didn't have to keep fighting. She could give up and give in to the lunacy scratching at her brain. It would be easier than clinging to her scraps of sanity.

She heard someone coming down the hallway, but she didn't care. There was no point in caring what happened next because everything was up to Dr. Carrow.

She heard snickering above her. She opened her eyes and looked to the side. She saw bare feet and a white hem. It was just another loonie. The snickering lunatic reached down and tickled her back. She flinched and the loonie laughed even harder.

"See. It's not dead." It was a man. "Just sleepy."

Lina turned her head again. He was alone. He was talking to himself.

"Hello," he said.

Lina didn't know if he was talking to her or the voices in his head.

He lay down on the floor next to her and poked her nose. "Hello."

"Go away."

"It talks too!" he said to himself. "It's kind of ugly though." He shook his head and stuck out his tongue.

"Bye ugly," he said, patting her cheek before he stood up and walked away.

Lina rolled over and pushed herself into a sitting position. She watched the man until he turned a corner and she couldn't see him anymore. She stood up and walked in the direction he had gone. She walked hoping to find food to fill her stretched out, empty body.

She entered the dining hall. It was empty except for a few nurses.

"Is lunch over?" Lina asked them.

"We're not doing lunch anymore," one of them said.

"What?" Lina was confused.

"We aren't feeding you lunch anymore. Breakfast and dinner. That's all there's food for," the other nurse said, clearly annoyed at Lina's presence.

Lina could feel pangs of hunger stabbing in her stomach. She looked at the nurses and tried to process this information. The nurses looked at Lina disdainfully.

"There's no food. Leave," another said.

Lina obeyed.

She didn't know what to do now. There was nothing to do. She had nowhere to be. Anders had said he would come find her, but she didn't know if he really would, and she didn't know if she wanted him to. She was too exhausted and hungry for conversation. She didn't want to miss dinner, so she sat in the hallway just outside the dining hall, waiting. She knew dinner wouldn't be for hours, but there was nothing better to do. She let her mind wander and drift into corners of her head that she rarely visited. She allowed herself to reach out for the few memories she had of her parents. There weren't many, and they usually made her sad, sad because she missed her parents desperately, but today she wanted to remember them even if it hurt. She pulled forward a memory of a day at the park with her parents. Lina had been very young at the time, so the details were foggy, but she remembered there were ducks. Ducks and a chunk of bread. Her mother had helped her feed pieces of the bread to the ducks and laughed loudly when Lina pretended to be a duck herself. Her mother had never seemed crazy to her, Lina had always thought she was perfect. Her father had been drawing. Looking back, she was fairly certain it had been a picture of her and her mother. She wished she had the picture. She wished she had anything that had belonged to her parents. She let the memory of the day dance in her mind, trying her hardest to remember more details. None came, but she continued to replay the memory because it was pleasant, and it would bring her a bit of happiness until she let it go away, after which there would only be sadness and longing.

"There you are." Anders' voice interrupted her thoughts.

"Hi," she said.

"What are you doing here?"

"Waiting for dinner."

"That's not for hours."

"I know."

He looked at her with pity, and that made her angry. It shouldn't have – she had spent more than enough time pitying herself after all – but it did.

"Did you know they don't serve lunch anymore?" she asked.

"Well…yeah…they haven't for about a week."

"I didn't." She was feeling grumpy.

"I'm sorry."

"Did you eat lunch?" It was more of an accusation than a question.

He seemed reluctant to answer. But he did anyway.

"Yes, I did."

Lina glared at him. "Lucky you."

"I can find you some food."

"Another wrinkled, sour apple? No thanks."

She was getting angrier. All of the anger she felt towards Dr. Carrow was boiling up inside of her. It started to erupt and it hit Anders in the face.

He didn't try to avoid it. "I'm sorry, Lina. I can find you something better."

"Don't bother," she said. "I'll wait."

"Did I do something to upset you?"

"No."

"Did it go okay with Dr. Carrow?"

"Yes. Why wouldn't it?"

"Lina, I know you aren't very fond of him, but he's here to help you."

Lina wanted to both laugh and cry over the absurdity of that remark. But instead she shrugged, not wanting to speak.

"I think we should take a walk outside. The fresh air will do you some good."

"I'd rather not."

She could tell Anders was growing uncomfortable, and that made her happy. It was sick of her, but she wanted to upset him because she didn't want to be the only one filled with darkness.

"You don't have to babysit me anymore. Sam's gone. You don't have to feel bad about upsetting him so much that he almost killed me," she said.

This time her anger made Anders flinch. Lina regretted saying it, but only a little. Her anger and fear prevented her from regretting it as much as she should have.

"Lina, I'm sorry... so very sorry."

Seeing the pain in his eyes softened some of her anger

"What Sam did to you was horrific. You didn't deserve any of it, and what happened yesterday was my fault. I shouldn't have left you alone. I wasn't thinking straight. I was just so mad. I wanted to find Sam and make him pay right away. But, I couldn't find him. I went to look for you. When you weren't in the rec room and you weren't in the dining hall, when you weren't somewhere safe, I was beside myself. And when I finally found you, and I saw what that monster had done to you, I wanted to die. Leaving you alone, letting that happen, it's not something you can let me off the hook for. I don't think I can ever forgive myself. But I'm also not going to stop taking care of you. And not because I feel guilty. I'm going to take care of you because I care about you, and you deserve to have someone watching over you. You deserve to be kept safe."

Lina started to cry.

"I didn't mean it, Anders. It wasn't your fault. Sam would have done it anyway. He always had murder in his eyes. It was going to happen soon enough, and I would be dead if you hadn't come looking for me. I was going to die."

And at that, this day's fear and anger was replaced with the utter terror she had felt the day before. She closed her eyes while the hot tears spilled out, and she tried to push away the feeling of knowing she had been about to die. Anders knelt beside her and put his arm around her. She sobbed into him, and he once again kissed her gently on top of her head. And as Lina sat there with Anders and tears streamed down her face, a memory from long ago began to make its way into her head, something she hadn't thought of in a very long time. It was the day her mother had washed her hands until they bled. How had she forgotten that? Lina remembered feeling scared and confused that day. She remembered her father sitting with her in their hallway and holding her until she stopped crying, just as Anders was doing now. She also remembered how much her father loved her mother. How caring and kind he was. How hard he worked to take care of her mom and make their life happy. Anders was like that. Anders was good like her father.

She realized then that she loved him.

Chapter Sixteen

Lina didn't see Anders for several days after that. He wasn't at work. She spent those days thinking about him. She focused on him instead of her fear and loathing of Dr. Carrow. She had known she cared about him, but love was more. It was stronger. Loving Anders was good. It didn't matter that he didn't love her back. That wasn't important to Lina. What mattered was that her love was valuable, and it offered her an escape from the horror that was her life.

Lina found herself staying awake at night thinking about Anders. At first, the thoughts were occasional, but after a couple nights, they consumed her. She couldn't get him out of her head. She imagined what it would be like to kiss him. She imagined what it would be like to spend their lives together. Her head and body felt restless. She got out of bed and walked into the dark hallway. She roamed the halls. She wondered where Anders was right now. She wondered if he was sleeping. She walked through the entire asylum. She walked outside. The wind slapped her in the face. She spent the night pacing the grounds of the asylum. She spent the night thinking about Anders. When the sun rose and more loonies started stumbling outside, Lina walked back inside.

Lina could not hold still all day. She ate her food while her knees bounced up and down. She ate it quickly, needing to move. That night, she could not sleep again. She went outside. She imagined Anders was there with her. She laughed out loud, picturing his wonderful face. She bounced on her toes and named their children. She was so enthralled with her fantasy that she didn't notice when daylight broke. She ran into a loonie and he barked at her. She glared at him, upset that he interrupted her fantasies. Her mind soon drifted away from the encounter. She thought of Anders again, and she wondered if he would come back to work today. She walked quickly to the showers. She wanted to look her best in case he did. She scrubbed her body until it was red. As she washed her hair, her fingers touched her stitches. She had forgotten about them. She had forgotten all about the missing hair on the side of her head. She was suddenly embarrassed. She wanted her hair to look good. She wanted Anders to think it looked pretty. How could he think it was pretty when most of it was missing? She tried to move it around, to cover the bald section. It wasn't working. It made her angry. She stepped out of the shower. She yanked her gown over her head. She raked her fingers repeatedly through the hair she still had, willing the rest to grow back. A powerful surge of anger filled her body. And then it was gone. Her mind wound back around Anders. She very calmly worked the tangles out of her hair. It was tedious because her hair hung down to her waist, but she did it for Anders. She felt that her heart would explode as she thought of him.

Lina left the showers. Her fingers drummed quickly in the air as she walked towards the dining hall. She wasn't sure what time of day it was, but if it was breakfast time and Anders was at the asylum, he would probably look for her there. She peeked into the room. It looked as if breakfast was just ending. She slipped inside and scanned the room. There he was. He was helping an old lunatic man stand up. He spotted Lina. He smiled at her. She felt her cheeks blush. She smiled back at him. She got a bowl of food and sat at a table. She pushed the food around while she clicked her feet together under the table. She wanted him to come over. She needed him to come over. She couldn't sit still anymore.

He made his way over to her.

She stood up quickly. "Do you want to go for a walk?"

"Aren't you hungry?" he asked, looking at her plate.

"No, I'm not. I haven't really . . . let's go for a walk," she said, and she headed for the door.

Anders followed behind her. She made her way outside. Anders had to walk fast to keep up with her. Right after they stepped outside, he reached forward and touched her arm. Her heart swirled around in her chest.

"Is everything okay?" he asked her, his eyes focused on her face.

"Yes...I just...I...I missed you," she said as she closed her eyes tight for a moment. She was feeling dizzy.

She must have been swaying back and forth because Anders tightened his grip on his arm.

"Do you need to sit down?"

Lina opened her eyes and the dizziness was gone.

"No, I'm fine."

She started walking again.

"Did you want to talk about something?" Anders asked, walking beside her. He was studying her. She instinctively reached up and tried to cover the bald spot that surrounded her stitches.

"Is your head hurting again?" Anders asked, sounding concerned.

"Mmm, no I...." She stopped

Anders was standing very close to her. She could feel her heart pounding wildly in her chest. Dreams of the two of them together swam through her mind. They pounded against the side of her head begging to come true. Anders was her destiny. Lina could feel it. Anders had to know that too. He had to feel it. The air around them was buzzing. Lina grew excited. The excitement in the air seeped through her skin and bubbled up inside her. She began laughing. She couldn't help herself. She was feeling her destiny falling into place. Everything was right in the universe. The wind tickled her ear and whispered to her that this was meant to be. Her laughter increased. She felt tears of joy trickle down her cheeks.

Anders looked at her. He looked confused, maybe concerned. He smiled uneasily. Lina wasn't aware of any of this. She wasn't aware that to him her laughter sounded unhinged. When Lina saw his smile, she saw only light. To her it was only an acknowledgment from him that he felt the joy too. She laughed and laughed until she couldn't laugh anymore. When she stopped, she stepped closer to Anders.

"You felt it too?" she asked.

Anders opened his mouth, but she cut him off. She already knew the answer. "Our destiny is written in the wind." She smiled widely and looked up at the sky.

Lina imagined their wedding day. Her mother's dress had to be packed away somewhere. She would wear it. She would wear gloves too. She remembered her mother wearing gloves. She remembered thinking she looked like a princess. She smiled at the thought of Anders in a tuxedo, smiling when he saw her in the dress. He would twirl her around.

Lina was so lost in her dreams that she was hardly aware of Anders guiding her toward the wall. She walked blissfully beside him. He sat underneath a tree, and she sat next to him. There was no one around. Her fingers played with the grass.

"Has anything happened since I last saw you?" he asked gently.

"No. I've just missed you. Have you missed me?"

"Of course. Have you been feeling okay?"

"I've been feeling wonderful." She smiled.

"That's good."

"Will your aunt let Bird leave school for the wedding?" Lina asked.

"The wedding?" Anders looked confused.

"Our wedding. Didn't you feel it? It's our destiny. You and me . . . ."

Lina's mind wandered away from her. She was beginning to feel a little panicked. Anders had looked so confused. Why was he confused? He had been there. He had been there when the universe opened up and then whispered the truth.

"Lina, are you sure you're feeling okay?" Anders asked softly.

"Yes, I'm okay." She stood up. She couldn't sit still anymore. "Why are you saying that? Why are you acting like this?"

Anders stood up too.

"Lina, don't be upset. I'm just worried about you."

"Why?" her voice was loud. "Everything is perfect."

"Do you remember where we are?"

Lina felt anger flare up inside her. "I'm not stupid, Anders. Of course I know where we are. I know we are in the asylum, but I'm leaving soon. I'm not supposed to be here. We are supposed to be happy."

"Oh, Lina," he said and his eyes looked sad. "I know you're not stupid. I want you to be happy. Why don't you sit back down?"

"No."

"Please," he said, and his eyes swallowed her up. She couldn't stay mad at him, not at her Anders. He was her everything.

She sat down and Anders sat beside her. He began telling her a story. It was a funny one about his nephew. Lina smiled. She was excited to meet Anders' family. She continued to smile and let him tell her stories until another orderly walked by and told Anders they needed help inside.

"I'll see you later," he said to her as he stood up to leave.

"Okay," Lina said as she watched him walk away.

Nothing much happened during the next few days. Whenever she saw Anders, he told her stories. They were all very good stories. When she wasn't with Anders, she spent her time waiting for the universe to release her from the asylum. She knew it was going to happen. She knew it was all part of the plan.

Instead of sleeping, Lina spent her nights planning her and Anders's wedding. She would invite the baker and his wife, and they would bring peanut butter cookies and a cake. Bird would come too. She would be Lina's maid of honor. Lina wasn't sure if she would invite her aunt and uncle. They were the ones who had made the huge mistake and sent her to this place, so she wasn't sure they deserved to come on her special day. Then again, if she hadn't come here, then she never would've met her true love. She put them down as a maybe. She would probably invite her cousins. She wanted them to see her looking radiant in her mother's dress. She wanted them to see how handsome Anders was; they would be so jealous. She imagined dancing with Anders. He would spin her around and everyone would clap. She couldn't wait to get out of the asylum. She couldn't wait for her life to truly begin.

Lina was watching Anders from across the dining hall when a nurse came and tapped her on the shoulder.

"The doctor is here to remove your stitches," she said to Lina.

Lina followed her to a room where Dr. Stevens waited.

"How are you doing?" he asked.

It took a while for his words to register. They had to tunnel their way through her wedding plans.

"I feel wonderful," she replied.

She knew Dr. Stevens was still talking to her, but she wasn't listening. She didn't have time to listen to him. She was somewhat aware of the stitches being removed, but only in regards to the fact she would need to find a veil that covered her scar.

"Lina," Dr. Stevens was saying her name loudly.

She looked at him annoyed.

"I need to know how your head has been feeling." He waited for an answer.

"Oh, it's fine. Great, really. Okay, I need to . . ." She stood up from the table ready to walk out of the room. She had wasted too much time here already.

"Wait," Dr. Stevens said, resting a hand on her shoulder. "Have you had any more nausea?"

"No. Now may I please . . . I have to see . . . ." She was wondering where Anders was. He was probably looking for her, no doubt upset that he hadn't been able to talk to her yet that day.

Dr. Steven's hand was still on her shoulder, and she was just barely aware that he was saying something to the nurse.

"She's not making sense, I think we should keep her here for observation to ensure there's no serious damage."

The nurse laughed unkindly. "Doctor, all the patients here are seriously damaged. This isn't like your hospital."

Lina didn't listen to Dr. Steven's response. She needed to go be with Anders. She threw his hand off her shoulder and hurried out of the room. She needed to ask Anders what kind of flowers he liked. She wanted to make sure he approved of the ones she picked out. She thought she saw him up ahead, so she picked up her pace. She lifted her hand and prepared to call out to him when a needle was shoved in her arm. She barely had time to turn and look at the nurse and Dr. Stevens before everything went black.

Lina opened her eyes slightly. Her head felt groggy. She could just make out the figure of Dr. Carrow and Dr. Stevens. They seemed to be arguing.

"I don't think she needs any more sedatives, Carrow. She needs to wake up so we can examine her," Dr. Stevens was saying.

"Isn't that sweet," Carrow snarled while injecting another needle into her arm. "You think you know what's better for my patient than I do."

Dr. Stevens opened his mouth to respond, but Lina was lost in darkness before his first word could reach her ear.

Lina was awake, but she was only slightly aware of that fact. She was only slightly aware of anything. Her head felt cloudy, and that was the only thing she felt. She turned her head and saw Dr. Stevens looking at her.

"Lina," he said.

She stared at him.

"How do you feel?"

She didn't respond. She didn't understand the question. She didn't feel anything. She opened and closed her mouth. Her tongue and lips were very dry. Lina looked at Dr. Stevens again and realized he was still talking to her. His voice sounded different. If Lina had been aware enough to comprehend, she would have known that he sounded worried.

"What did you give her?" she heard him say loudly to a nurse.

Lina didn't care enough to listen for the response. She continued to open and close her dry mouth, wondering if anyone would give her a drink.

Time no longer meant anything to Lina. She did not know if it had been hours or days since she had heard Dr. Carrow and Dr. Stevens argue over sedating her. She continued to drift in and out of consciousness.

When Lina was conscious, she only cared about whether or not someone was going to bring her a drink. They did that from time to time. A nurse came into the room with a cup. Lina tried to drink but half the water dripped down her chin and only some made it into her mouth. Lina tried to lick her chin to get the rest. She held out her cup for more water, but the nurse ignored her and left. Dr. Carrow came into the room. He was the only one there. Lina showed the cup to him. He slapped her on the wrist and the cup fell to the floor. She looked down at it. She tried to reach down and get it, and she fell off the chair and onto the floor. Dr. Carrow laughed. If anyone else had been in the room, they would have said that the laugh sounded cruel, but no one else was there, and Lina couldn't hear the cruelty.

Doctor Carrow turned as if he heard a sound and quickly shoved Lina back into her chair. "I've never liked you more," he whispered in her ear as a nurse entered the room.

The nurse was accompanied by Anders. He had a bowl of soup in his hands.

"I found an orderly willing to babysit this one," the nurse said to Carrow.

Carrow looked at Anders.

"How lucky," Carrow said. "I have so many other patients to attend to."

Anders started to respond, but Carrow cut him off. "Be careful feeding her. She might bite."

Carrow and the nurse left, leaving Anders alone with Lina.

Anders pulled up a chair and sat directly in front of her. "Sorry I didn't come sooner. I didn't know you were in here. What happened?"

Lina stared at the soup. She opened her mouth and drool spilled out.

"Lina?" His voice changed, but Lina didn't notice.

Lina focused as hard as she could. She opened her mouth.

"Soup." That was all she managed to say.

Anders gently lifted the spoon to her lips. She stuck out her tongue and tried to lap it up. Most ended up on her chin.

Anders tried again. His eyes were wet. He held Lina's chin steady as he poured the spoonful of soup into her mouth.

He kept feeding her. He didn't try to ask her any more questions. He stared at her face, and tears fell down his cheeks as he poured spoonful after spoonful into her mouth.

When the soup was gone, Anders stood up. He kissed Lina on the top of her head.

"I am going to fix this," he said.

Lina sucked on her hair.

A few hours or days or maybe even weeks later, Lina woke up and saw someone in her room. It was Dr. Stevens. He was taking vials out of a cabinet and putting them in his pocket. He turned and saw Lina looking at him. He smiled at her as he pulled different vials from his briefcase and set them in the cabinet.

It took several days, but slowly Lina began to return. The first thing to return was fear. She noticed it when Dr. Carrow walked into the room one afternoon.

"How is she doing?" he asked a nurse.

"No changes," the nurse responded.

Only Lina knew that was a lie. Her heart beat quickly as Dr. Carrow sneered at her.

When the nurse's back was turned, Carrow leaned down and flicked Lina hard in the ear.

"I think this time I finally found the cure," he said so softly that Lina could barely hear him.

She held very still hoping her wildly pounding heart wouldn't betray her.

As more of Lina returned, it became harder to hide it. The nurses started to notice. They told Dr. Carrow that she was recovering. He pretended to be pleased, but Lina knew that wasn't the truth.

Once most of Lina returned, she began trying to make sense of what she had seen Dr. Steven's doing. Had he really switched out the vials, or had that all been a dream? And if it wasn't a dream, why would he do it? Lina continued to ponder these questions until the final pieces of her personality returned, until shame took its usual place and overtook every other thought.

The return of the shame was overpowering, its weight so heavy that Lina could hardly stand. She remembered the things she had said to Anders. She wished desperately that she could shut off her brain so that she could stop picturing the look on Anders' face when she told him about the wedding. She couldn't bear the thought of seeing him again. The thought of having to face him now made her long for the drugged out stupor she had just escaped. The embarrassment burned in her chest and made Lina sick. She stumbled to a waste basket and vomited.

Just as Lina finished, a nurse came into the room.

"We need this room for a new patient. The doctor says you can leave."

The nurse looked at Lina as though she were a disease. Lina didn't blame her. She wiped a speckle of vomit off her chin and shuffled out of the room.

Lina didn't know where to go. She wrapped her arms around herself and tried to hold everything in place as the despair clawed its way out. She opened the first door she saw and stepped inside. It was a small dark room with nothing in it besides a dirty towel and a long-forgotten spoon. Lina dropped herself into one of the corners and hung her head between her knees. She listened to the lunatics on the other side of the door and chewed aggressively on her bottom lip. She noticed a dead spider by her foot. She stared at it until she fell asleep.

Lina stayed in the corner for days. Her dry throat cried out for a drink, but she ignored it. Water would bring life, and Lina only wanted to die. She lay on the floor with her knees pulled into her chest. Once another lunatic came into the room. He was talking loudly to an invisible companion and he hardly glanced at Lina. He stayed in the room for a short while, then picked up the spoon and left. Lina thought maybe that was two days ago. She wondered how much longer it would take for her to die. Anytime she slept, she had nightmares. Sometimes they were about Bird, and sometimes they were about Anders, but they were always about disappointing others. Sometimes Lina thought she heard singing, a sad tune off in this distance. The song played over and over in her dark mind, swirling around with self-loathing and sorrow. She knew she couldn't have much longer left. She laid in her own filth wondering how long it would be until they found her corpse.

Lina had just drifted off to sleep when she felt someone shaking her. She forced her eyes open and saw Anders kneeling beside her.

"Go away," she croaked.

"Lina," his voice caught in his throat. He lifted her slightly and cradled her in his arms. She was too weak to stop him. She felt a tear fall onto her head. "I've been looking for you everywhere."

"Leave," she begged.

"No, Lina. What's wrong? Why are you here? I've been so worried about you. I thought you were. . ." Anders didn't finish.

Lina wondered why he was lying to her. He wouldn't be worried about her. No one worried about Lina. She wasn't worth it.

"Leave," she said again as she made a pathetic attempt to free herself from his arms.

"Please talk to me," pleaded Anders. "How can I help?"

"Leave," she croaked out one last time. Soon enough he would give up. Soon enough he would leave. She doubted he could stand being around her very much longer.

"I'm not leaving you, Lina. I don't want to leave you. Don't you understand that? I'm not going to give up on you."

"Just let me die." Lina moaned.

"No, Lina, no. I don't want to lose you, okay? Please. I just got you back. It was bad enough seeing just a shell of you. I don't know what they had given you, Lina, but it was awful. It wasn't you . . . but, I mean, at least I knew that you were still somewhere inside. If you were really gone, if something happened to you, I wouldn't be strong enough to handle it. I'm so sorry for everything that has happened to you. You don't deserve this. You deserve so much better. All I want to do is help you. All I want is to take care of you. I know it's hard for you. I honestly don't know how you do it, how you manage to pull yourself back together when your mind tries to tear you apart, but you do it and it's astonishing. You've done it before, and I know you can do it again now. And if you're willing to let me, I want to be there for you. I want to help you. I know you can do it on your own, but you don't have to. If you let me, Lina, I will hold you together when you feel like you're falling apart because I love you. I love every part of you." Anders stopped, and his words pounded in Lina's ears.

He lifted up her chin and kissed her softly on her cheek and his kiss and his words broke her heart. It broke her heart because it couldn't be real. The things he said – they couldn't be true. Lina was broken, and people didn't love things that were broken. No, things that were broken got thrown away, not put back together. Lina wasn't worthy of this; she wasn't worthy of happiness. Her shame screamed in her head, demanding to be heard, demanding to be obeyed. She pulled away. Tears streamed down her cheeks.

Anders was staring at her. She lowered her eyes, unable to bear looking at him. Her throat felt tight, and the darkness inside was suffocating her. She wanted to die even more than before. She loved Anders, and it ruptured her heart to have him pity her like this, because that's what this was. It wasn't love. It was pity. No one could possibly love Lina.

She was too ashamed to speak to him, and he didn't say anything else. She kept expecting him to leave, but he didn't. He stayed with her. He stroked her hair and held her and eventually she fell asleep.

When Lina awoke, she was no longer on the floor of the small room. She was on a bed and there was an IV in her arm. She looked around and saw several other beds. A few nurses were huddled in a corner. She could hear them talking, but didn't pay attention to the words. She felt darkness and disappointment at being alive. She looked at the traitorous needle in her arm and watched as life-giving fluids were pumped into her body. She hated Anders for bringing her here. She knew it was him. No one else would have done this. Any other nurse or orderly would have been more than happy to let her die. She moved to pull the IV out and realized for the first time that she was strapped to the bed. More shame rose up inside of her. Wasn't it bad enough that she was still alive? Did she have to be strapped to a table, lying exposed for anyone to come and gawk at her pathetic form? Her eyes burned and she squeezed them shut. There was nothing she could do. Life had been forced back into her, and she had no way to escape the all-consuming degradation that chipped away at her.

Lina felt someone standing next to her; she didn't care who it was.

"Everything is going to be okay," she heard Anders say softly.

The crushing weight of his pity forced her deeper in the bed. She wished she could disappear entirely. She turned her head to the side so that Anders wouldn't see the tears washing down her cheeks and pity her even more. Flashes of the things she said to him during her episode trampled over her weak mind. She had been so sure that what she had said was true, so sure that they were destined to be together. She imagined what he must have thought when she rambled on about their wedding, about the universe, about so many things. It made her sick to think about it. She recalled him pouring soup into her miserable, drooling mouth and the pain of the memory was more than she could bear.

"Why are you doing this? Please just let me die." The words hurt as they pushed their way out of her mouth. Lina was desperate, desperate for an escape from the misery that consumed her.

"I'm doing it because I love you. I know you don't believe me, but it's true. I noticed you before we ever even spoke. I saw you and Bird together many times and you always seemed so kind. I've admired you ever since the first real conversation we had, when your only concern was Bird. That's when I truly realized how big your heart was. My admiration has only grown the more time I've spent with you. You're smart and strong and a fighter. You have to fight against your own mind and you overcome it every time and I'm in awe. When I thought I had lost you to Sam, that's when I realized it was love, because I realized how terrible it would be to never see you again. I realized how much you truly mean to me, how important you are to me. I would be miserable if you died… and so would Bird. Despite what you may think, she hasn't forgotten about you. She misses you. I have a letter from her. She wanted me to give it to you." Anders slipped the letter into her pocket. "I can't stay much longer. My shift ends in a few minutes, but I'll be back tomorrow night. Please, for me and for Bird, don't give up."

Lina still refused to open her eyes. She didn't want to see Anders.

Anders leaned down and whispered. "The world needs you in it. My world needs you in it."

Then she head him walk away.

Her shame cracked open just enough to let his words in. She wanted to believe him, but before she had time to even try, the shame sealed the crack and forced out any competing emotion. Lina was a slave to the demons inside her, and she didn't know how to escape.

After he left, Lina opened her eyes just slightly. There was no one in the room. Lina was left alone with her darkness. She stared helplessly at the ceiling as somewhere, buried deep beneath the shame, the tiniest part of her cried out for help.

Chapter Seventeen

Anders had lied. He didn't come to see her the next day. Lina wasn't surprised. He had appeased his pity by keeping her alive, and now he was never going to see her again. Why would he? How could it possibly benefit him to spend time with her? She stared up at the ceiling and let her mind wander. It wandered down dark paths to deep corners of her mind. She recalled every instance of disgrace and embarrassment, every time her sick, twisted mind had made her act like a fool. The memories banged around inside her head, and she felt as if her mind were melting away. She felt it dripping down the back of her head until it started to clog her throat. She felt as if she were choking, but she didn't care. She was so tired and angry at her broken mind that death was what she wanted.

For days, Lina longed for the release of death. She cursed any time a nurse refilled her fluids. She was swimming in darkness, consumed with despair.

One morning, Lina awoke and noticed that Bird's letter weighed inexplicably heavily on her leg. She had forgotten it was there. It almost seemed as if it were demanding to be noticed. The letter felt as if it were crushing her leg, and a tiny part of Lina couldn't help but think that maybe Bird really did care about her. Maybe Bird was one person who would miss her if she died. Why would Bird have gone to the trouble of writing Lina a letter and giving it to Anders if she didn't care about her at least a little? Bird was gone. She didn't encounter Lina every day. It would have been easy for her to forget all about the asylum, to forget all about Lina. The tiny part of Lina that was crying out for help, the part she wasn't even aware of beneath all the shame and despair grabbed a hold of this sliver of hope and started to pull itself free from the darkness.

More and more of Lina's shame began to fade away. As the days passed, the nurses deemed her healthy enough, and she was released from her bed. She walked the asylum hallways leaving droplets of darkness and self-pity behind her. She settled back into a routine and slowly returned to her normal self. When that happened, when she finally felt she was worthy, Lina found a quiet, secluded spot and pulled out Bird's letter.

Dear Lina,

I miss you every day. I wish you were here. I haven't seen you in months and it still hurts. I never even got to say goodbye. I don't really know what happened or how I ended up in the hospital. Anders visited me when I woke up. We talked about you. He said you wanted me to go to his aunt's school, that he was going to make it happen. I didn't think he really could. I thought I would go back to the asylum. I was scared of that, but I knew it would be okay because I would be with you. I cried when they told me I wasn't going back. I asked if I could say goodbye to you, but they said that wasn't a good idea. I went straight to the school. I like it here. The people are pretty nice. They don't know I came from the asylum. Anders' aunt didn't think we should tell them. I share a room with a girl named Jill. She is quiet. I would much rather share a room with you. I miss talking to you every day. You are my best friend and my sister. I didn't even have a name before I met you. I hope you know how much I miss you and how much I love you. I didn't ever want to leave you. I know you wanted me to come here and I know you want everything good for me and I want those things for you too. I'm going to find a way to get you out. I'm going to find a way to come see you. I hope you haven't forgotten how remarkable you are. I hope you don't let people make you think you aren't important, because you are important and you deserve to be happy. Thank you for being my friend and thank you for always taking care of me. I am going to see you soon. I love you. I don't know when I will write again. This letter took me almost two weeks to finish and it was hard getting it to Anders, but know that I think about you every day and that I owe you everything that is good in my life.

Love, Bird.

When she finished reading, Lina clutched the letter close to her chest.

Tears trickled down her cheeks. She missed Bird so much that she felt that her heart might explode. She read the letter again and her fingers traced Bird's carefully written words. She was so proud of her friend. She looked at Bird's letter and imagined the work Bird must have put into it. She imagined Bird dutifully checking the spelling of every single word, and she imagined Bird hunched over her paper, her deliberate penmanship spilling from her pen. Lina felt happier than she had felt in a very long time. Bird was becoming the person she was meant to be. She was out of the asylum and flourishing in the real world. Lina suddenly realized that Bird's room at the school was probably the first real room she had ever had. She wondered what it was like for Bird to fall asleep in a real bed that first night, and she wished she could have seen her face.

Lina carefully refolded the letter and slipped it into her pocket. The letter was her most treasured possession, the one bright gift in her miserable life. She went to take a deep breath, but realized she couldn't. She began hyperventilating…what was it that Carrow had said in his office that day? *"You think Bird is safe from me just because she's not here anymore? You think I can't get to her in that little school? You think you're so clever for getting her there? I could pay her a visit anytime I want."* His words came crashing back to her, hitting her like stones falling from the sky. Carrow could never see this letter. He would punish her for having it, and he would punish Bird. Lina needed to protect Bird. That job still wasn't done. Lina knew she would have to follow Carrow's rules and not make any mistakes. She had no doubt that he would carry out his threat against Bird the moment she stepped out of line.

Lina gripped the letter in her pocket. She wanted to hide it, to keep it safe from Carrow's evil, lunatic eyes. Making sure she wasn't being followed, she walked outside and towards the asylum wall. She looked carefully around, and when she was sure no one was looking, she began digging a hole. Her fingernails filled with dirt as she dug the hole deeper and deeper. When she was finished, she pulled the letter out of her pocket. She looked at it one last time, memorizing the words, then tore it apart and buried it. Now her treasure was safe. Dr. Carrow wouldn't find the letter. He wouldn't read about Bird's happiness and then snuff it out just to torment Lina.

Once her task was finished, she headed back into the asylum. She wandered the halls, having no real destination. She wondered where Anders was. Now that most of the darkness was gone from inside her, she wanted to see him. She remembered his words to her and wondered if maybe they could be real. Maybe it was more than pity, more than a sense of duty. But if that were true, wouldn't he have come to find her? Wouldn't he have come to check up on her by now? Hadn't he promised to take care of her? These thoughts filled her mind and kept her unpleasant company throughout the rest of the week. Each night she ate dinner in troubled silence and then headed to bed quickly after.

Lina was standing on the sidewalk. She looked into the restaurant across the street and saw Anders. He was wearing a suit and tie; he looked so handsome. Lina began to cross the street so she could talk to him. She was halfway there when someone joined Anders at the table. The someone was tall and gorgeous with thick brown hair. She whispered in Anders' ear and the 2 of them laughed. Lina stopped walking. Her feet were too heavy to move. She looked down and noticed for the first time that she was wearing a wedding dress. Wasn't she supposed to be getting married to Anders? Wasn't that why she was looking for him in the first place. Lina looked back up at him and the girl. She watched as Anders reached into his pocket and took out a small black box. He opened it and the girl squealed in excitement. Anders took a ring from the box and slipped it onto the girl's finger.

Lina looked down at her own hands only to discover them raw and bright red. Tiny specks of blood have dripped from her fingers and onto her dress. Lina cried out for Anders, hoping for an explanation. The sound of a horn honking reached her ears just as the front of the car crashed into her.

When Lina woke up the next morning, she could only remember pieces of the nightmare, mostly the end. She knew she had more important issues to worry about than the mysterious absence of Anders, but it still bothered her. Why would he say all those things to her and then just disappear? Had it even happened? Maybe she had dreamed it all up. That must have been it. There had been no kiss, no declaration of love. It had only been a delusion.

Even though she didn't really believe that, she tried to force her mind to accept it because it hurt less than what might be the truth, the truth that Anders hadn't meant what he said, or that Lina had finally driven him away. Could she really blame him for doing what she had begged him to do so many times before? No, she was the only one to blame if he had finally listened and given up on her.

Lina tried to forget about Anders, but it was not easy. Her only other options for thought were Carrow and Bird, and so she desperately tried to focus on Bird. She worked to fill her mind with thoughts of what Bird's life must be like. She tried to picture what the school might look like, as well as Bird's classmates. Lina could focus on those thoughts for a while, but inevitably her thoughts of Carrow or Anders would come knocking and her mind would grow much darker.

Lina wanted to feel relieved that she hadn't seen Carrow in a while, but instead she only felt worried. It was unlike him to stay away, especially after an episode. He usually liked to taunt her and rip at her fragile mind. She feared what he might be planning. Had he found out about Dr. Stevens switching the vials? Did he know that Lina saw Stevens do it? Was he planning to punish her for that? Perhaps he had finally tired of the game and was plotting how he wanted to get rid of Lina for good. Lina doubted he was ready to end the game, though. He had her just where he wanted her, alone and vulnerable. She believed a part of his twisted mind loved having someone to tell bits of his secrets to, someone he knew could never tell them to anyone else. Carrow knew that he owned Lina. He knew that he controlled her. She doubted he would be done playing his sick game for a very, very long time.

Chapter Eighteen

It had been three weeks since Lina had seen Anders, and even longer since she had seen Carrow. She hadn't spoken to anyone in all that time. She avoided other people as much as she could. She reverted to the life she led when she first came to the asylum – silent days spent in the corners. It was harder to do this time around. It was harder because this time she actually knew what it felt like to have a friend. She was haunted by the memory of Bird. Before Lina came to the asylum, she hadn't really had friends. There had been Stewart, but he had been taken away by the war. Aside from him, Lina had mostly spent time with her books. There were books in the asylum, but she didn't feel like reading anymore. She didn't feel like doing much of anything. Merely existing took all of her energy. Her thoughts tumbled around in her mind and drained her strength. Sometimes, she didn't have any thoughts at all. That was a recent development. It would last for a few hours, and Lina wouldn't even notice until she suddenly snapped out of it. She wasn't entirely sure how she felt about that. She supposed it would be easier if she forgot all of the things inside her, but as much as she had claimed she wanted to disappear, the thought of losing herself entirely frightened her.

Lina wondered how she would be able to keep track of herself when she spent her time every day being ignored by hundreds of people. No one spoke to her. No one had spoken to her in weeks, and she was getting used to it. When someone did finally acknowledge her, for the first time in nearly a month, Lina was startled. She was walking down the hallway when someone tapped her on the shoulder. She gasped loudly and whipped her head around. It was an orderly.

"Dr. Carrow wants to see you," he grunted. "Follow me."

Lina silently obeyed, her body shaking. When they reached Carrow's office, the orderly shoved her inside and quickly left. Lina looked warily at Carrow, who smiled eerily in return. Lina could feel sweat dripping down her face. She stood rooted to her spot, afraid to even move. This was the moment she had been dreading. What horrors did he have in store for her?

"Have you missed me?" he asked coolly.

Lina made no response.

Carrow put his head down slightly and massaged his temple with his fingers, "You know, I thought we had an understanding. I thought I made myself clear what would happen if you stepped out of line. Was I *not* clear? Or, are you just too stupid and insane to understand?"

He stared at Lina with a look of venomous disgust on his face. She had no idea what to do.

"I . . . " she started to say, but she didn't know how to finish.

Dr. Carrow rested his elbows heavily on his desk. "I thought you were finally getting better. I was finally making progress in my work, and then your little boyfriend ruined everything."

"What do . . ." Lina started to ask.

Carrow cut her off. "Don't play dumb. Do you think I don't know that that orderly of yours messed everything up? Do you think I don't know he talked Dr. Stevens into stealing my cure? I know everything. This is my asylum, not yours. Whatever sick tricks you played to get that idiot to care about you stop now. It all stops now."

"I didn't know. I didn't ask him to..." Lina began to shake.

"SHUT UP," Carrow bellowed. "I don't want your excuses or your lies."

His eyes were burning with lunacy and Lina started to cry. She couldn't help herself. Carrow got up from his seat and walked over to her. He gripped her chin so forcefully that she feared her jaw would break. "Look at me and pay very close attention." His breath was hot against her skin, "I'm giving you one last chance. Stay away from the orderly."

Suddenly Carrow began to laugh, wildly and horrifyingly. "I almost forgot to tell you the best part. Consider it a gift – something to help you follow the rules. The orderly, Anders is it?" He lowered his voice and his eyes sparkled excitedly. "I ran him over with my car."

Lina gasped. She felt panic and despair flooding every inch of her body. Was Anders dead? Had Carrow killed him?

Carrow slapped her across the face.

"Don't look so shocked, Lina. I warned you what would happen." Carrow walked back to his seat. "If he survives and if he returns, you will not speak to him. Do you understand?"

Lina bit her cheek and nodded. Did that mean Anders was still alive?

Carrow was rummaging through his drawer, clearly looking for something. A moment later, he pulled out dirty shreds of paper and threw them at her feet. Kneeling to pick them up, she recognized the tattered pages as the letter Bird had written to her. Standing again, her knees began to buckle and she felt that she was about to faint.

"Mess up again and you lose everything," Carrow hissed. "Now get out."

Lina turned and fumbled with the door knob, making it only a few feet away from the room before she fell to the floor.

This was hell, it had to be, and Carrow was the devil.

Lina was catatonic, sprawled helplessly on the asylum floor. If there had been even the tiniest speck of hope left inside of her, it was gone now. She wanted to move, to pull herself up, but she couldn't. Carrow had destroyed her. There was nothing left inside to fight anymore. Was Anders going to survive? Carrow must have thought so, or why would he have warned her to stay away? She could only imagine what kind of shape he was in. She pictured him lying mangled on the side of the road and she felt bile rising in her throat. *Please, Anders, be okay.*

She still couldn't move. She didn't know how long it had been. Carrow hadn't come out of his office yet. She knew she needed to get away before he did. She couldn't handle seeing him again so soon. The thought of having to look at his evil, monstrous face made her feel as though life was draining out of her. She needed to move, to get further away from his office. She tried to move so that she was sitting, but she couldn't. She remained face down on the floor. She mustered every single ounce of strength in her pathetic body and was finally able to lift herself slightly so that she was now resting on her elbows. *I need to move*. Those words banged around in her head over and over again, willing her body to obey. Slowly and deliberately, she began inching herself forward, her body dragging across the stained floor. After what felt like weeks, she made it to a door that led outside, but she couldn't lift herself any higher to open it. She rested her body directly in front of the door, desperately wishing for someone to come open it. She felt something crawl across her legs, but she couldn't turn to look. It was probably a rat. She had been noticing a lot of them lately. She remembered something she read in a book once about rats eating the bottom of people's feet while they slept. She wondered if the rats would eat hers. Lina supposed this thought should frighten her, but really, how could that make her life any worse? Rat-chewed feet or not, Carrow was going to torture her until he got bored, and then he would kill her, and she couldn't tell anyone because then he would kill them too. This was her truth. This was her reality.

Hadn't she once planned on going to Columbia? It felt like a lifetime ago that she had had that dream. She wondered who had received the scholarship that was supposed to be hers, who was living the collegiate life that would have been hers, had her mind not betrayed her. How long had she been in the asylum? It must have been over a year, but she no longer had any real concept of time.

Lina didn't even realize that she was crying until the tears began to fall onto her skeletal fingers. She cried silently as she thought of the life that could have been hers and of the lives that would be ruined if she tried to do anything to get it back.

"Hey, you need to get out of the way," an angry voice yelled at her.

She tried to obey, but there was nothing left of her strength to give.

"Did you hear me?" the voice yelled again, and after a moment of waiting for a response, "Stupid loon."

Lina supposed the person must have left because the voice didn't yell at her again, or at least not for a while. Eventually the voice returned, accompanied by another.

"See, right here like I told you," said the old voice.

"I see it," the new voice responded.

"Well, can you get her out of the way now?"

"Sure."

Suddenly Lina felt herself lifted quickly from the floor. With his arms under her armpits, an orderly (she could tell by the sleeves) dragged her into one of the rooms where the patients slept. He dropped her carelessly onto a mat and then walked away. Lina laid on the mat and stared up at the ceiling. She wondered if she would ever be able to move again. She stayed helpless on her mat and eventually fell asleep.

When Lina awoke, she still couldn't move. For the entire day she was stuck on the mat. Her mind drifted in and out of focus and she stared up aimlessly. The loonies came back in, which meant it was night again. She still couldn't move, and since there was nothing else to do, she slept. Morning came, and still she was frozen. She wet herself, and the warm pee smelled rancid as it coated her back. She would have tried to call out for help if she thought anyone would listen, but she knew nobody would. She spent another day stuck on the mat. Her tongue felt dry and swollen. Night came and she slept again. Another morning and she was still stuck on her back. She wouldn't survive much longer without water. She didn't really care. It would be better to die now than to have Carrow torture her indefinitely. A few times during the day she dozed off, but not for very long. Her throat was on fire. She closed her eyes and tried to ignore it.

"Lina," Anders said.

Lina looked up and saw him standing over her. They were in a field somewhere. She could feel cool grass tickling her arms.

"Hey, it's time to get up." He smiled at her.

She moved to push herself up and realized she couldn't. Panic started to take over.

"I can't move," she tried to say, but no sound came out.

"Lina?" Anders looked concerned.

She stared up at him with fear in her eyes. "Please help me," she tried to say, but her lips didn't move.

Anders knelt down, picked Lina up, and cradled her against his chest. She began to cry.

"Lina, don't cry," Anders said as he wiped away her tears. "We'll fix this. We always do."

He stood up and began carrying her. They approached a small white house. In the front yard was a magnificent garden with all sorts of flowers swaying majestically in the gentle breeze. They got to the house and Anders opened the door.

"Oh good, you're still home," Anders said to someone. Lina tried turning to look, but she couldn't move her head.

"What? Oh no! It happened again!" Bird's beautiful voice reached Lina just as her dear friend came into view.

Anders carried Lina to a bed as Bird followed alongside him.

He rested her gently on her side, and he and Bird kneeled in front of her.

"We're going to fix this," they promised.

"Bird," Lina wanted to say. Her friend looked beautiful. Her hair hung in a long braid and she was wearing what appeared to be a school uniform. Her face was no longer sallow and angular. It was full and healthy, and her scar was barely noticeable.

"Lina, do you remember where we are?" Bird asked. "This is our house. Do you remember our house?"

Lina's eyes scanned the area. Nothing looked familiar, but she saw a picture of the three of them hanging on the wall. Lina was in a wedding dress and Anders was in a tuxedo, Bird was next to them smiling brightly.

"I don't think she remembers," Bird said to Anders.

"Don't you remember?" Anders asked. "Don't you remember how we got here? Don't you remember how you saved us?"

Bird looked at her hopefully. "Come on, Lina. Try to remember."

Lina stared at them, unable to speak. She wanted to ask them what they meant. What had she forgotten?

Anders and Bird both smiled reassuringly at her. "You're going to do it," they said. "Lina, you can save us. You're going to save us. But first you have to get up."

Lina's eyes shot open. She blinked as the asylum ceiling came into focus. It had only been a dream. She wanted to go back. She wanted to go back to the white house, and the flowers, and Anders and Bird. Their words echoed in her mind. *"You have to get up."* She wondered what Bird would think if she saw Lina lying here like this. She was sure it would break her heart. Lina couldn't do that to her friend. She had to at least try to survive, even if there was no hope. Lina took a deep breath and tried to sit up. She felt her back rise briefly off the mat before it fell back down. She tried again. It took five tries, but eventually she was able to sit up. Her urine-coated gown was stuck to her back, and her mouth was drier than she ever remembered it being. She got to her feet and began shuffling toward the showers. It took forever, but she made it. She stepped under the shower head, too weak to even remove her gown. She turned on the water and let it rain down on her; she opened her mouth and gulped it down. She stayed in the shower for what felt like hours. When she was finished, she knew that Anders and Bird would be proud of her. Soaking wet, she made her way outside where she stood in the sun and let the heat wrap around her. She knew that somewhere Dr. Carrow was probably watching her. He was probably gazing down on her in cruel delight, but there was nothing she could do about that. There was nothing she could do about Dr. Carrow's plans, but she could at least do Anders and Bird the honor of not giving up.

The memory of her dream and the love she felt for Anders and Bird were the two things that sustained Lina. She woke, she ate, she shuffled, she sat, and she slept. It was all she had energy for. Each new day was a repetition of the day before. She had no sense of time. How long had it been since her encounter with Carrow? Five days? Ten? A month? The haze of lunacy that surrounded her made it impossible to keep track of anything concrete.

Every time she fell asleep, she hoped for another dream, another glimpse of the white house and the flowers, but it never came. It was hard to keep herself going, but Lina was determined not to let herself slip away. She was determined to keep living and playing until Carrow finally stepped in and ended the game. Some days she did worse than others; on those days she would drift away for a few hours at a time. She was worried by the increasing frequency of these occurrences but didn't know how to stop them. It took all her energy just to do the minimum each day. She couldn't fathom expending any more effort. If she could just know for sure that Anders was okay, or if she could somehow be certain that Bird was safe at her school, she felt that would help, but there was no way for her to learn anything about either of her friends.

Lina knew she needed to do something to keep herself from becoming completely insane. She knew that the mere dream of her friends would not be enough, not in the long run. She couldn't just spend her days waiting for Carrow to finish her off. She needed to fill them somehow. She needed something tangible, something in the asylum to help keep her grounded, to help keep her sane. She thought of the library. She hadn't been there in quite some time, but today she would go.

When Lina arrived at the library it was even more pathetic than she remembered. There were now only three books to be found, and one of them appeared to be half eaten. Lina grabbed the two uneaten books and carried them out of the room. She hid one, *Teeftallow,* under her mat and took the other one, *Macbeth,* outside and spent the rest of the day reading. When it became too dark to see the pages, she went back inside and hid *Macbeth* under her mat as well. She didn't trust them in the library. She didn't want the other lunatics to destroy them and leave her with nothing.

For the next week, Lina filled her hours with the books. It helped. She knew she would grow tired of reading the same two books eventually, but it was better than having nothing to do besides wait for whatever horrors Carrow had in store.

Lina sat in the shade of the tree reading her book. She tried hard to focus on the words and forget where she was. She was succeeding a bit, which is why when someone tapped her on the shoulder, she nearly screamed.

"Come with me." It was the lunatic man, the one with ominous warnings about the doctor.

"I..." Lina didn't know how to finish.

"Come with me, I need to show you where it is."

Lina looked up at him. She looked into his large brown eyes. They were lucid. They were sane.

"Hurry, please, before I forget." He sounded desperate.

Lina stood up and followed him as he began walking. She studied him as they walked. She had never registered his age before. She had always just assumed he was much older than she was because of how haggard he looked, but now she wasn't so sure. He had pale blonde hair and was balding, and the asylum had no doubt taken a toll on him physically, but Lina suspected he was younger than he seemed.

"Where are we going?" she asked.

"To his room. I need to show you his room." He glanced around nervously as he spoke.

"What room? Whose room?" she asked.

"The doctor's room, his secret room," he hissed.

Lina was silent as she followed behind him, not sure what to say. The doctor had to be Carrow. She was sure of it. But what was the room?

"My name is Richard," the lunatic said suddenly as he led her down a hallway. "Please remember it for me."

Before Lina could think of a response, Richard stopped walking.

He turned and stared at her intently. "We are almost there. I'm scared, I don't want to go back."

"It's okay. I'm with you."

"I can't do it." Richard's eyes began to fill with tears.

"Please, I need to know what Carrow is doing." Lina was desperate. She was so close to getting some understanding, some proof, just something to explain what Carrow was up to. Something that might explain the bruises and the games he played with her mind.

Richard gripped his hair and closed his eyes. He began to rock back and forth, "I can't, I can't, I can't" he whispered.

"Richard, just tell me where it is. I'll go alone. You don't have to come. You can stay safe."

"Who's Richard?" he asked suddenly as his eyes shot open. Lina's heart dropped to the floor as she watched his eyes, which only a moment ago had been clear and bright, become clouded with lunacy.

Richard began squeezing his fists together as he walked around in a circle. "Don't trust the doctor. No, no, no. You'd better listen. Don't try to run." He glanced at Lina and then shuffled quickly away. She knew better than to follow him. He was too far gone. He couldn't help her anymore.

Lina remained rooted to the ground. She felt heavy, too heavy to try moving right now. For a few brief moments she had had hope, hope that she would figure out what Carrow was doing. She had even allowed herself the briefest thought that perhaps with proof of something nefarious she could make it stop. That somehow she could show someone, maybe Dr. Stevens, what she found and end Carrow's game. But that thought hadn't lasted long, and she felt stupid for even allowing it to cross her mind; she pushed the thought away because allowing it to linger would only lead to further misery. The only end to Carrow's game was death.

Lina slowly made her way back outside. It seemed to take forever to get there. She plopped down beneath the tree and rested her head between her knees. She breathed in deeply through her nose, and her body shivered as she released the air through her mouth. She didn't feel like reading anymore, so she picked at the small patch of grass next to her. Her mind kept drifting down dark pathways and it was hard to stop it. She almost found herself longing for another episode because at least during the high she would be able to forget everything for a while, even though the crash back to reality always hurt too much for it to be worth it.

Lina went to bed still feeling defeated, and she was still so downtrodden in the morning that she didn't have the energy to worry about the dark bruise covering her arm. Carrow had struck again, and all she had to do now was wait and see what was in store.

Nothing happened for the rest of the day. She didn't hear any voices screaming, and she didn't get sick. She wondered how closely Carrow was watching her. She wondered if he was growing more and more irritated as the day progressed and Lina stayed the same.

She went to sleep feeling slightly triumphant that for at least that day, she had won.

Her victory was short-lived.

When she awoke the next morning, there was a new bruise, and her body felt as if it were on fire. Sweat poured down her face and back. She could feel it dripping from her fingertips as she made her way to the showers. She needed to cool down. She turned on the water and stripped off her gown. The ice cold water did nothing to lessen her discomfort. Her temper flared and her body heat continued to rise. She stepped out of the shower and threw on her gown. She swung the door open and stepped into the hall. She was walking very quickly with no real direction in mind. The only thing she could think about was cooling down. Suddenly another patient ran into her.

"Watch where you're going!" Lina screamed at the man.

The lunatic was tall and hairy. His skin was splotchy and his gown looked brand new. Lina looked down at her own gown. Compared to his crisp white one, hers looked gray and pathetic.

"Where'd you get the fancy clothes from?"

He looked down at his gown and then back at Lina. "Dunno."

"You don't know? How do you not know?" Lina felt inexplicably annoyed at how much cleaner his gown was than hers. She couldn't stand to look at it. She shoved him and then stormed away. She stopped the first nurse she saw.

"I want a new gown," Lina demanded.

"You have a gown," the nurse responded.

"I want a *new* one! This one is old and grimy and gray. I want a fresh, clean one. Get me a clean one!!" Lina's skin felt as if it were on fire, and she imagined that there were blisters forming on her arms.

The nurse folded her arms across her chest and her face fell into a scowl. "You already have a gown. You need to calm down."

The nurse stared at Lina for a moment longer and then turned and started to walk away.

Sweat dripped into Lina's eyes. It hurt. Tears of anger and frustration began to slide down her cheeks. Rage flared up even stronger inside of her.

"Get me a new gown!" she shouted as she rushed after the nurse.

When the nurse turned and saw her, she too began to run. "Help!" the nurse shouted, "I need an orderly! Help!"

The nurse turned a corner and Lina hurried to catch up to her. She managed to tackle the nurse to the ground just as a large orderly appeared. He pulled Lina off the screaming nurse and held her tightly in his arms. His arms were hairy and he smelled like beef. The scent made Lina sick.

"Let me go!" she shouted as she fought against his hold. "You reek!"

Once the nurse regained her composure, she glared at Lina as she spoke to the orderly, "I'll get a sedative for this one. Take her to Room 18."

Lina tried her hardest to free herself from the grasp of the odorous orderly, but her efforts were for naught. He carried her into the room and dumped her on the ground. He then positioned himself in front of the door and watched Lina with disgust.

Lina glared at the orderly. She was growing lightheaded; she couldn't stand the heat coursing through and around her body any longer. She desperately needed a drink of water.

"I need water," she demanded.

"No."

"Give me some water!" she shouted.

The orderly stared at her without responding until the nurse came into the room.

"You got it?" he asked the nurse.

"Yep," the nurse replied as she showed him the needle.

"Good," he grunted as he once again grabbed Lina.

"I need water!" Lina yelled desperately at her two captors.

"Hold her arm steady," the nurse said.

As the needle pierced Lina's burning skin, she felt immense and immediate pain.

She screamed, and even the callous nurse seemed concerned by Lina's reaction. Lina looked down and saw that her arm was bleeding heavily where the needle had just been.

"What's going on?" the orderly asked. "Is she supposed to bleed like that?"

"I don't...I....no, she's not!" The nurse looked into Lina's eyes, and Lina saw alarm and perhaps even a hint of pity. She wondered what the nurse was going to do next, but she passed out too quickly to find out.

Chapter Nineteen

When Lina woke back up, she was surrounded by people, her hair was drenched in sweat, and she felt so hot that she could hardly breathe.

"Water," she squeaked out.

No one seemed to hear her. They were all very busy discussing something above her.

"Water," she said a little louder.

"She's awake!" someone said. "Get the doctor."

Before Lina had time to register what was being said, Dr. Stevens appeared at her side.

"Lina, it's me, Dr. Stevens. Do you remember me?" he asked.

She nodded weakly.

"Everything is going to be okay," he assured her. "You're in the hospital, but everything is going to be okay."

"Water," she pleaded once again as her sandpaper tongue sat swollen in her mouth.

"I'll get you some right away."

When Dr. Stevens brought back the water, Lina drank it very slowly, allowing it to cool her burning throat as it slid down. The relief it provided was all too wonderful and all too short lived; the moment she finished the cup, she was once again acutely aware of the heat coursing angrily through her.

She could feel Dr. Stevens watching her, so she turned to look at him. His eyes looked tired and sad. Sweat dripped into Lina's eyes as she stared at Dr.

Stevens. She felt exhausted and confused. She was aware of most of what had happened, but remembering it felt like remembering a dream, or more accurately, a nightmare.

"I'm glad you are awake," Dr. Stevens said kindly, though his eyes were still sad.

There was a blanket covering Lina. She tried to push it off, but the movement exhausted her. She also discovered that her legs were shackled to the bed; the metal cuffs felt like pokers that had been left too long in the fire.

"I'm so hot," she said, and started to cry.

Stevens quickly removed her blanket.

"Thank you."

"I've never seen someone react to a sedative like this before," Stevens said, scratching his chin.

"It wasn't the sedative." The words spilled out of Lina before she realized what she was saying.

"What?" Stevens asked, his eyes narrowing in confusion.

Lina panicked, and as she did her temperature rose even higher. She couldn't stand the heat. Her entire body seemed to be on fire. Tears poured out of her eyes and her breathing became short and desperate. Terror welled up inside her.

"Breathe, Lina. Just breathe slowly." Stevens took her hand, and even though his added body heat felt terrible, she felt immensely grateful for the comfort. "We don't have to talk now. Just breathe."

Lina worked to steady her breathing. She opened her mouth wide to let air in, and sweat trickled onto her tongue. It tasted salty and dirty.

As the terror subsided and her breathing returned to normal, Lina felt exhaustion taking over. She closed her eyes and fell asleep with Dr. Stevens still holding her hand.

When Lina awoke again, there were two small fans blowing on the table next to her. They helped, but not enough. She became fixated on her hot scalp. The heat had nowhere to go because it was trapped beneath her sweat-soaked hair. Her hair clung to her face, neck and shoulders, acting as an unbearable blanket. The skin beneath the shackles on her ankles felt as though it was melting onto the metal.

Lina breathed heavily through her open mouth. She couldn't think about anything other than how uncomfortable she felt. There was water on the table next to her, and she drank it greedily, but it did nothing to ease her discomfort. Nurses came by periodically to check on her and bring her more water. She didn't want to spend the energy to try to speak to them.

Finally, Dr. Stevens came to see her again. His eyes filled with concern as he looked at her. She could tell he felt sorry for her and could sense how miserable she felt. She stared at his round, grandfatherly face and silently pleaded for him to provide some sort of relief. He looked at her blotchy red face and sweat-soaked hair and rested his hand gently on hers.

"Don't worry, Lina. We'll fix you."

The atmosphere in the hospital was very different from that in the asylum. It took her a while to put her finger on what exactly the difference was, but when a nurse stopped by and wiped the sweat off Lina's face, she figured it out. They treated her like a real person here. Not everyone, of course. She had noticed some nurses and doctors who looked at her with a mixture of alarm and disdain, but all the people in charge of her care made her feel human. It was a feeling she had missed immensely.

Over the next few days, Dr. Stevens tried several different remedies to bring her body temperature back down to normal. Finally, he was able to find a cure for Lina's condition. Lina was ecstatic. As her temperature returned to normal, Lina took her first pain-free breath in six days.

"How is everything feeling?" he asked.

"Much better, thank you."

Stevens looked at her with a slight scowl. "I don't like not knowing what caused such a reaction."

They sat in silence for a moment and then Dr. Stevens said, "If you're feeling up to it today, one of the nurses can help you take a shower. I'd also like to take you on a walk around the hospital. It will give you a chance to stretch your legs a bit and give you a change of scenery. Not that the rest of the hospital looks much different than this room does, but we could go around lunchtime and head to the cafeteria and maybe get a sandwich. How does that sound?"

Lina smiled and nodded. "That sounds great."

Dr. Stevens smiled, stood up and said, "Okay. I'll send a nurse over, and then I'll be back in a bit for our walk."

Shortly after Dr. Stevens left, a nurse appeared. She unlocked the shackles around Lina's ankles and led her over to the bathroom. The nurse waited on the other side of the wall as Lina showered. It was a glorious shower. The water was warm and there was actually soap Lina could use to scrub herself clean. The showers at the asylum didn't have any soap, so this was the first time in over a year that Lina was able to feel truly clean; it was a wonderful feeling, a feeling that Lina had never realized how much she had taken for granted during her former life.

After Lina was finished with her shower and dressed in a clean hospital gown, the nurse found a comb for her, and Lina began to comb out her hair. It was hard work. Her hair was far too long and it hung in tangled knots down to her waist. About a fourth of the way through, Lina was ready to give up. It seemed an impossible task.

She noticed the nurse watching her. She had the look of someone who was having an internal debate.

Lina continued to struggle to pull the comb through her matted mess of hair.

The nurse cleared her throat. "I don't suppose, um," she paused and rubbed the back of her neck. "I don't suppose you would like me to cut it?"

Lina set the comb in her lap. "Cut...my hair?"

The nurse nodded. "It might not be straight, but I could get rid of those tangles."

Lina looked at her and smiled. "I would love that."

The nurse smiled back and stood up from her chair "Well, let me just go get some scissors then."

The nurse returned a few minutes later with a large pair of scissors. "Okay. Here we go!"

A few minutes later, Lina's feet were surrounded by mounds of ratted red hair, and her head felt incredibly lighter.

"Thank you." Lina smiled. She had no idea how it looked, but she didn't care. She hadn't realized how much her hair had been weighing her down until it was gone.

"You're welcome," said the nurse. "Now let's get you back to your room."

Lina followed the nurse and got back into her bed, where the nurse redid her restraints. The nurse looked almost sympathetic as she shackled Lina to the bed, but, honestly, Lina didn't mind; a few restraints on her bed was worth it if it meant she could spend more time at the hospital and not at the asylum. Even with her legs chained to her bed, she hadn't felt this free in a very, very long time. Her body was clean, her head was light, and there was no Dr. Carrow lurking behind every corner. She lay back in her bed and waited for Dr. Stevens to come and take her to lunch.

When Dr. Stevens walked in, the first thing he did was smile and say, "I see you got a haircut."

Lina smiled and nodded. "The nurse did it."

"Well, it looks very nice," Stevens said as he began to undo her restraints. "Shall we head to lunch?"

"Yes. That sounds very nice," Lina responded.

Lina followed behind Stevens as he led her to the cafeteria. She stayed close as he chose two sandwiches and directed her to a table. "Lunch is served."

"Thanks," Lina said and took a bite.

They ate silently for a few moments and then Dr. Stevens began to speak. "Lina, you seem to be feeling much better. You seem even better than when I saw you this morning."

Lina smiled again. "I feel a lot better."

Dr. Stevens studied her for a few moments and then said, "Lina, how long have you been in the asylum?"

Lina chewed on her lip, thinking. "I'm not sure. Over a year, I think." She honestly had no idea anymore.

"Does your family..." Stevens began. "I mean, does anyone ever come to visit you or check on you?"

"No."

"Do you have anyone that could come visit you?"

"My aunt, uncle, and cousins could, I suppose, but they never will." She could hear the hollowness in her voice. She felt sad and ashamed as she answered.

"Why not?" he asked softly.

Tears trickled down her cheeks as she answered. "They're the ones who put me in there, and they don't care to see me"

She closed her eyes tight so that nothing else could escape.

Her eyes shot open when she felt Dr. Stevens' hand rest on top of hers.

"I'm very sorry," he said, and Lina could tell he meant it.

Dr. Stevens' eyes got a little more serious. "I need to ask you another question. Do you remember when you first got here…what you said about it not being a sedative that caused your reaction?"

Lina squirmed in her seat. The lightness she had been feeling began to dissipate. "I…uh, I don't know. I don't know why I said that. I was delirious."

He studied her. She was quite certain that he knew she was lying. "Was there something else they gave you at the asylum? Something that caused your reaction? You don't need to be afraid. You can tell me."

Lina curled her toes and looked down at the table.

"I know they've given you strange medicine before. Did they do it again? Is something going on? Has Dr. Carrow been giving you something? I want to help you." He sounded so sincere.

Lina really wanted to tell him, and she felt so much safer here than she did in the asylum. She played nervously with her ear lobe and looked up. "They try a lot of different treatments."

There, it wasn't the whole truth, but it was something.

"Can you tell me what kinds of treatments?" Stevens asked.

"I don't know – just a lot of different things," Lina was wringing her fingers.

Dr. Stevens looked at her intently and furrowed his brow. "They need to be more careful with their treatments, don't they? Dr. Carrow especially."

Lina shrugged her shoulders. What else could she do? She could tell there were a lot more questions hidden behind Dr. Stevens' words, and she could also tell that he was watching her reaction closely. She hoped her fear wasn't etched across her face. She couldn't remember if she flinched or not when he said Dr. Carrow's name. She thought maybe she had, but she hoped she was wrong. She tried to keep her face blank as she stared back at him. The silence was brutal, but Lina had no idea what to say in return, no idea what answer she could give that wouldn't put Dr. Stevens in harm's way. Lina doubted there were any limits to Dr. Carrow's web of horrors, and she didn't want this kind and good man to get caught in it. She couldn't give him any more information, and so she stayed silent and prayed he would give up and move on to a new subject.

Lina's prayers were answered when, after what felt like an eternity, Dr. Stevens sighed heavily and said, "You deserve to be well taken care of, my dear. That's all. I just want to make sure you are getting the help you need." Dr. Stevens cleared his throat. "How is your sandwich?"

Lina smiled faintly and replied, "It's very good, thank you."

"Well, I'm glad to hear it. Can I get you anything else?"

"Oh no, I'm fine, thank you. This was plenty."

And Lina meant it. Her body wasn't used to much food. Just the sandwich was almost too much. Suddenly a memory flashed into her mind. It was of Ruth, her nanny from so many years ago. She remembered sitting at the kitchen table while Ruth fed her sandwich after sandwich; she had forgotten she could once eat that much. She remembered that Ruth was singing a silly song. She couldn't remember where her mother had been. Had she been eating sandwiches too? Probably not. Lina felt that her mother had probably been locked away in her room during Ruth's silly song. Wasn't that why Ruth had started singing the song in the first place? To distract Lina? She was remembering things more clearly now, and the memory was bringing forth too many emotions, and Lina tried to shove it away, but it was too late. Lina could feel tears welling up and her head was spinning. She missed her mother and her father and Ruth so much it hurt. No, not just hurt. It tore and ripped and clawed at her soul. Lina could feel herself starting to panic. The excruciating pain of the longing she felt was unbearable...

"Lina dear, what's wrong?" It was Dr. Stevens.

Lina had almost forgotten he was there. She tried to steady her breathing, but she couldn't, and she started breathing even faster.

Suddenly Dr. Stevens was kneeling next to her chair and he had her hands in his. "Just breathe, Lina. You can do it. Breathe slowly. Breathe in and out." His voice was so soothing and his hands were so soft and warm. Lina tried to focus on his voice.

"Breathe in and out, Lina. Slowly."

Her breathing began to return to normal.

"Very good. That's very, very good." He gave her hands a reassuring squeeze.

Lina's head stopped spinning. The pain inside of her was subsiding.

"Thank you," she said.

"Of course, my dear. Would you like to go back to your room?"

Lina nodded, and Dr. Stevens helped her out of her chair and kept his hand on her arm to steady her as they walked back to her bed.

They got back to her room and Lina climbed into her bed.

She expected Dr. Stevens to lock her back to the bed and leave, but he did neither.

"Do you want to talk about it?" he asked.

Lina was shocked to hear herself say, "Yes." But she felt so safe with him. He seemed to genuinely care for her, and he treated her with so much kindness and respect. She found herself desperate to have him provide some sort of comfort for the longing and sadness that was still pulling steadily at her heart.

"I was thinking about my parents and Ruth, my nanny," Lina said. "I started remembering an afternoon when I was about five. It was when I still lived at home."

She paused for a moment not entirely sure what to say next. She hadn't talked to anyone about her parents, not like this.

"They died when I was five, my mother and my father. They had gone to a party. I remember we danced around the house together before they left. Ruth put me to bed, and I remember it being hard to fall asleep because I usually slept in my parents' bed, but I couldn't because they were out. My uncle was the one who woke me up and told me. He told me that my parents had died. I remember Ruth was standing by my door crying, I don't think I noticed she was crying at the time, but I can remember it now."

The words spilled out of her quickly and wildly and she soon had to stop because she was crying. She wrapped her arms around herself, trying to hold herself together. Talking about the night her parents died was hard. She wasn't used to it.

"Lina, I am so very sorry." Dr. Steven's eyes were filled with sadness. "That must have been very, very hard for you."

Lina's eyes were heavy with tears. "I miss them so much. I try not to think about it too much because it hurts, but earlier, in the cafeteria, I couldn't help it. I felt it all – everything I've tried not to think about – and it just hurt so much that I couldn't think straight."

"I lost a daughter," Dr. Stevens whispered. "I understand the pain. It can be unbearable and overwhelming. That I understand. But in time it gets easier to remember them without all the pain. I promise. I think you should let yourself remember them, Lina. Remember everything you can about them, even if you're worried it's going to hurt. In time the memories won't cause you so much pain. I promise."

Lina clutched her arms around herself even tighter and looked up at him. "I'm so sorry, That's terrible."

Dr. Stevens shifted in his seat. "It happened nearly 30 years ago. She was ten. She caught pneumonia. I felt like such a failure. I was a doctor, and I let my daughter die. I couldn't save her. It was unbearable. I was overcome with crushing guilt and heartache for a very long time. I shut out my family and my friends, and I tried to shut out memories of Daisy. That was her name. I didn't want to think about her because it filled me with such shame and grief. My wife helped to pull me out of it. She helped me realize that trying not to think about Daisy wasn't going to do me any good. I was never going to heal if I kept pushing all the feelings away. I'm not going to tell you it was easy, but I did it, and now I can talk about Daisy and think about her, and even though I still feel sad, the guilt is gone and I'm able to think about all the good times together and it helps me keep her close, and when she's close I don't have to miss her as much."

He was smiling at her with his sweet, grandfather smile, and Lina felt a surge of love for him.

"I guess what I'm saying is, don't push any memories of your parents away, even the bad ones. I'm sure they want you to keep them close."

How desperately Lina wished he were her real grandfather. This man with all of his kindness, Lina couldn't help but love him.

"I think my parents would have really liked you," Lina whispered.

"I bet I would have liked them too," he replied. "I've got some time. Do you want to tell me more about them?"

Lina was surprised to find herself nodding, but she really did want to talk about them. She wanted to feel close to them like Dr. Stevens said she could. She wanted memories of them to comfort her, not haunt her. Hadn't they used to bring her some comfort? Before all of this began? Before she became a lunatic? The good ones had at least. She wanted that again.

"They were perfect," Lina sighed. "Well, to me they were perfect. My father would tell the best stories. I remember waiting for him to come home from work so he could tell me a story. I think he made up a new one almost every day. He was so tall, and I remember his feet were huge. Sometimes I would try to walk around in his shoes, which always made him laugh. He laughed a lot. That was one of my favorite things about him. He could make almost anything fun. He used to make me and my mother laugh all the time. My mother used to let me try on her hats and gloves, and she would read to me all the time. Her favorite thing in our house was the bookcase. I think that some days we spent all day just looking at books until my father got home from work. She used to sing to me every morning while she made breakfast, or at least she did until Ruth took over."

Lina stopped.

Her memories were beginning to enter dangerous territory. She couldn't think about her parents for very long before having to acknowledge the truth about her mother. Lina didn't think she had ever said the words out loud. Her mother had been a lunatic too. Should she tell him? She was so used to defending her mother to her aunt, uncle and cousins. Would it be a betrayal to her now to admit the truth? But Dr. Stevens had said to allow all the memories, and if she wanted to stay close to her mother, she had to accept that her mother's insanity was part of the memories. Lina's mother was a lunatic, just like her, and she couldn't pretend that wasn't true.

"My mother was . . . " Lina took a deep breath, "well, my dad hired Ruth to help because my mom couldn't always take care of things."

Lina could feel anxiety coursing through her body, and her heart began to beat wildly. She interlaced her fingers against the back of her head and pulled her head towards her chest.

"My mother was a lunatic too." She whispered it and peeked at him through the hair that had fallen in front of her face.

Dr. Stevens placed a hand gently on Lina's shoulder. Lina began to cry. "I've never said those words before. I spent my whole life defending my mom to my aunt and uncle. They always said such horrible things about her. They hated her. But even if she was a lunatic, I loved her. I loved her so much." The last words came out with a sob.

"I'm sure she was a wonderful mother," he said gently.

Once Lina got control of her emotions, she continued. "She was. I never even noticed she was crazy. It never occurred to me that the things she did weren't normal. She was my mother and she loved me and I loved her, and my dad never treated her like she was a lunatic. He loved her so much. I know I was young, and I may not have been aware of everything that was going on, but I know with absolute certainty that my parents were in love, and my dad didn't love my mother any less because of what she was. If they were still alive, they would love me, too. My dad would take care of me the way he took care of my mom. I don't think he would have ever put me in the asylum. My parents would never have seen me the way my aunt and uncle did-the way most everyone does, as just another lunatic."

Lina took a deep breath and readied herself to continue, but before she could say more, Dr. Stevens interjected. "Before you say anything else, I want you to listen to me, Lina, because we need to get something straightened out. It's very important to me that you realize you are most certainly not just a lunatic. I may not know or understand everything about your condition, but of that one fact I am most certain."

Lina looked Dr. Stevens directly in the eyes, and she could tell that he deeply and truly meant what he said. She felt a fire burning inside of her. It was a fire of love and appreciation for this man and for her parents, but it was also a fire of anger— anger because if the circumstances of her life had been different, she never would have ended up in the asylum in the first place. She knew that what she had said was true. Her parents would never have sent her to the asylum. If they hadn't died, she would have been loved and taken care of even as she slipped into insanity. But they had died. It was a cold hard truth she had to live with. A truth she had never really been able to deal with because no one had been around to comfort her. Lina felt her anger rise even more. How was it that this doctor she hardly knew was a source of infinitely more comfort and support than Clark, Angela, Chrissie or Beth had ever been? Lina couldn't help but believe that if Dr. Stevens had been her real grandfather and she had been sent to live with him after her parents' death, he would not have been so hasty in sending her off to an asylum at the first signs of insanity.

"I wish my aunt and uncle felt the same way. I wish they saw me as something more than a lunatic. The whole time I lived with them they were just waiting for me to go insane. I heard them say it. They always suspected I would end up like my mother." Lina was crying again. How did she have any tears left? But somehow she did, and they burned as they slid down her cheeks.

"You've endured more sorrow than anyone should have to endure," Dr. Stevens said as he handed her his handkerchief. "Life has been unfair to you, but I want you to know that from now on, no matter what, you have me as an ally. I can't fix what you've gone through, but I hope I can help make your future a little brighter."

Lina looked up at him. "Do you really mean that?"

"I really do," he responded gently.

"Thank you. I don't know if I deserve this much kindness, but thank you so much, Dr. Stevens."

Dr. Stevens smiled at her warmly. "You can call me Walter."

Lina wasn't prepared for the flood of emotion that took over when Dr. Stevens told her to call him by his first name. Her eyes began to brim with tears. "Okay. Thank you, Walter, for everything."

Walter opened his mouth to say something, but just then a nurse came in to tell him there was another patient who needed his attention.

Walter smiled at Lina as he walked away. "I'll try to stop by before I leave today," he said.

The nurse turned to leave as well, but she noticed Lina was still unrestrained, so she quickly secured her cuffs and then followed after Walter.

Lina did not see Walter the rest of the day. She was visited by various nurses, one of whom took a few blood samples, but that was all. She was very tired and drifted off to sleep before she could eat dinner.

The next morning, Lina was just finishing her breakfast when Walter pulled up a chair and sat next to her bed.

"Good morning, Lina," he said with a smile.

"Good morning Doctor, I mean, Walter."

"I stopped by to see you last night, but you were already asleep, " Walter said. "I had some news I wanted to share. I talked to the officials at the asylum yesterday and told them we need to keep you here for a while for observation. They agreed to let you stay through the rest of the week."

Lina looked at him in amazement. The rest of the week? It was only Tuesday. That meant she had five days before she had to leave. Walter had just given her five days of freedom.

Lina could feel tears of joy and gratitude attempting to spill out. The way Walter was smiling at her with his crinkled, grandfather eyes, she knew that he had done this just for her benefit. He did rounds at the asylum, and even if he didn't know all of the horrors that went on there, he knew enough to know that this hospital was a luxurious vacation compared to the dark and depressing hell she had been living in.

Lina was so overcome with excitement that she couldn't speak. She simply stared at Walter with eyes full of admiration.

"I hope you slept well," Walter said, "and I trust the nurses have been taking good care of you."

Lina nodded her head, not ready to speak. She didn't want to start crying.

"I have to do my rounds, but I brought you something to help pass the time while you're here. " He had a mischievous smile.

He handed her a backpack. She opened it up to find a stack of books.

Walter smiled a large smile. "You mentioned all the reading you used to do with your mother, and I thought you might enjoy these."

There was no stopping it now. Warm tears of happiness poured down her cheeks.

Lina looked more closely at the books. They were all from the *Tarzan* series. She smiled and a small laugh escaped.

"I'm not sure how you feel about *Tarzan,* but I love them all and I thought it would be fun to share my favorites with someone else."

"I've read a couple and I loved them," Lina responded with a wide smile. "Thank you, thank you so very much."

The next four days passed by blissfully and far too quickly. The nurses ran various tests, ordered by Walter, and everything continued to appear normal, so Lina spent her days reading and chatting with Walter when he stopped by to check on her.

On the fifth day, her depression and fear began to creep back because Lina knew that tomorrow she would have to return to the asylum. Tomorrow she would have to wake up from this wonderful dream and return to the nightmare that was her life. She dreaded the thought of seeing Carrow. What horrors did he have in store for her? The memory of his sinister gaze was so intense that she could almost feel his hateful eyes staring mercilessly at her. She was trying in vain to push thoughts of Carrow aside when she felt a hand touch her shoulder. Her body convulsed in fear and surprise.

"Oh dear, I'm sorry, I didn't mean to startle you." It was Walter.

"No, I'm sorry. I'm just a bit jumpy today I guess." Lina hoped her eyes didn't betray her and reveal the terror that was storming up inside her.

Walter studied her for a moment and Lina offered up a weak smile. He cleared his throat and then began to speak. "I just got off the phone with the asylum. They are going to send someone to transport you tomorrow morning at 8:00 am." He took his glasses off, rubbed his eyes and sat down heavily in the chair next to her. "I tried to get you more time, Lina, I...." He trailed off.

Lina rested her hand on his. "I can't thank you enough for everything you've done for me. Your care has been wonderful. I feel better than I've felt in a very long time."

Walter smiled at her. "It has been an utmost pleasure."

Lina looked at him and worked to memorize his kind face. She didn't know when she would see him again, and she wanted to have a good, strong memory to call upon when her hell seemed too much to bear. She felt a small tear slip out of her eye. She tried to brush it away before Walter noticed.

"Lina, I wish there were more I could do for you. Having spent these last few days getting to know you makes me question many, many things. You don't deserve what life has thrown at you. You know that right?" His voice was soft. "Despite what you may have been led to believe, you do not deserve to suffer. You do not deserve to be treated as an inferior person. You do not deserve to be mistreated in any way."

Lina tried to take hold of every word he said. She wanted to take all of them and store them away so that she would never forget them.

"I'm going to come to the asylum as often as I can to check up on you, okay?"

Lina nodded. "I would like that." But she knew that Carrow would do everything in his power to prevent that from happening. She could only imagine the disgust he would feel if he heard the things Walter was saying to her right now. She could hear his cruel laugh echoing in her mind. *"On the contrary, Lina,"* she could hear him say, *"you deserve each and every misfortune that has come your way. You are a disease, an unsavory, horrible disease and unless we can kill off that disease you will never be anything more than a pathetic, slobbering lunatic."*

Walter spent as much time with Lina as he could that day. His goodness and care felt like warm rays of sunshine to Lina, but even the endless sunshine of Walter Stevens couldn't cast away the darkness that returning to Carrow and the asylum brought into Lina's mind.

When the asylum staff arrived to take her back the next morning, she noticed tears in Walter's eyes. She tried her best to smile at him as they escorted her away, but the fear and dread were already filling every inch of her body, and she wasn't able to trick her mouth into giving a smile.

Chapter Twenty

As they drove up to the asylum, Lina realized this was the first time she had actually seen the building from outside the walls. The first time she had come, with her aunt and uncle, she had been in such a deep depression that she hadn't even bothered to look at the building that would become her prison. As she peered through the barred windows of the automobile, she shuddered. The dark, gray bricks of the wall and building contrasted horribly with the clear, sunny sky. Even the sidewalk outside the building looked depressing. Lina noticed that very few people walked directly past the asylum. She saw them cross the street to walk along the other, more cheerful side. A group of boys on bicycles stopped and stared at the automobile as it pulled up to the gates. She saw them whispering and nudging one another with fearful eyes before they quickly rode away, perhaps worried if they stayed too long a lunatic would escape and attack them.

A pair of orderlies escorted Lina back into the asylum, and, without so much as a word, left her standing alone in the dreary hallway. The flickering lights and maniacal laughter she had once grown so used to now plagued her eyes and ears as though she had never before experienced them. A few days of freedom had seemed a relief at the time, but now her time away only served to keenly remind her of all she didn't have and made the hellish realities of the asylum all the more painful to bear.

Lina sighed and slowly walked down the hallway. She had no destination in mind, but she supposed she could try to find a spot farther away from the dreadful sounds of unhinged laughter. She walked along, letting her hand slide along the cold, white wall beside her. She wondered how long it would take Dr. Carrow to summon her, how long it would take for him to inject her with a new blend of horrors. After a while she moved outside, walked to the potato garden, and sat down. She had not been to the garden since Bird left. It had seemed too empty without her there. But remembering Walter's advice not to push away her memories, she decided this was as good a place as any to think about everyone she missed and loved.

She thought about Bird and allowed herself to remember how she felt when she first sat here with Bird, how much difference having a friend had made.

She also reached deep to pull out every memory of her parents that she could. Some of them were happy, some less so, and some were only half formed and hazy, but she could remember clearly how safe and loved she had felt sleeping between her parents every night. She thought of the soft smile that would appear on her mother's lips whenever Lina snuggled close, and she could hear her father's soft snoring and the "Good morning, little Lina" he whispered to her each sunrise as he kissed her forehead.

Lina allowed herself to sit in her memories for the rest of the day, and when night came, she lay down on a mat and prayed for dreams of her parents.

When Lina awoke, she couldn't remember any of her dreams, but she was almost happy, and so she felt that her prayers had been answered and her subconscious had been filled with joyful glimpses of her mother and father.

She got up and went to see if they were serving breakfast. Her stomach was growling. She had grown accustomed to eating three full meals a day at the hospital, and it would take her a bit to readjust to the meager offerings at the asylum.

Fortunately, she hadn't missed breakfast, and she took a bowl of gray oatmeal and sat near the door. She was nearly finished when she heard someone mention Dr. Carrow's name. Trying not to attract attention, Lina turned slightly and saw two nurses talking.

"That's what I heard," one nurse said. "He's gone. Apparently he's under some sort of investigation."

"Really?" the other responded.

"Yes. The word is that one of the hospital doctors that comes here for rounds filed a complaint."

"My lands! Dr. Carrow!" The second nurse put her hand on her cheek. "I never really liked him very much, but I don't know if that means he's a bad doctor."

"I suppose we'll find out soon enough," shrugged the first nurse and then began to share another piece of gossip.

Lina didn't listen to the rest of their conversation. She couldn't focus on anything other than what she had just heard. Carrow was gone. That's what they had said. Carrow was gone. He was under investigation. Did that mean he was in trouble? She was sure it was Walter that had filed the complaint. It had to be. She could tell he had questions about Carrow. But she hadn't expected him to do anything like this. She had never expected anyone to do anything about Carrow. What did this mean? What would they uncover in the investigation? Would Carrow be allowed to come back or would he lose his position at the asylum? With these thoughts rolling around in her head, her mind pulled forward the thought she had deemed stupid when it had first entered her mind – the thought that if she found his secret room, if she found proof of something, it could end his game. The thought grew stronger and stronger and didn't seem so stupid anymore. Her body shook with excitement. Was it really true? Could the game really be over? She couldn't allow herself to believe it entirely. It would just be too heartbreaking if the nurses' gossip turned out to be false. She kept a very watchful eye over the next few days, sure she would see Carrow lurking around the corner, disgust and loathing emanating from his lunatic eyes.

She never saw him. She never felt him. She allowed herself to get even more excited. Suddenly the asylum didn't seem quite as miserable. If Carrow were gone, Lina felt she might be able to find a way to survive. She felt stronger than she had in over a year. Maybe she would be assigned a doctor that would actually try to help her. Plus, she had Anders. Anders. Her hopeful thoughts stopped. She hadn't seen him since he came to visit her the day after he had saved her life. The day after he told her he loved her.

She hadn't seen him since Carrow told her that he had run him over. Would he be coming back? She had to believe that if Anders felt well enough, he would come back to see her. He had to. Everything she knew about Anders told her that he would return. So why hadn't she seen him? Had something gone wrong with his recovery?

As the days passed, Lina became consumed with worry over Anders. She eavesdropped on every conversation she could among the asylum workers, hoping someone would mention him, but no one ever did. The agony of not knowing was terrible.

Worry about Anders and excitement over Carrow's departure competed for Lina's attention. Most of the time, worry was the winner. When she thought about Anders, her chest ached. She hadn't realized how reliant she had become on seeing him regularly. She pulled the memory of the night when he told her that he loved her from the darkness and miserable abyss of her mind. *"I want to be there for you. I want to help you. If you let me, Lina, I will hold you together when you feel like you're falling apart because I love you. I love every part of you."*

With the threat of Carrow removed, she was able to let herself imagine, really imagine, what it might be like to have Anders love her, to have something truly good in her life.

Lina remained in her state of partial excitement over Carrow being gone and partial dread over the well-being of Anders for several days. Until something finally happened, finally someone returned.

She was eating breakfast when his voice reached through the hysterical chatter and nudged her ear. She turned and looked around slowly until she saw him. He was talking to an orderly just outside the door to the cafeteria. Her heart jumped into her throat. She wasn't sure what she should do. Had he seen her yet? Was he going to come to her right now or wait until he could catch her alone somewhere? She wiped her sweaty palms on her gown. She hadn't been able to look away from him. She just kept staring. She didn't know what else to do. She tugged nervously on the ends of her hair, rooted to her seat until finally his eyes found her. She felt her face flush as Anders' lips formed into a smile.

He made his way over to her and sat across from her at the table.

"Lina, he said, smiling wide, "you look so...healthy."

Lina smiled. The last time he had seen her, she had been strapped to a table close to death. She hadn't looked at herself because there weren't any mirrors at the asylum, and she hadn't bothered to look while at the hospital, but she was sure that with her matted tangles gone and a week of human compassion and kindness and satisfying meals she looked healthier than he had ever seen her.

"Thanks," she said softly as she studied his face. His eyes were just as bright and kind as ever, but he now had a scar running through his right eyebrow. His hair was longer than she had ever seen it and it curled a bit-like she thought it would.

They stared at each other, silently, across the table for a while, each wondering what to do now. They hadn't seen each other in over a month, and the weight from their last interaction was heavy in the air waiting to be addressed. Lina fiddled nervously with her fingers and Anders rubbed the back of his neck.

Finally Anders broke the silence. "Would you like to take a walk?"

Lina nodded and followed him out of the cafeteria. They walked in silence. Without discussing it, they went outside and walked towards the wall.

"I'm sure you've been wondering where I was," Anders said quickly. "I promise my being gone had nothing to do with you, nothing at all. I was in an accident and the asylum didn't clear me to return until yesterday."

"I heard," Lina responded.

"You did?" Anders seemed surprised. "Oh good, I was so afraid that you thought I had abandoned you or something, which is something I would never do."

"I know that," she said. "I'm glad you're doing better."

She smiled widely at him and shifted nervously from foot to foot. "I uh," she cleared her throat, "I never got to thank you for saving my life...again. I'm sorry you've had to do that more than once. I, um, well, I've been feeling a lot better actually. The best I've felt in a while. I had to spend some time at the hospital."

"What happened?" Anders looked worried. "Is everything okay?"

"Yes, yeah, I'm fine. It was a bad reaction to a sedative or something." Lina chewed her lip as she lied. "But everything is fine. Being in the hospital actually helped a lot. It helped me feel…human again."

Her eyes began to tear up. "It was just nice to be somewhere that wasn't here, you know? Somewhere where people treated me kindly. Do you remember Dr. Stevens?"

Anders nodded.

"Well, he was my doctor while I was there, and spending time with him helped me remember some of the good things I had forgotten about." Lina wiped tears from her eyes. "It was just really nice to escape all of this." She gestured at the asylum.

Anders' eyes were moist as he tentatively reached for her hand. "Lina, I…I wish you could feel that way all the time."

"Me too." She laughed nervously and looked down at her feet. "But I guess I would have to be sane all the time to have that happen."

She looked back up at Anders, and she could tell he was deep in thought.

"Lina, I've never asked, but how long have you been here, at the asylum?"

"Um, I think it's been about a year and a half? I was brought here when I was 18."

Anders studied her for a moment. "Your…um, episodes? Do you know how many of them you had before you came here?"

"Just one," she answered quickly. "I had one that made my aunt and uncle send me here."

"Your aunt and uncle?" Anders asked.

Lina realized then that Ander's knew almost nothing of her life before the asylum. She took a deep breath and gestured for him to sit beside her and she told him about her parents, who had taken care of her and had loved her and each other in spite of her mother's issues. She told him about the relatives she had lived with after her parents' death and how she had immersed herself in reading to cope with their cruelty and indifference.

"Did I ever tell you I was going to go to Columbia?" Lina asked.

Anders looked surprised and shook his head.

"Yes. I even had a scholarship. I was sent here the summer before I was supposed to start…the summer before my life was really going to start." Lina stopped as deep sadness set in as she thought about the life that could have been.

"I wish I had known all of this before," he said. "I'm sorry I never asked."

Lina smiled faintly, gave a little laugh and shrugged. "Who has time to learn the stories of all of the loons in this place?"

Anders looked at her. "You're even more amazing than I thought, you know?"

Lina felt her heart pounding.

They sat in a comfortable quiet after that, backs resting against the tree, their hands just barely touching.

Chapter Twenty-One

Lina and Anders developed a bit of a routine after that. Whenever he was working, he would seek her out and spend as much of his time with her as he could. They talked about his life, they talked about her life, they talked about a lot of different things. The only thing they didn't talk about was Anders' confession of love. It hovered nearby, always waiting to be addressed, with neither of them sure what to say about it.

It was an impossible situation, there was no way they could actually have any sort of real relationship. He was an orderly and she was a lunatic. Lina suspected that Anders would not have so readily admitted his feelings if he hadn't been so shocked by seeing her on the brink of death. And so, they talked around it, but Lina didn't mind. She was just happy to have anything at all. Being around Anders helped her remember the parts of her that were sane. It helped her feel real and alive, especially with Carrow being gone. Lina was afraid to ask if Anders knew anything about Carrow. A part of her believed that uttering his name would somehow summon him back to the asylum.

When she was with Anders now, she sometimes even joked. She had forgotten that she once had a sense of humor. Anders helped her write a letter to Bird and promised to deliver it to her in person to check up on her. She scrawled the letter quickly on a piece of paper with a pen Anders had brought in.

Bird,

My sweet, wonderful friend. I wish I could have written to you sooner. I am so happy for you, honestly. You are living the life you deserve and it brings me so much joy. I want you to know that I am doing quite well. I feel good and I feel hopeful. Anders is being a very dear friend to me so please don't worry that I'm alone. I love you, Bird, and hope to get the chance to see you again someday, but even if that doesn't happen, know that I love you and I want you to have a wonderful life. Do that for me and I will be happy, okay?

With All My Love,

Lina

Anders didn't work again for a few days after he took the letter, but when he returned, he told Lina with a big smile that Bird was doing very well and had written her a letter in return.

Lina,

It was so wonderful to get your letter! I am so glad you are feeling good and hopeful. It makes me feel better knowing you are feeling well. I love you so much Lina and I promise I will live the greatest life I can. And I will find a way to come visit you, and I'm not going to give up on finding a way to get you out of there either. You deserve to be out here too. Don't forget it.

Love,

Your Bird

Lina smiled as she read Bird's note. "Thank you for doing this, Anders," she said as they walked the asylum grounds.

"You're welcome."

"Thank you for everything, actually. You have made this place much less depressing for me, and I'm very grateful for it. I actually feel like myself these days, so thanks for, I suppose, letting me find myself again." Lina gave a little laugh.

"I still love you, by the way." Anders said it casually, so casually that Lina thought she must have misheard him, but he went on. "I know we haven't talked about it, but I thought I would mention it just in case you were wondering."

Lina tucked her hair behind her ear. "Well then, I guess I should let you know that the feeling is mutual…just in case you were wondering."

They both smiled and walked along in a blissful silence.

She felt that with no Carrow, maybe this could be enough, maybe just knowing that Anders loved her and knowing that Bird was safe and living a good life would be enough to carry her through the rest of her days.

Chapter Twenty-Two

Lina was just finishing breakfast when she felt a tap on her shoulder. She turned, expecting Anders, but it was an orderly she didn't recognize.

"It's time for you to go see the doctor," he grumbled.

Lina stood up to follow him. She had assumed, with Carrow gone, she would be assigned to a new doctor, and it seemed they had finally gotten around to it.

She followed the orderly who led her to a room, opened the door, shoved her in and then walked away. Lina stumbled and then looked toward the desk to see who her new doctor was.

When she saw his face, she felt instantly sick to her stomach. She doubled over and vomited the breakfast she had just finished.

"Disgusting," Carrow said with a sneer. "Absolutely disgusting."

Lina wiped the vomit from her chin as her hands quivered.

Carrow picked up the phone on his desk, called for someone to come clean up the vomit and then turned his hateful gaze back on Lina. "We have a lot to catch up on, but since your rancid bile is souring up my office. I'll keep it brief," He got up, walked over to her and slapped her hard across the face and said, "Never underestimate me."

Lina lifted her own hand to her cheek to feel the burning left by Carrow's monstrous slap.

"I don't know how you found someone dumb enough to help you, but you both failed. I'm back, and I'm not going anywhere, so stop trying to change the rules. You will never win." Carrow tugged roughly at the ends of her recently cut hair. "You look terrible. Get out."

Lina pulled the door open and got out as fast as she could. She walked swiftly away from the office, her mind buzzing and her heart pounding. She felt sick. She felt terrified. She felt stupid. She felt helpless and miserable. How could she have let herself feel so hopeful? Did she really think her life was one where things turned out in her favor? Her parents had died when she was five; her guardians had never cared about her; she had gone insane, been sent to an asylum and assigned to the care of a man even more psychotic than she was— a man who was hellbent on terrorizing her and destroying anyone who got in his way. No, Lina's life was not one of good fortune or luck, and she had been a fool to think she could make the best of her situation and find some hope. An insane and utter fool.

As her thoughts raced, so did her breathing, and she found herself growing lightheaded and dizzy. She quickly found an empty closet and shut herself inside. Once the door was shut, she dropped to the floor, pulled her knees to her chest and rocked slowly back and forth. Hot tears poured down her still stinging cheek as she tried to steady her breathing. After a while, and with great effort, she was able to get her breathing back under control. She took several deep breaths and wiped away her tears with her sleeve. With her mind calming down, her thoughts turned to Anders, and then to Bird, and finally to Walter. Meeting all of them had been lucky for her. They all had brought good into her life, right? Maybe she wasn't so stupid for thinking she could have hope. She had been blessed to have had a respite without Carrow lurking around every corner, waiting to pull her down into a mist of agony, fear and insanity. Her mind was the strongest it had been since coming to the asylum. She had been reminded of what she once was, and she wasn't ready to let that go. Defiance rose up in Lina. She wasn't going to let Carrow bury her in fear. She wasn't going to let him waltz back in and resume his reign of terror. She was stronger now. She was better. She had allies, influential allies. Walter already clearly distrusted Carrow. Perhaps Anders could get a message to him and get him to help somehow. But how? Walter had already reported Carrow, and Carrow had already been investigated and nothing had come of it. He had come back. Lina needed proof, tangible proof, because without hard evidence, the testimony of a lunatic would convince no one. She needed something that would incriminate Carrow and show the world the mad man that lurked beneath his sallow, unsightly exterior.

She needed the room.

She needed to find the room Richard was always muttering about. Clearly poor Richard had endured horrors in that room. There had to be something in there that Carrow didn't want found. But how could she find the room? Richard had only the briefest moments of lucidity, and from what she had witnessed, they were few and far between. She needed to find the room fast. She needed to find proof before Carrow unleashed his hellstorm of rage and insanity upon her and everyone around her.

Lina stood up. She didn't know how she was going to do it, but she knew that she was going to try her best. She was going to end the game or die trying. She took one last deep breath and then walked out of the closet and into the hallway.

As Lina walked, she worked to keep her fears at bay. The broken and weak parts of her banged around in her head desperately trying to be heard, but Lina wouldn't listen. She wasn't going to fall apart, not this time. She had to somehow stay stronger than her deranged mind. She centered her thoughts on one thing and one thing only. *"I'm going to find proof. I'm going to stop Carrow."* Over and over that thought replayed in her mind. She used it as a club to batter away any other thoughts.

She kept her eyes peeled for Anders, and also for Richard. She had no real plan, but she knew that any chance of success depended on help from both of them.

She saw Anders first.

"Lina," he said cheerfully, "I've been looking for you."

"Anders!" Her mind flashed to an image of him being hit by Carrow's car. She felt the fear rising. She shoved it away. "Anders, do you trust that I'm sane right now?"

He looked a little startled, but he studied her for a moment and then said, "Yes, Lina, yes I do."

"Okay, good." She exhaled, not even realizing she had been holding her breath. "Follow me." She led Anders to the same empty closet she had been in before, checking to make sure no one was watching them.

Anders followed her into the closet, clearly very confused but at least not doubting her sanity.

"Okay, I need you to know that Dr. Carrow is back, and that he is...." She searched for the right word. She didn't want Anders to do anything rash, but she needed him to listen to her. "He's unhinged, Anders. He's not safe, and you need to be very careful around him. When he's around he makes me worse. He makes me crazier. "

"What does he..."

Lina cut him off. "I don't know exactly, but he's doing something to me and I don't trust him. Remember Dr. Stevens? I don't think he trusts him either. I need you to find Dr. Stevens. His first name is Walter. I need you to find him and tell him that Carrow came back. Somehow, he passed the investigation and he came back. I need you to tell him that I said he was right – Dr. Carrow is doing things he shouldn't. I need him to try to get Carrow out of the asylum again."

Anders rubbed the back of his neck the way he always did when he was concerned or in deep thought. "If Dr. Carrow is a threat to you, I need to get him out of here right away."

Lina shook her head. "You can't. No one will listen to you. You're an orderly, he's a doctor and we have no proof."

"But you could tell somebody. Tell them what you told me. Maybe there are more patients he's trying to harm. I could get a list of his patients and we could talk to them."

"Anders, do you honestly think anyone would believe me – or any other patient here? My mind is a mess. We're all lunatics here." She could tell Anders wanted to interrupt again, but she put up her hand to stop him. "You've seen it yourself Anders. My sanity isn't constant. It isn't stable. Carrow would convince everyone I was having one of my episodes. You know he would."

"You never should have been sent here," Anders said. "What you just told me confirms it. You said yourself you had only had one episode before you came here - one episode in 18 years, but then you come here and have multiple in less than two years? Being here has made you worse, not better. I can see that so clearly now. Carrow is making you worse. This place is making you worse. I'm going to talk to some people and try to get you out of here. You shouldn't be here. I'm sorry I didn't see it before. But, Lina, your mind is so much stronger than you think, and I'm going to make them see that."

Lina felt herself tearing up. "I don't think you can possibly understand how much that means to me." The tears were falling now and she wiped them away. "But with Carrow here and with him as my doctor, that couldn't possibly happen. If there's any chance that you could get me out of here, we need to get rid of him first, and even then it's still a big if. My aunt and uncle sent me here, and they would have to approve my release and I assure you they never would. But it's a wonderful dream, and I love you for having it."

Anders looked at her, his eyes focused intently on hers, "One way or another I'm getting you out of here, whether or not we can get rid of Carrow."

"Okay, but right now I need you to focus on getting Walter to help. And be careful around Carrow." Lina took a breath; she hating saying this next part. "We can't spend time together anymore. Carrow is going to be watching me and he can't see us together.

"No." Anders shook his head. "I'm not abandoning you. How can I make sure you're safe if I can't be around you?"

"You won't be abandoning me, and if you're around me I won't be safe. And neither will you. Carrow doesn't want me to have friends. He's made that very clear. It's a game Anders. He's playing a terrible game, and if I don't follow his rules, things get worse for me and the people around me – the people I care about."

Realization dawned on Anders. "That's why you pushed so hard for me to get Bird into my aunt's school, isn't it? You weren't just protecting her from Sam, you were protecting her from Carrow too."

Lina nodded. "So you see Anders? I can't risk him hurting you to hurt me."

"I can take care of myself, Lina. Now that I know the truth about him, I'll keep my distance. I won't let him hurt me. But I can't just sit by, watching you from a distance hoping you're okay."

Lina hadn't wanted to tell Anders this part, but she saw his determination. He was going to do what he thought he needed to do no matter what she said, so she might as well give him the whole truth. He needed to understand how dangerous Carrow really was. "He already has hurt you Anders. He tried to kill you with his car."

Anders was stunned. "*Carrow* is the one who hit me?"

"Shhhh," Lina whispered, taking his hands in hers. "Yes, it was him. I broke the rules of his game by talking to you, and so he ran you over. So, please, listen to me and stay away from me. If he thinks we are still friends, he *will* kill you this time. I know he will. He's a monster, Anders, he's an absolute monster."

Anders was holding her now. She had begun to shake as she spoke, and now she sobbed into his chest, "Please, Anders, listen to me. Because if he does something to you, I'm sure my mind will break for good."

"Okay," Anders whispered as he rested his cheek on the top of her head. "I promise. I'll keep my distance from you. I won't do anything to upset Dr. Carrow. I'll be careful, okay?"

"Okay." Lina wiped her nose. "Thank you."

"I love you, Lina."

"I love you too, Anders."

They stared at each other in silence for a moment.

Anders leaned forward, hesitating for just a moment before he kissed her softly and quickly.

He pulled back and studied her face.

Lina felt her lips curve into a smile, her lips that had once so carefully whispered Anders' name alone in her padded cell.

Anders smiled back at her and Lina quickly locked away the memory of this tiny, perfect moment to keep it safe.

"Okay, so I'm going to talk to Walter and see if he can help," Anders said, pulling her back into reality.

"Yes," Lina responded.

"What if Walter can't get him out of the asylum?" Anders asked.

"I know there's something here at the asylum that would prove what he's doing, I just need to find it." Lina paused. "And I will find it. And once we have proof we can get rid of him."

Lina couldn't help but feel that this really was going to work. Here she was telling Anders something that sounded completely insane, and he trusted her. There wasn't any doubt in his eyes. He believed her. He loved her. And he was going to listen to her.

Anders left the closet first. Lina waited for a while after he left to make sure Carrow didn't see them together. She walked down the long hallway, wondering what her next step should be. She gnawed at her thumbnail, deep in thought. Everything depended on her finding the mysterious room. She had to find the room. There were many rooms and closets in the asylum, but there was no way it was anything as obvious as that. There had to be some sort of secret entrance to it, some long forgotten passageway that only Carrow knew about. She needed to try to follow Carrow to see where he went. It was a terrible plan, but so was her other option, catching Richard in a lucid moment and finding out from him.

Two horrible options – each with little chance of success, but Lina was going to try because the alternative was to let Carrow torment and abuse her, and she wasn't going to do that; she had only recently gotten the real Lina back, and she wasn't about to let Carrow destroy her.

Chapter Twenty-Three

Lina had not seen Carrow in three days.

Three days.

It was terrifying.

She had hardly slept. At night, she lay on her mat, silent and still, waiting for Carrow to come for her.

She had spent her days lurking around his office, hoping to see him before he saw her, but he never appeared. How had she not seen him? Was he not at the asylum? That seemed unlikely. He had just barely been permitted to come back; he was surely behind on his psychotic games. Was he somewhere watching her? Did he already know her plan? She paced around in a circle, her fingers clenched tightly around her arms. She was spiraling.

NO, she shouted in her mind. *No, this fear does not control me. Carrow does not control me. I'm not going to fall apart. I'm not.*

She was going to try to talk to Richard. Yes, that's what she would do. She would talk to Richard and follow Richard. Perhaps even in his unhinged mutterings and wanderings he would lead her to where she needed to go.

Focus on Richard, she commanded herself. *Find him and follow him. You're going to find that room.*

As she walked through the asylum looking for Richard, she passed Anders. They met each other's eyes for only a moment and then looked away. She wondered if he had talked to Walter yet, but there was no way she could risk asking him, not when she wasn't even sure where Carrow was or what he could or could not see. She couldn't risk Anders. She knew what she had told him was the truth; her mind would never recover if Carrow killed him.

His death would shatter her fragile hold on sanity.

Richard, she thought. *Just find Richard.*

She had to endure another nearly sleepless night and half a day before she succeeded. He was huddled against the outer wall, rubbing his cheek against the brick. As she got closer she saw there were tears streaming down his face.

"No, no, no," he moaned, his eyes closed. "Don't say it. No, no, no."

"Richard?" Lina asked softly as she approached him. "Richard, do you remember me?"

He didn't seem to hear her, so she rested her hand on his shoulder. His eyes shot open in terror.

"No," he shouted. "No, I can't. No. No. No."

As he spoke, he pulled his face away from the bricks and Lina saw that his cheek was raw and bleeding. His eyes were clouded with lunacy and fear. Lina's heart ached for him.

"I'm not making you go anywhere," she said. "We don't have to go anywhere, I promise."

His head was shaved and there were several scars etched across his scalp. She reached out tentatively to rest her hand on his unmarred cheek, Richard's broken eyes watching her intently.

"I know the doctor is bad. I know he hurts you. I will never take you to him," Lina said.

Richard tilted his head so that it rested more heavily on Lina's hand. His eyes were still pouring tears. "Can you make the voices go away?"

Lina felt tears in her own eyes. "I don't know, but I can stay with you and try." She moved closer and gently positioned Richard so that his head was resting in her lap. She stroked his head softly as her soul bled for him. What horrors had this poor man had to endure? Lina imagined that the hell she had been through with Carrow was only a tiny portion of what Richard had endured. Lina was sick with hatred. She had hated Carrow for a long time, but holding this wounded and broken man unleashed a deeper fury in her that she didn't even know existed. More than anything she wanted to take away some of Richard's pain. She wanted to lift and share his burden, and she wanted to destroy Carrow so that he could never do this to anyone else ever again.

"The voices want me to die," Richard cried. "They don't like me. The doctor put the voices there, and they don't like me. They say I'm no good. They say I should die. I'm no good. I'm just bad, bad, bad, broken like he said."

"The voices are wrong. You are good. I want you to stay here with me. The doctor is bad, not you, and I'm going to stop him," Lina said. "I'm going to find a way to stop the doctor."

"Don't trust the doctor, no, no, no, don't go with him no, no, no, doctor's no good, no, no, no." Richard almost sang the words. "Tell the voices to stop. Please."

Lina felt a deep sob in her very core. "You terrible voices leave him alone. Richard is good and you need to leave him alone."

Over and over she repeated those words for what felt like hours. Her throat was dry and she longed for a drink, but she didn't stop. Richard's gentle sobs kept her going. She knew what it was like to have a voice in your mind that you couldn't control, and she wasn't about to leave him alone with the ones that plagued him. The sun began to set. Her voice was hardly more than a whisper at this point.

"Leave him alone. He is good, leave him alone."

Richard began to snore. Lina leaned her head back against the wall, grateful for a chance to rest her voice. She continued to gently stroke Richard's head. Her legs had long ago fallen asleep, but she held still. This was how she could share some of his burden, she who only knew the smallest part of what he might have gone through. She would stay here against this wall and stroke his head and let him sleep and hope that when he awoke the voices would be gone. The sun was fully gone now and the moon shone in the sky. Lina stared at the moon until she too fell asleep outside by the wall.

Lina woke up with her face in the dirt. The sun was just beginning to rise and someone was tapping her shoulder.

"Hey, girlie. We should hide."

It was Richard.

She sat up.

"Come on, girlie. Let's go, go, go, go, gooooo." Richard was knocking his fists quickly but softly against his head.

Lina saw the fear in his eyes and got up to follow him. He took off running and she followed.

"Hurry, hurry, the wicked thing is coming, hurry, hurry, hurry, don't want to go, no, no, no, nooooo," Richard said frantically.

Lina looked over her shoulder. she didn't see anything or anyone, but still she followed. Richard opened a door and ran inside, Lina was right behind him. Almost everyone was still asleep, but a few loons roamed the halls. Some of them stared at Richard and Lina as they ran past, but most of them were too preoccupied with the madness in their minds to even notice them.

Richard tripped as he was rounding a corner. He fell hard onto his knees. Lina tried to help him up, but he started sobbing and collapsed on the floor. "No, no, no, no, no! Nowhere to go!" His cries shook his emaciated, wounded body.

"Come on, Richard, I'll help you," she said. "I'll take care of you."

"Girlie no! Kissed by the devil. He's coming for you." Richard looked at her with his watery, haunted, fearful eyes.

Lina felt a shiver creep down her spine. She took a shaky breath. "Let me help you up, I'll get you somewhere safe."

Richard wailed even louder. "Nowhere safe, nooooo, kissed by the devil doctor says." He reached up and took Lina's face in his hands, his eyes even more haunting than before. "The devil is coming for the devil in you, but the devil's in him and it never ends."

Fear snaked its way through every part of her body. Her face was still in Richard's hands, and she stared into his mad eyes. He was no longer wailing. He sat in silence as his tears ran down his face. Lina rested her own hands on top of his and continued to look into those sad, wild eyes. It seemed to her as if their souls were connected – his past and present could be her future; his madness could become hers. She knew the real Richard was buried underneath all the lunacy and fear; she knew he was deep in there, pleading for someone to pull him out. She could feel it in her soul.

She rested her forehead against his and the tears spilling from her own eyes mixed with his and fell to the floor.

"I'm going to stop him," she whispered. "I'm going to end it. I promise."

Richard dropped his hands from her face, making hers fall away as well. He blinked several times, and Lina thought she saw the tiniest speck of lucidity returning to his eyes, but before she had the chance to see it grow, she felt a needle pierce the back of her neck and everything started to go black.

When Lina awoke, she saw her mother standing in front of her. She wore a blue party dress and her hair was in sleek waves. She smiled at Lina. Lina smiled back. Her mother started walking away and beckoned Lina to follow. Lina did. Her mother led her through the asylum hallways, checking every few minutes to make sure Lina was still following.

"Where are we going?" Lina asked, but her mother said nothing. She just smiled and kept leading the way.

Suddenly, her mother turned around and her smile was gone, replaced by a look of horror. She started running, urging Lina to follow. Lina ran as fast as she could, trying to keep up with her mother. They dashed through the hallways, dodging patients and nurses as they ran. Her mother turned a corner sharply, and as Lina followed, a large hand reached out and grabbed her.

"Oy, slow down. You're going to hurt someone." An orderly gripped her tightly.

"Okay, okay, I'll be careful." Lina wriggled out of his grip, and as soon as he was distracted, she took off running again, hoping to catch up with her mother.

Lina couldn't see her mother anywhere; fear was welling up inside her. She needed to help her. Clearly she was terrified of something, and Lina needed to make sure she was okay. She pushed her way through the lunatics as her eyes desperately searched for her mother. She spotted the hem of a blue dress heading outside and she ran to follow. Lina flung the doors open and saw her mother running as fast as she could. Lina's chest burned as she strained to catch up. As she ran, she passed Anders. She slowed for a moment and looked at him. His eyes were wide and he looked at her with concern. He looked as though he wanted to say something, but his eyes scanned the area around her and he said nothing. Had he seen her mother? Had he been looking for her?

Wait, he didn't know her mother. He didn't know what she looked like.

Wait.

Her mother was dead.

Lina's mother was dead. But she could see her running frantically up ahead. She needed Lina to save her. Didn't she?

"Lina," Anders whispered, "is everything okay?"

He didn't look at her as he spoke. Why was he being so cautious?

Carrow.

He was being cautious because of Carrow, because Carrow couldn't see them together, because if Dr. Carrow saw them together, if he knew that Lina and Anders still talked, he would kill him.

Suddenly Lina remembered the needle in her neck. She remembered Richard. She remembered holding him in the hallway.

Carrow had done this. Carrow had given her something. This wasn't real. Her terrified mother running through the asylum wasn't real. Lina's mind struggled to process everything.

"Lina?" Anders was still there. His voice was full of worry.

"I'm okay, it's okay," Lina whispered. "I promise it's okay. Just stay away. I don't know if he's watching."

Anders clenched his fists and walked away.

Lina headed in the other direction. Her head was pounding and she felt nauseous, but she walked along steadily knowing that if Anders saw her struggling, he would try to help her, and she couldn't risk him doing that.

Lina could still see her mother. She had stopped running and she was standing, waiting for Lina with tears streaming down her face.

Lina closed her eyes tight, hoping that when she opened them this hurtful apparition would be gone.

She wasn't.

Lina's mother opened her mouth. "Help me, please."

"You're not real," Lina whispered. "This isn't real."

But her mother didn't leave. She just continued to cry and plead for Lina's help with terror-filled eyes.

Lina turned to head back inside. She needed to find Richard.

Her mother followed.

Had Carrow taken Richard to his secret room? Or had he merely injected him and left him in some hallway as he had Lina. There was no way for Lina to know, but she had to look for him. She had to find the poor broken, battered and shattered Richard. Lina opened every door she passed.

Her mother followed behind her, her haunting tears wreaking havoc on Lina's mind.

From time-to-time, Lina had to stop and sit. The energy it took to remind herself that her mother wasn't real was entirely draining. Hearing the desperate cries of her beautiful, beloved mother and being powerless to do anything about them ripped at her heart. Lina took several slow and steady breaths and tried her best to ignore the apparition. There was nothing she could do for her mother. Her mother was dead. This scared and sorrowful presence wasn't even a ghost. She was the result of whatever Carrow had plunged into her neck. She was nothing more than a terrible side effect from the doctor's latest batch of poison.

"You're not real," Lina whispered once again as the apparition reached out for her. "You're not real. I can't help you. You're not real. I need to find Richard."

Tears slipped down Lina's cheeks as she continued to search for the missing lunatic.

Lina opened another door to check for Richard. He wasn't there. Her mother wailed. Lina vomited bile onto the floor. She wiped her mouth and kept on looking.

It was nightfall before she finally found him. He was sobbing on the floor just outside the rec room. His arms were covered in what appeared to be self-inflicted scratches.

She sat beside him. "Do you remember me? I'm here now. I'm here to take care of you."

Richard looked at her with blood shot eyes. "They hurt, they hurt, they hurt."

"What hurts?" Lina asked.

He held out his arms to her. "The rats, so many rats. They won't go away."

She ran her hands down his forearms, hoping she could wipe away the invisible rats.

"See, they won't leave," he cried.

"I'm so sorry," Lina said, her heart aching because she had no idea how to save him from the delusion.

Richard cried into her shoulder while her mother continued to sob on the other side of her. Lina's head throbbed with the stress of it all. Her vision grew blurry as she tried to keep her delusion at bay while helping Richard bear his. She could feel sweat slipping down her forehead and her eye began to twitch.

Her mother wailed even louder, and her tears now looked like blood dripping from her eyes.

Lina shut her eyes tightly and wrapped her arms around Richard. "We're going to be okay. It's going to be okay. I'll stay with you and you'll stay with me."

They stayed like that for what felt like hours, Lina with her eyes closed, no longer able to stand the sight of her phantom mother with the bloody tears, and Richard sobbing into Lina's shoulder as he scratched at his invisible rats.

Lina didn't know how long it had been silent before she noticed.

No one was crying.

She slowly opened her eyes. She didn't see her mother. She looked around. She didn't see her anywhere. She looked at Richard. He was asleep on her lap. Lina gave a huge sigh of relief, and overwhelmed with exhaustion, she, too, fell asleep.

Someone kicked Lina awake.

"Is they dead?" a voice said.

Lina opened her eyes and saw an old lunatic woman standing over her. Lina sat up and looked around. She saw Richard sitting next to her. He appeared to have just woken up as well.

The woman scowled at them. "I don't like you," she said and walked away.

Lina looked over at Richard again. He was already staring at her. His eyes were clear.

"Thank you," he said simply.

"You're welcome," Lina replied.

Lina knew there was no time to waste. She had no idea how long Richard would stay lucid. "I need to find Dr. Carrow's room. I'm going to find proof of what he's doing and get rid of him. Can you show me where it is?"

Fear appeared in Richard's eyes, but he nodded and stood up. Lina stood up too and they started walking.

Richard was shaking as he walked. Lina could feel his fear in the air around him.

"You don't need to go in with me. You don't even have to get close. I just need you to show me where it is. I don't want you to ever have to go in there again," Lina said, hoping to ease some of his fear.

Richard looked at her with his scarred head, his scabbed face and his scratched-up arms. "I don't want you to go in there either," he shuddered.

"I have to," Lina said firmly. "I have to stop him. I have people who can help me. People in and out of the asylum who can help get rid of him, but I need some proof."

Richard turned a corner. "We're getting close."

She could feel the panic rising off him more quickly and wildly than before.

She took his hand. "Stay with me. I need you to show me the way."

Richard took several breaths and gripped her hand tightly. "I'm trying."

They started walking again. "He really hates you," Richard said, "even more than he hates me. He talks about you a lot. You need to be careful."

Lina shuddered.

They walked a bit further and turned a corner. Richard's head began to twitch to the side.

"We're here." He was beginning to shake so hard he could no longer walk. Lina knew she was about to lose him. There were at least six doors along this stretch of hallway.

She took Richard's shoulders to steady him. "Which room? How do I get there?"

She could see the panic exploding in his eyes. She knew he also knew his time was running out.

"Under the carpet, in the corner, hidden stairs."

He was sobbing hard now and pounding his head with his fists.

"Which room?" she asked desperately, but it was too late.

"No, no, noooooo," Richard yelled as he turned and ran in the opposite direction.

Lina wanted to follow him to try to comfort him somehow, but she knew if she walked away now she would forget which hallway she needed to be in. She walked to the end of the hallway and back. She was right – there were six doors. She looked around and then knocked on the first door. She wasn't sure if Carrow would say anything if he heard a knock, but if he did respond, she would know to get far away before he opened the door.

No one responded to her knock. She slowly opened the door. The room was unoccupied at the moment, but it was clearly someone's office. She ran to the first corner and tugged at the carpet. It didn't move. She tugged harder and crawled around the entire room tugging each inch of the carpet's edge. Beads of sweat were dripping down her neck and her hands were shaking with nerves. No part of the carpet lifted. She opened the door just a crack to make sure the hallway was empty before she walked out. She saw a couple of lunatics trudging along but none of the staff, so she pushed open the door and slipped out. She knocked on the next door and waited for a moment to see if anyone responded. No sound came from the room, but she heard the clack of shoes coming closer.

He really hates you. Richard's words popped into her mind.

None of the patients had shoes. Panicked, she opened the door and slipped inside. It was a closet. She wiped the sweat from her forehead and berated herself for being so rash and stupid. If those shoes did belong to Carrow, and if this had been the room that led to his secret room, she would have been hand delivering herself to him and his den of horrors.

He talks about you a lot Richard had said. What did that even mean? What did he say about her? What plans did he make as he wreaked havoc on Richard's mind and body?

She waited a few minutes before she cracked open the door to check the hallway. It was clear, so she darted out and walked to the next door. She heard someone cough behind her, and she jerked her head to see who it was. It was just another patient. He scowled at her, barked and then walked away. Her heart was beating fast, and nervous sweat was pouring into her eyes. Her nerves were shot. She needed to calm down before she kept searching. She walked out of the hallway and carefully memorized her path as she made her way outside.

The sun shone brightly outside, and she took a deep breath and raked her fingers through her hair. She paced back and forth nervously. She needed to collect herself. What if she actually encountered Dr. Carrow as she searched for his room? She needed to keep herself together.

She couldn't crumble into a pile of quivering fear and sweat.

He really hates you. Richard's words continued to bang around inside her skull. They crashed into her tiny wisps of courage and attempted to beat them into submission.

She knew Dr. Carrow hated her. This wasn't new information. She couldn't let it rattle her so much. But in reality it wasn't those four words that made the bile rise up in her throat. It was the fact that they were followed with *even more than he hates me* uttered by a man who looked as if he had clawed and climbed his way out of the hands of a monster. A monster who hated her even more, who wanted to hurt and torture and mutilate her even more than he had that poor soul. Lina reached to feel the scar that was on the side of her head. The one she had gotten when she banged her head into the wall to silence the screams Carrow had put in there. If Carrow had his way, this scar would soon be one of many. She could almost feel the knife slicing into her scalp. She wrapped her arms around herself, fell to the ground and rocked herself back and forth.

She closed her eyes and tried to search through the darkness and anxiety that was consuming her for some of her conviction and drive to stop Carrow. A tiny, brave part of her fumbled its way through the mist filling her mind looking for something to grab onto.

"I know there's something here at the asylum that would prove what he's doing. I just need to find it...and I will find it."

Hadn't she said that to Anders? She had said it with so much surety. The tiny part of her pulled that memory forward and out of the darkness. She clung to those words as she stood up and began to walk back inside.

She had four more doors to open.

Chapter Twenty-Four

Lina woke up strapped to a table.

Her head was throbbing. What was going on? How did she get here? Where even was here?

Then she remembered.

It had been the fourth door. She had opened the fourth door. She had pulled at the carpet. It had come up when she got to the third corner. She remembered her heart pounding in her ears as she pulled it up enough to find the trap door in the floor. The door opened to reveal a staircase. She remembered walking down the staircase. A rat had hissed at her when she got to the bottom. The ground had been cold and damp. She remembered looking at the door in front of her and she remembered carefully pulling it open.

She had found the room.

Lina walked into the room. No one was inside. She looked around, wondering why this room even existed. Who had built it? How many people knew it was here? What had been its original purpose? Surely it had never been intended to become what it was. A large medical table was in the middle of the room. She could see streaks of dried blood on its legs. Various tools lay strewn on a tray next to the table. A small desk sat in the corner piled high with notebooks. There was an entire wall lined with boxes. Lina opened one of the boxes. It was filled with syringes as were the next two boxes. The rest of the boxes held vials and bottles, some empty, some full.

She walked over to the desk, picked up a notebook and looked inside. Her heart leapt, and she opened up another notebook. Dr. Carrow had detailed his illicit experiments in these notebooks. She didn't have time to read them thoroughly, but she knew there was enough here to get someone to take her and Anders seriously. Enough to convince them to at least check to see if the room was real. Lina grabbed five of the notebooks and stuck them underneath her gown. She pressed her arm against her chest to keep them from falling and then rushed out of the room and ran up the stairs.

Dr. Carrow had been waiting at the top. His eyes were black with rage as he shoved her back down the stairs. Her head had smacked into the wall as she rolled back down to the cold, damp ground.

Lina opened and closed her eyes and tried to sit up. Maybe it had been a nightmare. Hadn't she endured sleeping horrors before? But she knew it wasn't a nightmare, not this time. She was awake, and she was strapped to the blood splattered table in the cold, secret room.

She rotated her head from side to side; she saw a jar on the tray next to her that appeared to be filled with her hair, but she didn't see Carrow anywhere in the room. She struggled against her restraints, but it was no use; she was strapped securely to the table and there was no escaping. She began to scream and yell although she knew the chance of anyone hearing her was almost nonexistent. Her throat was dry and burning, but she screamed and screamed and screamed because she didn't know what else to do.

Her screams turned hoarse and she felt as if she had been yelling for hours when the door finally opened and Dr. Carrow appeared before her.

"It's about time you woke up," he sneered. "You've been out for days. I was worried that I had given you too strong a dose and we wouldn't be able to do any more experiments."

Lina stared at him. Had she really been on this table for days? Had anyone noticed she was missing?

Dr. Carrow picked up a vial and rolled it between his hands. "I wasn't planning on bringing you here yet, but I guess you just couldn't wait." He laughed coldly. "That's okay. I can move up the schedule a bit."

Carrow filled a syringe with the liquid in the vial and injected it into an IV Lina had not realized was in her hand. Lina's eyes grew wide and Carrow laughed again, "This isn't anything fun – just a little something to make sure you stay awake. You and I have a lot of work to do."

Carrow sniffed and began to check her vitals. When he was finished, he walked away. Lina heard a chair scrape against the floor and assumed he was sitting at his desk. Her heartbeat was speeding up and her arms and legs felt itchy. She blinked her eyes rapidly as whatever Carrow had given her began to take effect. The light above her seemed to grow brighter, and when Dr. Carrow coughed the sound was like a bomb exploding in her ears. Lina winced as she heard the chair scrape again. The sound was almost unbearable. Carrow walked over to her and checked her pulse. "Very good," he seemed to shout. "Let's begin."

For what felt like hours, Lina endured agony after agony. Carrow scraped skin off various parts of her body and put the specimens in different cups. He removed a toenail from each of her feet and injected something that felt like fire into the exposed raw flesh. He poured something vile down her throat, and when she turned her head moments later and vomited it out, he forced her mouth open and did it again. Lina's eyes flooded with tears as he held her mouth shut and plugged her nose until she swallowed the second round of vomit back down. Once the horrible liquid was inside of her, Carrow pulled his chair close to the table and sat down with a notebook and pen in hand and stared at her. Lina sobbed as the sound of him tapping his pen pounded in her ears. Lina knew Carrow was waiting to see what her reaction would be to the liquid, and she lay trapped and full of terror as she too waited for it to take effect. It didn't take long before she began to convulse. She felt her airways closing and she gasped desperately for breath. Carrow sat, unmoving, still observing as Lina felt herself heading for death. She was seeing spots when Carrow finally shoved a needle into her neck that allowed her to breathe again. Lina watched him write rapidly in his notebook for a moment before she passed out.

This time when she awoke, Carrow was standing over her wearing a surgical mask. A foul odor and the disgusted look in Carrow's eyes made Lina believe she had soiled herself. When she turned her head and saw a cup full of what looked like excrement, she knew she was right.

"Why?" Her own voice sounded foreign to her. Lina hated how broken she sounded. She didn't even know what exactly she was asking. She looked over at the containers holding her hair and her waste. Carrow was clearly out of his mind.

Carrow ignored her and poured what smelled like bleach all over the bottom half of her body. It burned terribly on the skin he had cut.

"Disgusting," he said as he poured something even stronger on top of the bleach.

Lina tried not to cry. She didn't want to cry anymore, but she had never felt more broken or degraded in her life. She felt her legs blistering as whatever substance Carrow had poured on her ate away at her skin.

"I heard him asking about you," Dr. Carrow said as he took off his surgical mask.

Lina didn't respond. She didn't know what to say.

"Your little orderly. He was asking the nurses if they had seen you. I thought I warned you about that."

"I don't talk to him anymore," Lina said. "I don't know why…"

Carrow slapped her across the face. "Don't lie to me you lunatic trash. You broke the rules, and now I have to move everything up, and I have to take care of that orderly."

Lina bit her lip and forced herself to hold in her tears.

"Why anyone would notice you were gone is beyond me. I didn't want to bring you here yet. I wasn't ready for this stage of the experiment, but you just had to find my private room and force your way in. I wanted to try more variations before the final extraction, but now that bloody orderly is up there asking questions and looking for you." Carrow's spit hit Lina in the face as he shouted, "You are going to help me find the cure, you and your demons!" Carrow's voice was more wild and unhinged than Lina had ever heard it. "The madness is all over you. If we stop your madness, we stop it all. I don't like being rushed. WHY DID YOU HAVE TO BREAK THE RULES! I made myself clear, even for a stupid lunatic like you, did I not? I told you what would happen if you didn't obey. Do you not want me to eradicate lunacy?" Carrow was laughing a terrifying, mad laugh. "That's it, isn't it? You don't want me to find the cure?" He paused to flick her hard on the lips. "You want to spread your demons. Well, that's just too bad. I'm going to examine that broken brain of yours and find the cure."

Carrow lifted the jar that held her hair and studied it for a moment before he threw it to the ground. She heard him writing in his notebook and muttering to himself.

He was suddenly standing beside her again, and his voice became eerily calm as he said, "It's time to look inside."

Lina watched as he pulled on a pair of gloves and picked up a large scalpel. "This part is going to hurt, so scream all you want. No one can hear, and I need you awake."

Lina felt the scalpel slice into the top of her scalp. Blood ran down the side of her head. "Just a little deeper." Carrow now spoke in a calm, professional voice as the scalpel cut into her skull.

Lina screamed in agony and anger. All her nightmares were being realized. Carrow was going to kill her, but first he was going to cause her unbearable pain, all in the name of a cure – a cure he would never find because he himself was a lunatic. She was going to die, and Anders was going to die, and Richard was going to die, and Carrow would keep killing and killing and filling his notebooks with his horrible experiments. All of Lina's efforts to expose this maniac would be for naught. She listened to the sounds of his scalpel scratching against her skull.

"I need something sharper," she suddenly heard Carrow say as he set the scalpel down and walked out of the room.

Lina sobbed and closed her eyes as she waited for Carrow to return and bring hell with him.

Lina heard the door open. She braced herself. She heard heavy breathing as someone began undoing her restraints. She opened her eyes. It was Richard.

A wild sound flew from her mouth, something between a laugh and a cry.

"Let's go girlie," he said as he helped her off the table.

Lina nearly collapsed as pain shot up her foot and leg when she stepped onto the floor.

"Careful, careful," Richard said as he steadied her and led her towards the door. "We have to hurry. He'll be back soon."

"A notebook," Lina cried. "Get a notebook."

Richard grabbed one off the tray and dragged Lina through the door and onto the stairs.

Lina leaned heavily on Richard for support as they made their way up the stairs. When they reached the top of the stairs, Richard pushed the trap door open and lifted Lina up into the ground level room.

Lina fell to her knees and Richard pulled himself up next to her. "Here, take the book. I don't know how much more time I'll have, and I don't want to run off with it." He handed her the notebook and she clutched it against her chest.

Richard was shaking and his face was white. She knew how terrifying that room was for him and how hard it must have been for him to willingly go into it.

She gripped his hand and kissed his cheek. "Thank you for coming for me."

"Thank my mind for staying sane long enough for me to realize you were missing," he said as he helped her stand and led her toward the door. All they had to do was find anyone, any member of the staff besides Carrow. They could do that.

They stepped into the hallway and Richard began to run, dragging Lina along with him. They had just turned the corner when they came face to face with Carrow.

"Demons," he hissed.

Something snapped in Richard and he lunged at Carrow. He pushed him to the ground and punched him in the face. "I need an order…" Carrow began to shout, but then he looked at Lina. She could only imagine what she looked like. How could he explain this? And then his eyes fixed on the notebook. "You little…" he started to say just as Richard punched him hard in the jaw.

"Let's go," Richard said, and hoisted Lina back up.

From the emptiness of the hallways, Lina assumed it was nighttime. The staff was always less vigilant at night. Lina began to yell, "Help, help, help, I need a nurse." Her throat burned as she cried out desperately.

Richard continued to drag her along with him until she felt something sharp slice her side. She hunched over in pain, causing Richard to fall.

Carrow pulled her up and pressed his knife against her arm. "This ends now," he hissed as he pulled her back toward the room she had just escaped.

"Noooooooooooooo!" she screamed.

Dr. Carrow lifted his hand to silence her and Lina bit down hard on his fingers. He flinched and she flung her head backwards and heard his nose crack. Free from his grasp, she began to crawl away, but she knew she wouldn't be able to stand. She screamed wildly for someone to come. She was so filled with relief when she heard the sound of shoes heading toward them that she almost didn't see it happen.

She heard a roar and turned to see Richard jump between her and the now recovered Carrow. Carrow's eyes were glowing with madness and rage as Richard crumpled to the floor.

"What is going on?" A pair of stunned orderlies had arrived and were looking at Dr. Carrow and the bloody, mutilated Lina.

Lina was only mildly aware of Carrow as he spewed lies. Her eyes were fixed on the large knife stuck in Richard's chest. She cried out and pulled him into her lap. His blood was warm as it drenched his gown and hers.

"Help!! Help! He needs help!" She was shouting at the orderlies.

Richard managed to lift his hand and Lina grasped it in hers. "It's okay." His voice was raspy. "I'm okay dying for you. I want you to live."

"Richard, you can't die. Live! You have to live!" Lina sobbed.

"I thought I'd be afraid when I died. But I'm not. I'm not afraid at all," Richard whispered as his eyes began to close.

Lina could see the life leaving his body.

"Thank you, Richard. Thank you for my life," she cried.

"We stopped him. He'll never . . . ."

There were no more words.

While Lina was watching Richard die, several lunatics and a few asylum workers had gathered around. The orderlies were standing on either side of Dr. Carrow as he told one lie after another. Lina could see that the two men were doubtful. They had seen him throw the knife. They had seen Richard and Lina running away from him.

"He is a monster," Lina said simply.

Dr. Carrow sneered at her. "She is delusional. We need to get her sedated."

"No." Lina was still holding Richard's lifeless body in her arms. "He is the delusional one. Look at what he did to me. Look at what he did to Richard."

She picked up the notebook that was on the ground next to her. "Here, read it."

Carrow chuckled nervously. "She's lying. Of course, she can't help it. Self-harm and compulsive lying are two of her symptoms."

One of the orderlies put a hand on Carrow's shoulder. It was a warning. Lina knew it and Carrow knew it too. The other orderly flipped through the notebook. A few nurses came over and looked at it with him.

"This doesn't look good, doc," the orderly said.

"Take him to the office and call the police," an older nurse said to the orderlies as she gestured for the notebook.

They handed it to her and the two of them led Carrow away, while Carrow, with his lunatic eyes, tried to explain away the evidence.

The nurse knelt by Lina. There was a softness to her. She held the open notebook up to Lina. "Is this about you?" Lina saw tears welling up in the nurse's eyes.

Lina looked at the book.

Patient reacted poorly to #37.

—-lost consciousness and soiled herself.

Collected sample of excrement for further evaluation. Possible demonic presence in waste?

Stench of excrement required a combination of bleach and sulfuric acid to remove.

Lina could feel the nurse looking at her legs.

Due to unexpected variant in patient and likely complications, will begin final phase of experiment. Extracting brain in individual portions will allow me to determine which contains demonic lunacy. Once demon presence is found, experimentation on infected matter can begin.

Next to these notes Carrow had drawn an image of what appeared to be Lina with devil horns. Lina looked at the picture then looked up at the nurse and nodded.

"Oh dear," the nurse said. "He really is mad."

Lina cried silent tears as she continued to hold her dead hero.

"Should we," a young orderly cleared his throat, "um should we move her and the uh, body?" He looked at the nurse as he gestured toward Lina and Richard.

The nurse gasped as though she had just realized Lina was clinging to a dead body. "Oh, yes, yes." She began to assign tasks to the staff members surrounding her.

Lina's mind began to grow hazy. She was vaguely aware of the people moving around her. She heard herself cry out, "Be careful" as they lifted Richard's body onto a stretcher and carried him away, but it sounded like the voice came from far away. Another far-away voice of hers began shouting directions to the secret room. "Get the notebooks," she thought she screamed. After that, everything became even more hazy. She thought she might have cried in pain as they tried to wash away the blood, but none of it felt real. It all felt distant and confusing.

When she woke up and saw Anders sitting beside her, things started to come back into focus.

Anders choked out a sob when he saw Lina open her eyes. "I'm so sorry I wasn't there. I'm so sorry, Lina. I looked everywhere for you. I was desperate. You were missing for almost a week. Walter called me when they brought you in."

"Where am I?" Lina asked.

"You're in the hospital. They brought you to the hospital." Anders spoke quickly.

"Carrow!" Lina cried out, her memories flooding back. "Where is he?"

"I called the asylum. He's in police custody." Anders looked sick. "They told me what happened. They told me about the notebook."

Lina sat up quickly. "Richard! What did they do with Richard?"

Anders steadied her. "I…I don't know. Who is Richard?"

"Anders, you need to go make sure they take care of his body." Lina was desperate. "Please, Anders. He saved me. Richard saved me. He was my friend…he …." Lina was crying too much to talk any more. Richard, poor Richard. He needed a proper burial. He needed to be honored. He had suffered so much, and he had died saving her. People needed to know his name.

Walter came running over. "What's going on?" He looked at her and he looked at Anders. "How long has she been awake? Is something hurting?"

"She's talking about someone," Anders said. "I'm not sure who though."

"Richard," Lina blubbered. "His name is Richard. Anders, go make sure they know his name. They need to know his name. They need to take care of his body, please!!"

"Lina," Anders looked desperate. "I can't leave you, after what just happened. I can't leave."

"Please!" Lina felt her grief flowing out of her. She didn't have enough room to hold it all inside. "He died saving me, please."

She broke down sobbing.

"I'll take care of her," Walter said to Anders. "I won't leave her side until you get back. I promise."

Anders looked down at Lina, and Lina looked desperately up at him through her tears.

"Okay, okay." His blue eyes were bloodshot. "I'll go."

"Thank you." Lina's voice was watery. "Make sure they all know he's a hero."

"I will." Anders gave her a quick kiss on the cheek and left.

Lina watched him walk out and then looked up at Walter. He pulled a chair close to her and sat down. He rested his hand on Lina's.

Lina's body ached. "I held him while he died. Carrow was going to kill me, but he jumped between us. He saved my life, and I don't think they even know his name."

He nodded at her with understanding. "Richard was a hero, and that Anders of yours will make sure they know that."

"I'm so tired." Lina rolled to her side and folded her chin into her chest.

"I'm sure you are," Walter responded gently. "You just sleep. I won't go anywhere. I promise."

Lina cried soft tears until her pillow was soaked and she was fast asleep.

Chapter Twenty-Five

"I read some of the notebooks. I couldn't read them all. It made me sick. The things he wrote about her, the things he did, the things he planned to do." Anders was speaking. He didn't know Lina was awake. "How did we not know? How did no one know what was going on? I knew she was scared of him, before she told me everything, I knew she was scared of him, and I thought," his voice cracked, "I thought it was probably some sort of delusion. What's wrong with me? How did I not know sooner? How was I so stupid? The books were awful. The things he wrote were so awful."

"It's not your fault," she heard Walter reply. "It's not your fault that man was a monster."

"But how did I not know?" Anders groaned. "I should have known something was going on. You did, and you didn't even work with him."

"I never suspected it was anything like this." Walter spoke quietly. "No one would have suspected it was anything like what it was. Don't blame yourself. It won't help. You took care of her. You helped her. You were there for her, and you made her feel safe enough that she was able to confide in you. You need to remember that. You were the only person she told, and when she did tell you, you listened and you trusted and that is what matters."

They were both silent for a moment, and Lina kept her eyes closed and her breathing steady. She wasn't ready for them to know she was awake.

"They want to know when she will be well enough to go back," Walter said.

"She can't go back," Anders was firm. "She doesn't belong there."

"You're right," Walter responded.

"Her aunt and uncle are the ones who had her admitted. They can have her released. I can get their phone number from the office," Anders said.

"I already called them." Walter said, "I called them when she first got here. I wanted them to be aware of the situation. They don't care. They didn't care at all. *That lunatic is not our problem anymore* – that's what her uncle said to me."

Anders made a sound that could only be described as a growl. "They're heartless and disgraceful."

"My thoughts exactly," Walter sounded equally disgusted, "I don't believe they will ever request for her to be released."

"She's not going back there," Anders said firmly.

"She doesn't belong there," Walter responded.

The two men sat together in silence until a nurse arrived to inform Walter he was needed in surgery. When he left, Lina heard Anders sit down in the chair beside her. She waited a few moments and then rolled over and opened her eyes.

He smiled at her, but his smile was weak and his face was etched with worry.

"I called Richard's family," he said. "I called them and told them what happened. They came down to collect his body. I told them what Carrow did. I told them that Richard was a hero. His mother cried for a long time." Anders choked on a sob. Lina could sense the pain he felt. She could only imagine how hard it must have been to talk to Richard's parents, to try to comfort them when he also needed comfort.

"Thank you. Thank you for doing that," Lina said softly.

Anders looked up at her with his bloodshot eyes. "I'm sorry. I'm so sorry for it all."

"You have nothing to be sorry for," Lina began.

"No, please," he interrupted her. "The last thing you need to do is to worry about my feelings, not after…not after everything you have been through."

Lina could tell he was struggling to hold back tears.

"But what if I want to? What if after surviving that hell all I want to do right now is tell you that you have nothing to be sorry for. None of it was your fault. Nothing bad that happened to me was ever your fault. And it's over now. The game is over. Carrow can't hurt me anymore."

"I thought I lost you, that I really lost you this time." His face was in his hands and his shoulders shook as he tried to control his sobs.

"But you didn't. I'm here," Lina said

Anders looked up. He stood up from his chair and came and rested his hand on her shoulder. "Can you tell me about Richard? I want to know about the man who saved your life."

Lina nodded and began to tell him everything she knew about Richard. She told him about his moments of lucidity when he tried to warn her. She told him that he had endured even more of Carrow's horrors than she had, and finally she told him about him dragging her from the room and jumping between her and Carrow's knife.

"His mother said he had always dreamed of being a hero. They seem like good people. They'll see to his burial." Anders took a breath, "I saw the room. I saw the room and read some of his notebooks. He was sick, Lina. He was so sick and terrible and completely insane. I can't believe what he did to you, what he did to Richard. I'm so sorry. I feel horrible. I couldn't even read everything he did to you, and yet you managed to endure it."

"I just told you that you don't ever need to be sorry." Lina smiled a tired smile.

Anders ran his hands through his hair. "Okay, okay, but you don't need to take care of anyone but yourself right now. I'll be okay. I'm here to take care of you."

Lina could tell he was struggling to maintain his composure. "Thank you, I love you."

"I love you too." He paused for a bit and then asked, "Is there anything you need or want right now? Anything I can get for you?" Anders asked.

Lina thought for a moment. What did she want? She hadn't eaten in days, but she didn't feel hungry at all. Her body ached, but she was sure she was already full of medication. She thought of Richard's blood that had coated her as he died and she thought of all the terrible things Carrow had injected her with and covered her with while she was strapped to that table. She thought of his madness and hate that had dripped all over her as he tortured her. "Do you think they'll let me take a shower?" she asked.

"Let me find out," Anders said, and he left quickly on his errand.

He returned a short while later with a nurse in tow.

"I hear you want a shower," the nurse said kindly.

Lina nodded, "Is that okay?"

"We need to see if you can stand first, and I'll have to take the bandages off your legs, but it's almost time to replace them anyway." As the nurse spoke, she began unwrapping Lina's legs. She then helped Lina sit up and held out her arms to help her stand. "Let's take this nice and slow," she said.

Lina put her feet on the floor and gripped the nurse's arms. Anders steadied her from behind. It was painful and it took a while, but Lina was finally able to stand. The nurse and Anders supported her from both sides as they walked to the bathroom. When they got there, the nurse took over while Anders stayed on the other side of the door.

"Okay, dear. Hold onto the bar while I get your gown off, okay?"

"Okay," Lina said.

Lina held herself up as the nurse removed her gown and placed it in a hamper. She then took Lina's hands again and helped her turn around to head into the shower. But before they were able to complete the turn, Lina came face to face with her reflection in a large mirror.

She let out a gasp.

She wasn't prepared for what she saw.

Her head was completely bald, and a large row of black stitches stood in stark contrast to her white scalp. Her legs were an angry red that she knew instinctively would never go away. There were cuts all over her arms that she didn't even remember getting, and a yellowing bruise covered half of her face. She could see each of her ribs through her skin – her unhealthy gray skin. There was a row of stitches along her side where Carrow had sliced her. She looked like a character from a horror film.

The nurse had stopped and stood quietly by Lina, holding her steady as she took everything in.

Lina watched as a tear ran down her bruised cheek. She felt ashamed.

Ashamed of how she looked and ashamed for feeling ashamed. Richard had saved her life at the expense of his own, and all she could do was bemoan her wretched appearance. She wanted to look away, but she forced herself to keep staring. She wanted to stare until the image didn't horrify her anymore.

"Surviving isn't always pretty," the nurse said quietly with a soft, understanding smile, "but it's always something to be grateful for."

Lina turned to look at the nurse's kind face and then back to her mutilated body in the mirror. She had survived. She was alive when she should have been dead. The nurse was right. That was something to be grateful for, not something to be ashamed of. Lina stared hard at her reflection. She was alive thanks to a heroic friend who no longer was. She was ugly and broken, but it didn't matter. She was alive. That's what mattered.

"You're right," Lina said to the nurse. "I'm alive. The rest doesn't matter."

The nurse helped her into the shower and stood off to the side, ready to assist if needed. Lina sat on a small stool and scrubbed herself clean. The water stung as it hit her red legs, but Lina didn't mind. She was washing away Carrow, and nothing else mattered.

As soon as Lina was clean and dry and in a fresh gown, Anders came back in to help the nurse get Lina back into bed. After putting fresh dressing on Lina's legs, the nurse left to check on another patient.

"Is there anything else you need? Anything I can get you?" Anders asked.

Lina looked around. A tray of food had been left on the table by her bed. She still didn't feel hungry, but she forced herself to eat a few bites and drink some water.

Anders sat silently in the chair beside her. She could feel him watching her as she ate. She turned and looked at him. He looked exhausted.

"You need to get some sleep," she said to him.

"I'm fine. Really, I am."

Lina sighed. "I thought of something I need."

"What is it?" Anders sat up.

"I need you to go home and get some sleep."

"Lina, no, please don't make me leave again. I just need to be here making sure you're okay." Anders looked at her with desperate, tired eyes. "Please."

Lina looked back at him. She imagined how she would feel if she were in his position. If he had been taken and tortured and she hadn't been able to find him. She pictured him lying in a hospital bed covered in wounds and bandages. She wouldn't want to leave his side either. She knew she wouldn't. "Okay," she said. "I'm going to go back to sleep, though, so will you at least try to sleep here? I promise I will wake you up if I need anything."

Anders smiled a tired smile. "Okay. I'll try."

Lina closed her eyes. She didn't feel all that tired, but she kept her eyes closed because she wanted Anders to fall asleep and she knew he never would if she were awake. But soon her deception became a reality and she drifted off to sleep.

Her mother and father were sitting at the kitchen table. They were still in their pajamas. Her father was reading the paper and her mother was eating breakfast.

"Good morning, love," her mother said when Lina walked into the room.

"Good morning, Mama," Lina responded.

Lina helped herself to some scrambled eggs and bacon.

"I'm finished with the paper. Would you like to read it?" her father asked.

"Yes, thanks." Lina took it and smiled.

Lina read and ate while her parents chatted beside her. Lina was only half listening to what they were saying. Something seemed off about this newspaper. A tingle went down her neck. Something was definitely not right.

"Lina, honey, do you still want to go shopping with me later today? There are a couple things I still need to get for the party."

"Mmm. What?" Lina tried to focus on her mother's words, but the newspaper was screaming at her to uncover its mystery.

Lina's head was pounding and sweat was dripping down her forehead.

"Hey, sweetheart, can I have the paper back?" Her father was asking.

Lina tried to hand it to him, but her body wouldn't let her. They were going to realize she was crazy...any minute they were going to realize it and send her away. Tears fell onto her breakfast. Her father gently took the paper from her hands and her mother came over and wrapped her arms around her.

"It's going to be okay," her parents said in unison.

"Please don't send me away. Please," Lina begged.

"Oh, honey, we would never send you away," her mother said.

Lina looked up at them with sad, scared eyes. "You promise?"

"We promise," her father said. "We love you. We'll figure this out."

Lina woke up and it seemed she could still feel her mother's arms around her. She looked over and saw Anders asleep in his chair. Her heart ached for both how much she loved him and how much she missed her parents. She had tried not to think too much about what she had overheard Anders and Walter talking about – about how the asylum wanted her back. She couldn't even begin to imagine going back. The thought made her sick. Had she assumed that revealing Carrow's monstrous deeds would lead to her release? She must have, because she was in no way prepared to return to the asylum. She knew Anders and Walter would never send her there willingly. They were like her parents. They cared about her, but what could they do? Her aunt and uncle had signed her over to the asylum. That's where she was to live out her days. That hadn't changed. Granted, it would be better without Carrow there. Maybe she would get a doctor who actually cared about her, and she would still get to see Anders. That would be nice. She and Anders would never actually be able to be together, not with her as a patient and him as an orderly, and she couldn't expect him to put his life on hold for her. No, Anders had already done all he could for her. She would have to convince him to move on and find someone outside of the asylum. Anders was going to be a great husband and father, but he couldn't be either of those things with Lina, and Lina loved him too much to let that happen. The memory of Anders' love would have to carry her through. She could have dreams of what might have been. She could create a fantasy world to escape to. It would be okay. It would have to be okay. She had to go back, and neither Anders nor Walter could change that.

Lina sat up in her bed, shifting carefully and quietly so that she didn't wake Anders. She knew it wasn't going to be easy convincing him to move on, but she knew it was the right thing to do. She would wait for a while though. She would wait until she was back in the asylum and things were settled and Anders could see that she wasn't in danger anymore. That's when she would tell him. That's when he would move out of her reality and into her memories and dreams. He would live inside there with Bird and her parents, and when Lina got too lonely, she would reach inside her mind and visit them.

A nurse came by to check on her. Seeing Anders asleep in the chair, she spoke in a whisper. "I'm just checking your vitals."

The nurse worked quickly and almost silently. "Is there anything I can get you?" she asked when she was finished.

"May I have something to drink?" Lina asked in a whisper as well.

"Of course, I'll be right back."

The nurse returned moments later with a large cup of water. Lina whispered a thank you and the nurse nodded and then left. Lina drank her water slowly and wondered how long she had before she had to go back to the asylum. Walter had gotten her nearly a week before. Perhaps he could get her a little longer this time. That would be nice. Maybe he could bring her some books to read again. Maybe she could even sneak some into the asylum with her. She would have to ask Anders for help with that one, but she was sure he would oblige.

Anders shifted in his chair and yawned. He was awake. He smiled at Lina and she smiled back, but neither of their smiles reached their eyes for they both knew the asylum was waiting and that made true happiness impossible.

Anders stayed with her for the next two days. Walter had given him special permission. Lina spent her time talking to Anders and reading some books that Walter had brought her. (She hadn't even needed to ask, he had just appeared with them.) The nurses were kind and took good care of her. Lina was content.

On the third day, Anders had to leave.

"I have a few things I need to take care of, but I'll be back as soon as possible." His face was still etched with constant worry, even when he tried to appear calm.

Lina was about to respond when they heard a knock on the door to her room.

Anders smiled the most genuine smile she had seen in a while. "Oh good, sounds like she made it."

"Who?" Lina began to ask, but Anders had already opened the door, and Bird was smiling at her with misty eyes.

"Bird!" Lina gasped, "Oh, Bird, come here!"

Bird walked up to the bed and took Lina's hand. "Lina," she said as her voice cracked, "Lina, I have missed you so much."

"Come here. Come sit with me." Lina scooted over to make room on her bed for Bird.

"Are you sure? I don't want to hurt you." Bird looked at her with concern.

"I'm sure. Please. I have missed you so much."

Bird smiled and carefully placed herself on the bed next to Lina. Lina rested her hand on Bird's cheek. "Oh, Bird, you look wonderful."

Anders cleared his throat; Lina looked up. In her joy and surprise at seeing Bird, she had nearly forgotten he was there.

"Sorry. I just wanted to let you know I'm leaving, but you're in great hands, and I'll be back later today." Anders turned to Bird. "Bird, I'm so glad you could make it. Take good care of her while I'm gone, okay?"

"Of course," Bird responded.

"Thank you," Anders said and headed out of the room.

Lina focused her attention back on Bird. Bird really did look wonderful. Her skin was still pale, but now it was no longer the nearly translucent color it had been in the asylum. Her blonde hair was cut to her chin and her face had filled in a bit, giving her a much healthier and happier appearance. Lina thought she looked radiant.

"My Bird," was all Lina could manage at the moment. She was just so happy to have her friend with her.

Bird smiled at her with silent tears sliding down her face.

"Oh, Lina, I'm so sorry. I'm sorry I left you alone. If I had stayed maybe..."

Lina cut her off. "No, no. I promise your staying would not have made anything better. It wouldn't have stopped Carrow and it would have put you right in his line of fire...and I wouldn't have been able to bear it. Knowing you were safe saved my life, okay? I mean it. So, you need to promise you will not feel the least bit guilty about anything that happened, because I don't want to let Carrow cause me or the people I care about any more pain, understand?"

Bird was still crying, and Lina felt her eyes brimming with tears, ready to join her.

"Okay," Bird finally responded, and she wiped her cheeks.

After that, Lina steered the conversation towards what had been going on in Bird's life. She wanted to know everything – what the school was like, what she was learning, if she had any friends, how she liked her teachers, had she read any good books. Bird obliged and filled Lina in on all the details of her post-asylum life. It felt good to talk to Bird. With Carrow gone, Lina could ask Bird to come and visit her occasionally when she was back in the asylum. She knew that with school Bird might not be able to come very often, but Lina was sure that she would visit whenever she could; it would be something to look forward to.

Lina was just about to ask Bird about visiting her when Anders returned. Lina was shocked how her time with Bird had flown by.

"Did you have a nice time?" Anders asked them both when he entered the room.

They nodded simultaneously. Anders smiled widely. Lina didn't want to dampen his spirits by bringing up the asylum. She hadn't seen such a genuine smile on him in a while. Bird had given her the number to the school. Lina would find a time to call her before they sent her back to ask about visits.

"That's great," Anders said, still smiling at Lina. Then he turned to Bird. "It's time to get you back to the school. I have a car waiting for you out front. I promised my aunt I would have you back before curfew." Anders scratched the back of his neck. "I'll wait outside and give you a minute to say goodbye."

He walked out the door. Lina pulled Bird quickly into a hug. "Thank you for coming. It means the world to me. I love you, Bird."

"I love you too, Lina. So very much."

"Bird, do you think that once I'm back in the asylum you can come visit me occasionally? I know it won't be very often with school and everything, but if you ever have time, could you stop by?" With Anders out of the room Lina felt it was safe to ask.

"I hate that you have to go back," Bird sighed. "It's ridiculous. You don't belong there."

"It's okay. I'm really okay. Carrow's gone, and maybe this time I'll get a doctor who can actually help me with my episodes. It will be better, so much better." Lina tried to sound as positive as she could.

"I wish I could be as brave as you," Bird responded, "and of course I will come visit you. I will visit you as often as I can."

"Thank you, friend." Lina gave her a kiss on her forehead.

Bird smiled at her. "I will always do anything for you."

They gave each other one last hug, and then Bird got up and went outside to find Anders and head back to the school.

Lina's heart ached as she watched her friend leave. She took a deep breath and tried to focus on the joy she had felt reuniting with Bird and not on the despair of her best friend's departure and her own ever closer return to the asylum.

It will be so much better this time she told herself, and she tried her hardest to believe it.

Two more days went by and Lina was feeling better each day…at least physically. Despite her daily mantra of *It will be better this time,* her imminent return to the asylum was a constantly looming cloud over her mental state. She knew it wouldn't be much longer before she had to return, and anytime there was an uncomfortable lull in conversation with Anders or Walter, she felt certain they were thinking about it too.

It will be better this time

It will be okay

Carrow's gone. It will be okay.

It will be so much better this time.

It will.

It has to be.

You survived Carrow. You can survive a life in the asylum.

These thoughts flowed constantly through Lina's mind, doing their best to keep the darkness and fear at bay. She pictured herself snuggled up between her mother and father.

"It will be okay," her father reassured her.

"We promise," her mother said as she kissed her on the cheek.

Chapter Twenty-Six

Lina could feel her anxiety rising. It was like an unstoppable fire burning within her. She had not seen Anders since that morning. Walter had come in before his shift started to keep her company, but something felt off. There was an energy about him. There had been an energy coming from Anders as well. They knew something, something they weren't telling her.

She was going back.

She knew it.

Her chest felt tight and her whole body was tense. When were they going to tell her? Was Walter waiting for Anders to come back? Maybe Anders was trying one last desperate plea to the asylum or to her aunt and uncle. That would be like him.

She tried to focus on what Walter was saying, but her mind was buzzing, and it was hard to hear him with all the noise from her own mind. She felt her breathing becoming faster and shorter, and she tried to take deep breaths to calm herself. If today was her last day outside the asylum, she didn't want to spend it in a state of panic. She drummed her fingers along the table next to her bed and continued to focus on steadying her breathing until she was finally able to hear some of what Walter was saying.

"My wife made chicken and dumplings last night. I meant to bring you some. She even put together a plate for me to bring you, but I forgot. I'll have to bring it to you tomorrow."

Lina's head shot up. Did he just say "tomorrow"? Was she wrong? Would she still have a few more days of freedom? She allowed herself to cling to that hope and have a pleasant conversation with Walter.

Anders returned shortly before dinner time. He smiled his wide smile again and took a seat next to her bed. Walter stood up from the chair on the other side of her and announced that he was officially on duty now and had to check on some other patients.

Lina thanked Walter for sitting with her and then turned back to find Anders still smiling at her. His eyes were brighter than she had seen in a while, bright and kind, and it reminded her of the first time she had seen him. He had been so kind and good to her during her first episode at the asylum – during all of her episodes actually – and he was good to her still. She wished desperately that they had met under different circumstances, that they had met outside of the asylum, that she had never had an episode, that they had fallen in love in the real world. She imagined them older, dancing around their living room like her parents used to. Life with Anders would have been glorious. Lina was sure of that.

Lina was so lost in thought that she didn't even realize she was crying until Anders was wiping her tears away. "What is it, Lina? Did something happen? Does something hurt? Is there anything I can do?"

Lina blinked her eyes a few times in an attempt to stop the tears. "Oh no, it's okay. I was just thinking about my parents." It was a partial truth at least. "I just got lost in some memories."

Anders nodded understandingly and put his arms around her. He held her and kissed the top of her bald head.

Dinner soon arrived and they ate in a safe silence. Lina knew that Anders would wait for her to talk when she was ready.

After they finished eating, she smiled softly at him. "Thank you…thank you for always taking care of me."

"You're welcome, but you don't need to thank me for taking care of you. I do it gladly."

"I know, but I still want to say it."

"Okay, well, in that case, I'm going to thank you as well."

"For what?"

"For everything." He smiled, and Lina locked the memory of his smile away safe so that she could pull it out when she felt herself slipping away in the asylum.

* * *

Lina couldn't remember falling asleep, but Anders was shaking her awake. Lina had no idea what time it was. It felt like the middle of the night. She opened her eyes and looked up at him confused.

"What's going on?" she mumbled.

"We're getting you out of here."

"What?" Lina rubbed her eyes. "Are they here to take me back?"

"No. You're not going back to the asylum. We're leaving the hospital and we're going to my sister's house in Philadelphia."

Lina sat up straight, suddenly wide awake. "What? What are you talking about?"

"You don't belong in the asylum, Lina. We both can see that." That was Walter. Lina hadn't even realized he was in the room, "So, we're taking matters into our own hands and getting you out of here."

"But you'll get in trouble. Won't you get in trouble?" Lina felt jittery.

"We'll be fine. I've already signed the discharge orders transferring your care back to the asylum," said Walter.

"And I made sure those papers made it into the files at the asylum before I resigned so that no one can blame this on Walter or the hospital," Anders added.

"But won't they come looking for me?" Lina asked.

"I honestly don't think they will," Anders said. "You're not dangerous, and the asylum isn't going to want to publicize that they lost a patient, a patient that poses no risk to the public and was in the hospital because she had been attacked by one of their doctors."

"But what..." Lina's head was spinning. "This is crazy. I can't let you two do this."

"Too late. We're already doing it." Anders pulled some clothes out of a bag.

"Put these on. You can't walk out of here in your hospital gown."

He dropped the clothes in her lap. Lina looked down at them. Was this real? Was this really happening? She looked up at Walter and Anders. Neither of them seemed nervous. They were calm, incredibly calm as they waited to sneak her out of the hospital.

She looked at Anders. "How would this even work? I just stay at your sister's house and hope she doesn't notice the next time I have an episode? Won't she wonder why you're bringing a strange woman to her house? This is too much. I can't let you do this for me."

"First, it's not too much. Second, I've already talked to my sister. I told her everything." Lina began to interject but Anders held up a hand to stop her. "Yes, I really mean everything. She knows it all, and she has a room waiting for you. And as far as another episode goes, I'll be there to take care of you. And when it ends and the sadness comes I'll be there to take care of you as well. I know what I'm getting into, Lina. Nothing we might go through could ever be anywhere close to the horrors of the asylum, and we made it through that. You made it through that, and now you deserve to live your life. Whatever you want to do, wherever you want to go – all I ask is that you let me go with you."

Lina felt tears stinging her eyes. She looked down at the clothes again and then back up at Anders. "Anders, I…I believe you when you say you will take care of me, but that doesn't mean it's fair of me to let you carry my burden…"

Anders opened his mouth to respond, but Walter cleared his throat and spoke first. "If I may interject here, Lina, there's no reason for you to feel you have to carry your burden on your own. You can rely on other people, and it's not unfair and it doesn't make you selfish. Do you think your father felt that taking care of your mother kept him from the life he wanted?" Lina shook her head and Walter continued. "Exactly. Taking care of the person you love is part of life. It's a part of life for everyone who loves. You have an illness, but that illness does not define you. Do not let it define you. Please let us help you because you are a wonderful, smart, remarkable woman, and we are most certainly not letting you go back to that asylum."

Lina wiped away tears and stared at the two men in front of her. Could she really do this? Could she really let them do this?

"Yes, dear, you can." Her father kissed the top of her head.

"You absolutely can." Her mother smiled.

Lina took a deep breath. "Okay."

Anders and Walter smiled and then walked out of the room to give her privacy.

Lina took off her gown and put on the sweater, skirt, hat and shoes Anders had given her. She opened the door a crack, and Walter and Anders came back into the room.

"Okay, so how does this work?" Lina asked, "How do I get out of here?"

Lina glanced at the front doors.

"You just walk out." Walter smiled.

"I just walk out?" Lina asked.

"Yes, dear. I'll walk the two of you out of here and then you get in the car and drive away. Simple as that. This is a hospital, not a prison. Visitors come in and out all the time."

Lina could feel excitement rising within her. This was real. She wasn't going back to the asylum. She was going to walk out of the hospital with Anders and go to Philadelphia.

"I just walk out." She couldn't stop the smile that was forming.

She walked toward Walter and gave him a hug. "Thank you," she said. "Thank you for everything. I love you."

Walter hugged her tight in return. "I love you too, my dear."

Lina stepped back and straightened her shoulders. "Okay, I'm ready."

Anders took her hand in his. "Here we go."

Walter led the way, and the three of them headed for the doors.

Lina felt her body tense up as they walked past a group of nurses chatting, but they didn't pay her any attention.

She held her breath as Walter pushed open the door. Anders squeezed her hand reassuringly as they stepped outside.

Chapter Twenty-Seven

The night was dark and the air was so cold it stung, but Lina made Anders drive with the windows down so she could feel it on her face as they drove to Philadelphia and freedom.

Epilogue

The anxiety and sadness filled every inch of her body, leaving no room for anything else. A sharp pain seared her chest as the depression tore at her heart, demanding the space for itself. Her sorrow and fear weighed her down too much for her to possibly get off the floor. She curled into a ball and sobbed as the pain of it all threatened to destroy her.

Anders laid down beside her and rested his arm gently over her. Lina choked on her sob.

"I'm sorry, I'm so sorry," she cried.

"You have no reason to be sorry. None at all. I love you. I will always love you," Anders responded.

Lina didn't believe him. How could she? She had just spent the last month in a complete delusion. A horrifying, embarrassing, hideous delusion. How could he love her?

"I know you don't believe me right now, but I promise you, I love you. Nothing that happens will ever make me love you less." He sounded so sincere.

Lina gagged as the pain in her chest worsened. She sobbed hard, painful tears. This had been her first episode in over a year, but that did nothing to lessen her shame.

"Mama sad?" A small curly head peered into the room, and Bird came rushing after her.

"Sorry. I tried to keep her in the kitchen," Bird said.

"It's okay," Anders said as he picked up their two-year-old daughter and gave her a kiss. "Mama's a little sad right now, but she'll be okay."

Lina choked on her tears as Anders carried their beautiful daughter out of the room. Now Bird lay down next to her and stroked her hair. "It's all going to be okay. You'll get through this pain and it will all be okay."

Lina couldn't do anything except cry, and so Bird laid next to her until she fell asleep, exhausted from all the crying.

When Lina awoke she found herself in bed with her daughter, Marie, snuggled up close to her, snoring softly. Anders was there too, watching her with his kind, but tired, eyes.

"I love you," he whispered.

Lina tried to believe him.

* * *

Her depression lasted for about three weeks. Bird was home from the university for the summer holiday, so she helped take care of Marie when Anders was at work so that his sister, Anne, could have a break. Most of Marie's care had fallen to her during Lina's episode, and that shame ate at Lina, but her sister-in-law continued to reassure her that watching her niece and helping Lina was never a burden. She loved them both.

The more Lina's depression dissipated, the more she was able to believe that the people around her meant it when they said they loved her.

It had been six years since she escaped from the asylum, and in those six years, she had had only four episodes. Lina tried to remind herself that it could be worse. It had been worse while she was under the "care" of Dr. Carrow—the same Dr. Carrow who had been lobotomized and locked away in an asylum for the criminally insane. Lina had finally stopped having nightmares about him a year ago.

It had been five years since she and Anders had exchanged vows in a small ceremony. Walter, his wife, and Bird were the only people there other than Anders' family. Their wedding portrait hung in their bedroom next to a portrait of Marie as a baby.

When Lina was finally up to leaving the house, Anders took her and Marie to the park. Lina smiled for the first time in nearly a month as she watched her daughter stick flowers in her hair. Anders put his arm around Lina and kissed her head.

"She's perfect, isn't she?" Lina said softly.

"She certainly is," Anders responded.

Lina had been afraid to have a child, afraid to pass on her insanity, and Anders had never pushed her. During the first years of their marriage, Lina had helped to tutor Anne's children. She worked with them on their math and reading. She thought about becoming a teacher but was worried it would cause her too much stress. And so she kept tutoring her niece and nephew, but at night she found herself yearning for a child of her own to teach. She dreamt of her parents and thought often about her mother – thought of herself snuggled close to her mother every night. She never once resented her mother's illness or blamed her for her own insanity. Would a child of her own feel the same way? If her child inherited her unsound mind, would he or she still love Lina? Lina hoped they would.

One night after dinner, Lina finally shared her thoughts with Anders. "If we have a child, would you be willing to take care of them the way you take care of me?"

Anders had dropped the dish he was drying. With tears in his eyes, he had spun Lina around the kitchen.

"I take it that's a yes." Lina smiled.

"That's absolutely a yes." Anders kissed her and then set her down.

"The child might be insane. I might become more insane. I might not always be able to care for a child the way a mother should."

"Any child would be lucky to have a mother as strong as you," Anders said.

Lina put her hand on his chest. "I know how much you believe in me, but for right now I need you to imagine the worst-case scenario. Imagine I have more and more episodes and I eventually can't take care of our child. Imagine our child has issues of their own and needs you to protect them," Lina took a deep breath, "even if that means protecting them from me sometimes. Would that be too much for you? I know you promised to take care of me always, but I'm asking if you can take care of another person too, another person that I need you to promise me you would put first. Because they only way I can do this, and I do want to do this, is if I know that you will be able to put our child first, put our child before me."

Anders scratched the back of his neck, the way he always did when he was deep in thought. "When I married you, I promised I would do anything you asked of me and I meant it. So, yes, Lina, I can promise to put our child first, and I promise to do my very best to give our child a wonderful life."

Lina nodded solemnly. "Thank you. I needed to hear you say that."

Anders grinned and picked her up again. "But, that doesn't mean for a second that I think you are going to make anything other than an exceptional mother."

Lina smiled as she thought about that night, and again when Marie brought her over a handful of flowers.

Lina knelt down next to Marie and helped her twirl the flowers into her hair. Anders looked down at them and laughed. Marie began to giggle and Lina kissed her on the cheek.

Lina's life wasn't perfect and it wasn't always happy. There were still times when the mania took over and she would lose herself for a while, and she didn't know if that would ever stop. But, at the end of every episode she had people there, people she loved, waiting to pull her out of the darkness and back into herself; and for someone who had thought she was going to die alone in an asylum, for someone who had endured and survived hell, it was a more beautiful life than she could have possibly imagined.

Dear Reader

After I finished writing *The Unsound Mind* I couldn't shake the feeling that I needed to know more about Richard.

And so, one night, I sat down and wrote his story.

If you have emotionally recovered from Lina's story, I invite you to turn the page and read more about the man who sacrificed himself to save her.

My Name Is Richard

A short story companion to *The Unsound Mind*

Before

Richard first met Margie when they were 12 years old. She and her family moved into the house across the street. The first time he saw her she was riding her bike down the street and she had chocolate smeared on her chin. It was love and first sight...well, at least it was for him.

When they were both 15, Margie noticed how handsome Richard was getting.

At age 16, they sat together at the park reading comics and Richard finally worked up the nerve to kiss Margie. It was a wonderful first kiss.

When they were 21, Richard proposed and Margie started planning the wedding.

At age 23, Margie had her first miscarriage...

And then again at age 24. Richard held her and cried with her on their bathroom floor both times. He kissed her and told her he loved her and then after she fell asleep he cleaned the blood off the linoleum.

When they were both 27, Richard watched Margie bleed out and die during childbirth. The child, a boy, died as well.

A few months later, Richard suffered a complete mental breakdown. His parents did everything they could to help him, but they didn't really know what to do. After a year of Richard showing no signs of improvement, his parents took him to the asylum so he could receive professional help. His mother sobbed for a week after they had him admitted.

After

Richard never spoke, not to the other patients, not to the nurses, not to any of the doctors. The only time he made any sound during his first 2 years at the asylum was when he cried himself to sleep every night. His parents came to visit often, they would smile at him and try to get him to talk, but he couldn't-he just couldn't. Something had broken in him when he watched Margie and their son die on that table and he didn't know if it could ever be fixed. Margie had been his world and with her gone, he had no idea how to carry on. Deep inside, a part of him really wanted to speak, to do anything besides sit and stare. But he didn't know how to find his way to that part, and so day after day after day he sat in complete silence, and at night when he lay down to sleep and Margie wasn't there beside him, he sobbed because the pain of her absence was more than he could possibly bear.

During his third year at the asylum, he noticed the arrival of a new patient. She had red hair and she didn't speak either, at least not at first. After a few months a very young patient arrived, and the red-haired girl talked to her.

Every so often, Richard would have days he couldn't remember or bruises he couldn't explain. But, that didn't worry him too much, there wasn't enough left of him to worry about that...until, miraculously, there was.

Richard's parents were sitting across from him for their weekly visit. His father was talking about some sports game and his mother was smiling at him, and suddenly Richard was overcome with just how much he loved his parents. How much he loved these 2 people who refused to give up on him.

Every week, for 3 years, they came and visited him. Maybe their unending love and hope could help him find his voice again.

"Mom...Dad," it hurt to speak.

His mother gasped and his dad smiled widely.

"Yes, honey, it's us. It's Mom and Dad. We love you so much, Richard. So, so much." His mom cried as she spoke.

Richard couldn't say anymore but he began to feel something he had thought was lost returning to him.

The next time Richard saw his doctor, he was able to force out, "Help me."

"Of course, that's what I'm here for," Dr. Carrow replied.

Trial And Error

Dr. Carrow had told him he could make him better. He said he had been working on some new treatments and he was going to test them on Richard. Richard was lucky, Carrow said, he was getting a chance that no other patient was getting. A chance to be cured, a chance to go home.

It wasn't until Richard's third visit to the room that he realized Dr. Carrow had lied.

The first 2 times it hadn't been that bad. Carrow had collected a sample of his blood and given him a small dose of something that made him vomit.

"Trial and error, it's trial and error," Carrow muttered as he made some notes.

Richard should never have gone that third time. He should never have let Carrow strap him to that table, but Carrow was his doctor and Carrow said he wanted to cure him. Three days later, when Carrow let him leave, Richard could barely remember who he was.

And then he couldn't remember at all....

* * *

An orderly came to take him to the visitation room, someone was here to visit him. But who could that be? A strange couple sat across

from him. The women had blonde hair and the man was mostly bald. They kept calling him Richard and asking him if he wanted to talk. Was his name Richard? He couldn't remember. He looked around with panicked eyes and sweat began to slip down his forehead. He was supposed to know these people. Why didn't he know these people?

An uncontrollable fear welled up in him, "Who are you?" He asked the people.

Their faces instantly crumbled, "Richard," the woman said tentatively, "it's us, it's Mom and Dad."

"I don't..." he began. He was going to say 'I don't know you,' but a sudden intense pain exploded in his head. He felt like his head was bursting open, he cried out in agony and had to be carried away by 2 orderlies.

Very Afraid

Most of the time he didn't know who he was, he only knew that he was very, very afraid of the doctor.

The doctor laughed coldly and told him he was stupid. He told him he was disgusting and talked often about how only he could cure him...about how even though he hated him, he was a doctor and it was still his job to cure him.

Sometimes he talked about someone else. He called her the devil girl. "Kissed by the devil, there's a demon in that one." The doctor would say as he cut him open with his blade.

And so, he didn't know who he was; but he knew he was scared. And because the doctor liked to tell him all of his plans for the girl, he knew that she should be very, very scared too.

Things Remembered

Richard remembered *all* the terrible things Dr. Carrow said and did to him while he was lost.

His parents still came every week, at least for a while. But, sadly, he was never himself and the lost version of him was scared and confused whenever they came. Eventually Dr. Carrow came with him to one of his parents' visits. He told them their presence was putting a lot of strain on Richard's mind and that perhaps it would be for the best if they stayed away for a while. When Richard finally found himself again after that visit, he cried out in agony and begged for a nurse to call his mom. The nurse didn't listen, and it wasn't long before he forgot who he was again.

Once when he was himself, Richard saw Dr. Carrow with the girl. The girl he always talked about, the girl he claimed was kissed by the devil. He knew it was her by the way Carrow looked at her. He could see the hate so clearly marked on his face. It was the girl with the red hair. He would have to try to warn her. He couldn't just sit back and watch somebody else endure the same fate as himself.

Anytime he was lucid, Richard would look for the girl, but those moments were usually very brief. "Find the girl, warn the girl, save her from the doctor," he would repeat to himself, hoping the other part of him, the part that only knew fear, might be able to help...

Don't Trust The Doctor

He didn't know who he was again, he only knew the living nightmares that flashed around his mind, he sat on the floor and rocked back and forth. He tried to tell the nightmares to go away, he just wanted to be alone, but they wouldn't listen, just like the doctor never listened to him. Suddenly, there was a flash of red and a girl sat by him. Something inside of him yelled and screamed that he needed to tell her something. But who was she? What did he need to tell her? And then somehow he remembered, he needed to warn her. She was the girl that needed to be afraid of the doctor too.

He turned to look at the girl, she looked scared. Scared like him. He reached out and grabbed her arm.

"Don't trust the doctor." He continued to stare at her, willing her to listen, to save her from the nightmares.

He tried to think if there was more he needed to say but everything went blurry inside of him and so he let go of her and started rocking again. The rocking would help hold him together.

Beautiful Margie

He was eating breakfast when he remembered who he was. It had been a while...had it been a month? Richard searched his mind for memories of Margie. He wanted to remember her while he could. He sat and thought about her for as long as he could. He pictured her on their wedding day and on the first day she learned of her first pregnancy. She had been so happy then. Richard had been happy too. He had carried her joyfully around the house and told her he was taking her out to dinner. They had been so very, very happy. After she lost that baby, she stayed in bed for a week. It had broken Richard's heart to see his beloved Margie so sad. He would have done anything in the world to make her smile.

Far too quickly, Richard's memories of her began to blur and he knew he was going to go away again, he cried and wailed and screamed apologies to his beautiful Margie. His beautiful Margie that he hadn't been able to save.

Walking The Halls

It was night and Richard was walking the halls. He had been in the room again and his skin felt like fire. But he wasn't thinking about that, in his mind he was with Margie, at the park, reading comics. They were going to kiss soon, for the first time; this was one of his favorite memories.

Suddenly he saw the red-haired girl coming in from outside. She tripped and fell to the floor with her hands on her head. He came close and nudged her with this foot.

"Girlie," he whispered, "Girlie, hide. Don't walk alone where the Doctor can find you."

The girl looked up at him, studying his face.

"Get back to bed," Richard urged, "Don't let him find you, he wants to find you."

"Don't let who find me?" the girl asked, sitting up.

"The doctor." He responded and his hands started shaking.

She reached forward to take one of his hands in her own, "Which doctor? What will he do?"

He wanted to answer, he really did. Carrow had been talking about her a lot while they were in the room and he knew she was in danger, but he was slipping away again and reason was fading into fear. He closed his eyes and tried to stay. *Help me Margie, help me save her, he prayed,* but it was too late, Richard was gone.

* * *

He opened his eyes and had no idea where he was, but he saw that red-haired girl again. Something inside him screamed, it wanted him to do something, to say something. *Warn her*, a voice whispered in his mind, *warn her about the doctor*.

"Don't trust the doctor," he croaked out and then ran away because he was scared and confused and he wanted to hide.

Poison

He was Richard and Dr. Carrow was laughing wildly. He was talking about some of the things he had done to the "demon girl."

"I poisoned her little pet because she was misbehaving. She's not as compliant as you," Dr. Carrow paused to inject something into Richard's arm and then he leaned close and dropped his voice, "She's even more demented than you are." And then he began laughing so hard tears spilled from his eyes.

Hiding

He couldn't remember why he was hiding, but he knew he was hiding from the doctor. A pair of orderlies found him and dragged him into a room. The doctor was there waiting, the orderlies left.

"That was very bad of you, very very bad of you to run away. We have a lot of work to do." The doctor threw a vial at him and the contents splattered all over his face, "He stole my cure, that idiot doctor stole my cure and now we have to start all over again."

"No, no, no, no" he sobbed as he fell before the doctor, "no more."

"Oh, shut up," the doctor said as he stepped on his hand so hard he heard his bones crack.

Remember It For Me

Richard hadn't been himself in a very long time. It was probably the longest he had ever been lost. He immediately set out to find the girl. He needed to warn her about Carrow and his room. Carrow was growing angrier by the day and he knew he was running out of time. Soon it would be too late and the girl would be lost like he was. He ran around frantically until he finally found her sitting under a tree. He bent down and tapped her on the shoulder. She jumped and looked up at him.

"Come with me," he urged.

"I..." she began to respond.

"Come with me, I need to show you where it is." he implored. "Hurry, please, before I forget."

She stood up and he began walking with her following closely behind.

"Where are we going?" she asked.

"To his room, I need to show you his room." He glanced around nervously as he spoke.

"What room? Whose room?"She asked.

"The doctor's room, his secret room," he hissed.

He didn't know how long he had before he lost himself again, and he didn't know if he would ever find his way back once he disappeared again.

"My name is Richard," he said suddenly as he led her down a hallway, "please remember it for me."

Richard stopped walking, fear began to claw at his back. He turned to look at the girl, "We are almost there. I'm scared, I don't want to go back."

"It's okay, I'm with you," she soothed.

"I can't do it," Richard's eyes began to fill with tears.

"Please, I need to know what Carrow is doing," her voice sounded desperate.

Richard gripped his hair and closed his eyes, he began to rock back and forth, "I can't, I can't, I can't," he whispered. He was helpless again, helpless like the time he watched Margie and his son die. He couldn't save Margie, he couldn't save his son and he wasn't going to be able to save the red-haired girl either. Dark clouds began to fill his mind and he felt himself falling away.

* * *

"Richard, just tell me where it is. I will go alone, you don't have to come, you can stay safe." Someone was talking to him. Why was someone talking to him and why were they calling him Richard?

"Who's Richard?" he asked.

He didn't like being out in the open, he wanted to hide. The doctor was going to find him, he just knew it. He began squeezing his fists and walked around in a circle, "Don't trust the doctor...no, no, no. You better listen, don't try to run."

He glanced at the person standing next to him, but he had no idea who she was and so he left, he needed to find a place to hide.

The Voices

The voices started as a whisper, but as the days dragged on they grew louder and louder. The doctor had put the voices in there and he wouldn't take them away. The voices were mean. The voices were cruel. The voices said he should die. He covered his ears and tried to scream at them to leave but they wouldn't listen. He walked around barely aware of where he was going until he ran into a nurse.

"Watch out," she hissed at him.

"Make the voices stop" he begged, but she just looked at him in disgust and walked away.

He made his way outside and screamed up at the sky until finally, exhausted from screaming, he rested against the big wall. He scratched his face and the voices cheered. He scratched it again and they laughed. *We hate you*, they said, *everyone hates you, you're very bad, we wish you were dead.*

"No, no, no," he moaned, his eyes still closed, "Don't say it, no, no, no."

He felt someone come close to him and he heard them whisper something, but he didn't want to look, what if it was someone coming to take him back to the doctor? He didn't want to go. He felt a hand on his shoulder.

"NOO," he shouted, "no, I can't, no, no, no, no."

He pulled his bloody face away from the wall. He saw the red-haired girl.

"I'm not making you go anywhere," she soothed, "We don't have to go anywhere, I promise."

She reached out and rested her hand on his cheek. He stared at her, wondering what she was going to do next.

"I know the doctor is bad, I know he hurts you, I will never take you to him." she said.

He leaned against her hand and cried, "Can you make the voices go away?"

"I don't know, but I can stay with you and try." She moved closer and positioned him so his head was resting in her lap. And then she began to softly stroke his head.

"The voices want me to die," he sobbed, "they don't like me. The doctor put the voices there and they don't like me. They say I'm no good, they say I should die. I'm no good, I'm just bad, bad, bad, broken like he said."

"The voices are wrong. You are good, I want you to stay here with me. The doctor is bad, not you and I'm going to stop him," the girl said, "I'm going to find a way to stop the doctor."

"Don't trust the doctor, no, no, no, don't go with him no, no, no, doctor's no good, no, no, no." he crooned, "Tell the voices to stop... please."

He felt the girl's tears falling onto his head, "You terrible voices leave him alone, Richard is good and you need to leave him alone..."

He didn't know who Richard was, but he liked her kind voice. He liked that she was telling the voices to leave him alone.

Over and over she repeated those words, "Leave him alone, he is good, leave him alone..."

And finally he fell asleep.

When he woke up the voices were so quiet he could barely even hear them. He turned and saw the red-haired girl asleep by the wall. He tapped her on the shoulder, "Hey girlie, we should hide."

She sat up. "Come on, girlie, let's go, go, go, go, gooooo," he knocked his fists against his head as a warning to the voices not to come back.

He waited for the girl to stand up and then took off running, hoping she was following. He needed to find somewhere for them to hide. He didn't want the wicked doctor to find them.

"Hurry, hurry, the wicked thing is coming, hurry, hurry, hurry, don't want to go, no, no, no, nooooo." he said frantically.

He opened a door and ran inside, he could hear the girl running behind him. He turned a corner and tripped. His knees slammed into the floor. He wasn't going to make it, he collapsed on the floor and started sobbing. "No, no, no, no, no! Nowhere to go!"

"Come on, Richard, I'll help you," she soothed, "I'll take care of you."

"Girlie no! Kissed by the devil, he's coming for you," he looked at her and cried for her because he knew the doctor was going to hurt her too.

Her voice was shaky, "Let me help you up, I'll get you somewhere safe."

"Nowhere safe, nooooo, kissed by the devil doctor says," he took the girl's face in his hands "the devil is coming for the devil in you, but the devil's in him and it never ends."

The girl stared at him and then rested her forehead against his and covered his hands with hers.

"I'm going to stop him," she whispered, "I'm going to end it, I promise."

He dropped his hands from her face and blinked, he felt something happening. Hadn't she called him Richard? That name sounded familiar.

Unfortunately, he didn't have time to figure out why because the doctor was there and he had just stabbed a needle in the girl's neck.

The doctor looked at him, his eyes enraged, "What a disgusting pairing," he rushed forward and plunged the same needle into him.

The Rats And The Room

He awoke to find a dozen rats clawing at him. He tried to brush them off, but his hand went right through them. Their teeth pierced his flesh and he cried out in pain. A nurse walked past and he yelled to her, "Help, help, stop the rats."

She barely spared him a glance before she turned the corner.

He spent the rest of the day and into the night trying to wipe them away, but his efforts were futile, for some reason his hands kept passing through them.

He was sobbing in agony when the girl suddenly appeared again.

She sat beside him, "Do you remember me? I'm here now, I'm here to take care of you."

He turned to her "They hurt, they hurt, they hurt."

"What hurts?" she asked.

Confused how she could possibly have missed them; he held up his rat covered arms, "The rats, so many rats, they won't go away."

She wiped her hands down his forearms, but her hands passed straight through them as well. What kind of rats were these?

"See, they won't leave," he cried.

"I'm so sorry," she responded.

He buried his face into her shoulder and cried because he didn't know what else to do. He didn't know how much more he could take, the rats had torn so much of his flesh that he could see his bones showing through.

The girl wrapped her arm around him, "We're going to be okay; it's

going to be okay. I'll stay with you and you'll stay with me."

What felt like hours later, he began to fall asleep. He assumed the rats would finish him off, but there was nothing he could do to stop them anyway.

* * *

Richard felt someone kicking him, he moaned as he opened his eyes. How long had he been asleep? The woman who had kicked him began to kick someone else and that was when Richard realized the red-haired girl was asleep on the floor next to him; suddenly he remembered what had happened. He looked down at his arms and saw they were covered in scratches, he must have done that to himself when he thought the rats were on him. He seethed when he thought of all the horrors Dr. Carrow had forced upon him.

The lunatic woman who had kicked them said, "I don't like you," and then walked away.

He stared at the now awake red-haired girl.

"Thank you," he said simply.

"You're welcome," she responded, "I need to find Dr. Carrow's room. I'm going to find proof of what he's doing and get rid of him. Can you show me where it is?"

Richard felt a shiver in his soul but nodded and stood up so he could show her the way. He shook as he walked, but he knew it had to be done. And it had to be done now; he could disappear at any minute.

The girl spoke softly behind him, "You don't need to go in with me, you don't even have to get close, I just need you to show me where it is. I don't want you to ever have to go in there again."

Richard turned to look at her, "I don't want you to go in there either."

"I have to," she said, "I have to stop him. I have people who can help me. People in and out of the asylum who can help get rid of him, but I need some proof."

Richard turned a corner, "We're getting close." His body began to shake harder the closer they got. The room was where his nightmares began, where Dr. Carrow worked to erase him. He could feel himself slipping and he pleaded with Margie to help him once again. *Marg, let me help her, I couldn't save you, but I can save her. Don't let me leave yet.*

The girl took his hand, "Stay with me, I need you to show me the way."

Richard took several breaths and gripped her hand tightly, "I'm trying." He could feel Margie bracing him from the other side as well.

They started walking again, "He really hates you," Richard said, "even more than he hates me. He talks about you a lot. You need to be careful."

They walked a bit further and turned a corner. Richard's head began to twitch to the side.

"We're here," he was beginning to shake so hard he could no longer walk.

The girl took Richard's shoulders, "Which room? How do I get there?"

You can do this, Margie seemed to say, *just tell her where it is.* He quickly shouted, "under the carpet, in the corner, hidden stairs."

* * *

He opened his eyes, once again lost and confused.

It's Okay

Richard awoke outside by a tree and based on the flashes he could remember, it had been several days since he was last around. He pulled forward memories of Margie and worked to memorize her face, he wanted it so ingrained in his mind that even if he never came back again, he would still be able to see her. Even if he didn't know who she was when he was gone, he still wanted to be able to see her face. He was picturing Margie in her favorite red dress when he remembered. The red-haired girl. He had been with the red-haired girl.

He had been leading her to the room.

He quickly stood up and began searching for her...

He searched.

And searched.

And searched.

In what could only be described as a miracle, he was still himself as the sun began to set. He was never around this long. *You need to find her,* he seemed to hear Margie whisper. And that's when he realized where the girl had to be. She had to be in the room. He took several deep breaths and began walking toward the nightmares.

Stay with me, Marg, I can't do this without you, he begged.

He pictured Margie with her brave, determined face; the face he had fallen in love with when he was 12-years-old and he knew she was by his side.

He was getting close when he saw Dr. Carrow rush past him. He was in such a hurry that he didn't even notice Richard. Richard picked up his pace, the girl was in serious danger. He entered the room, pulled up the carpet and descended the stairs.

The first time Carrow brought him to the room, he told him how he had found it.

"I was sitting at a desk when I heard something scratching beneath me, it wouldn't stop so I tore up the carpet to find what it was. Imagine my surprise when I found a door. I pulled it open, and found a little mouse clinging to the other side. I had to explore, and when I discovered what was at the bottom of the stairs, I knew it was a sign for me to begin progressing my work. I knew it would be the place where I found the cure."

Richard could never have known then what Carrow had in store for him as he joyfully told him about his discovery. At the time, he had been given no reason to distrust his doctor. And when that finally changed, it was too late for him to do anything about it.

He just hoped it wasn't too late for the girl.

He pushed open the door and looked inside. There was a rancid smell of human waste and something else he couldn't place that burned his eyes. The girl was strapped to the table, her head was shaved and her scalp was sliced open. Her blood dripped to the ground next to what appeared to be jars of her hair. He swallowed down vomit and terror as he walked forward and began to unstrap her from the table.

The girl turned to look at him and the relief in her eyes gave him the boost of courage he needed.

"Let's go, girlie," he said as he helped her off the table. She nearly collapsed to the floor and that was when Richard noticed how terrible her legs looked, they were red and blistered and her feet seemed to be bleeding.

"Careful, careful," Richard said as he steadied her and led her towards the door, "We have to hurry, he'll be back soon."

"A notebook," the girl cried out, "get a notebook."

Richard looked to see what she was talking about and saw one on the tray by the table. He quickly grabbed it and began dragging her to the stairs.

The girl leaned on him as they made their way up the stairs. After they made it through the secret door, Richard lifted the girl up and handed her the notebook. "Here, take the book, I don't know how long I have left and I don't want to run off with it."

Richard was shaking and felt like he was going to faint, but Margie was still with him so he knew he could keep going.

The girl kissed his cheek, "Thank you for coming for me."

"Thank my mind for keeping it together long enough for me to realize you were missing," he said as they made their way into the hallway.

Richard began running and dragging the girl with him, trying to get as far away from the room as possible. As they turned the corner, his heart dropped to the floor.

"Demons," Dr. Carrow hissed when he saw them.

Richard could feel the fear flooding his body, but he refused to listen to it. He wasn't letting Carrow hurt anyone else. He shoved Carrow to the ground and punched him in the face. Carrow began to shout for help and then he noticed the notebook the girl was carrying.

"You little..." Carrow began to snarl before Richard cut him off with a punch to the jaw.

"Let's go," he lifted the girl back up and once again began to drag her.

"Help, help, help, I need a nurse." she yelled.

Suddenly the girl winced and slipped from his arms. Her collapse led Richard to trip and fall as well. During the time it took Richard to recover, Carrow pulled the girl up and pressed his knife against her arm. Blood was dripping from her side where Carrow appeared to have stabbed her.

"This ends now," Carrow said as he began to pull the girl in the direction of the room.

"Noooooooooooooo!" she screamed.

Richard watched in amazement as the girl bit down hard on Dr. Carrow's fingers and then flung her head back until she made contact with his nose. Richard heard the crack before he saw Carrow grab his nose in intense agony.

The girl began to crawl away from Carrow, and Richard went to help her.

The girl was screaming for help and didn't see Carrow raise his arm. She didn't hear him hiss as he released the knife from his hand.

With a roar of anger, Richard jumped in front of the knife; he wasn't letting Carrow erase another person. He wasn't going to watch another person die, not when he could save them this time.

The knife landed in his chest and Richard knew instantly it had hit his heart. He could hear people arriving and the murmur of commotion as the girl pulled him into her lap.

"Help, help, help, he needs help," she shouted.

Richard lifted his hand and the girl grasped it in hers, "It's okay," his voice was raspy, "I'm okay dying for you. I want you to live." He tried to focus on the girl, he wanted her to know he meant it.

"Richard, you can't die. Live! You have to live!" she sobbed.

"I thought I'd be afraid when I died. But I'm not. I'm not afraid at all," Richard whispered as his eyes began to close.

"Thank you, Richard. Thank you for my life," she cried.

He had done it; he had saved her. He hadn't been able to save Margie, or his son but he would be with them soon.

"We stopped him. He'll never . . . ." Richard was saying, but then the darkness left and to his abundant joy, he saw his sweet Margie and his son, waiting for him up ahead.

He ran to them.

At Peace

Richard's mother and father stood by Margie's parents. The mothers held hands as they watched the casket being lowered into the ground.

All four of the parents had tears in their eyes.

"They're together now," Richard's dad said solemnly.

The three others nodded in agreement.

"Your boy died a hero," Margie's dad offered.

"Our boy," Margie's mom corrected, "he was our boy, too. We loved him like he was our own."

Richard's mom smiled at her, "We loved Margie like she was our own, too. Those two were perfect together, weren't they?"

"They really were," they all agreed.

"And now they're together again so Richard can finally be at peace." Richard's mother cried and her husband took her in his arms.

Margie's parents joined the embrace and the four of them stood by the graveside crying soft tears of sorrow and relief. When the parents were finally ready to depart, they placed roses beside the newly installed headstone, which read: ***"Richard Green; beloved husband, son, father, friend and hero."***

They also placed another set of roses by the slightly worn headstone next to it, which read: ***"Margie Green: beloved wife, daughter, mother and friend."***

* * *

In the future, the four parents would visit the graves often. They would leave flowers by the headstones and remember stories together. They would talk about their son and their daughter and take turns reminding each other that Richard and Margie were together and that's how they were always meant to be.

Occasionally the red-haired girl would visit the graves as well. She would place her hands on Richard's headstone and she would thank him for saving her. She would tell him all about her life, the life she was able to live because of his heroic sacrifice.

Made in the USA
Las Vegas, NV
20 May 2023

72340785R00163